"This c...
he murmured darkly

as he slowly loosened her fingers from his wrist.

She stiffened and broke the eye contact. My God, did he think she was coming on to him? She opened her mouth to deny his assumption, but before she could speak, he pressed his finger against her lips.

The callused roughness felt erotically abrasive. "You don't know what I'm going to say," she finally whispered.

"I don't want to know."

"Cage, I can't let you think that by touching you I meant more than concern...."

"This—" he pressed their wrists together so that their pulses pounded, rich and full, against one another "—isn't about concern. It's about you and me."

Caught in his gaze and the sudden fire between their wrists, Haley felt her thoughts tumble wildly. When she realized the meaning in "you and me," she protested in a hushed voice. "No. That's not possible...."

Dear Reader,

This month starts off with a bang—and with a book that more of you than I can count have requested over the years. *Quinn Eisley's War,* by Patricia Gardner Evans, finally completes the cycle begun in *Whatever It Takes* and *Summer of the Wolf.* Quinn is a commanding presence, and every bit the American Hero he's featured as. This is a story torn from today's headlines, and yet timelessly romantic. I have only one word left to say about it: enjoy!

The rest of this month is pretty spectacular, too, but what would you expect when we're celebrating the line's tenth anniversary? It's hard for me to believe we've been around that long, but it's true. And because it's your support that has kept us flourishing, it seemed only fitting to reward you with one of the best lineups we've ever published. We've got *Ironheart,* the latest in Rachel Lee's bestselling Conard County series; *Somewhere Out There,* the followup to *From a Distance* by award-winner Emilie Richards; *Take Back the Night* by yet another award-winner Dee Holmes; *To Hold an Eagle* by yet *another* award-winner (Does this tell you something about the line?) Justine Davis; and *Holding Out for a Hero,* the first of the stories of the Sinclair family, by Marie Ferrarella, another of our bestselling authors. In short, we've got six books you can't resist, six books that belong on your shelves—and in your heart—forever!

We're also offering a special hardcover tenth anniversary collection featuring the first books some of your favorite authors ever wrote for the line. Heather Graham Pozzessere, Emilie Richards and Kathleen Korbel are regular fixtures on bestseller lists and award rosters, so don't miss your chance to get this once-in-a-lifetime collection. Look for details at the back of this book.

And, of course, I'll expect to see you back here next month, when Silhouette Intimate Moments will bring you more of what you've come to expect: irresistible romantic reading.

Leslie J. Wainger
Senior Editor and Editorial Coordinator

TAKE
BACK
THE NIGHT

Dee
Holmes

Silhouette® ™
INTIMATE MOMENTS®
Published by Silhouette Books New York
America's Publisher of Contemporary Romance

SILHOUETTE BOOKS
300 East 42nd St., New York, N.Y. 10017

TAKE BACK THE NIGHT

ISBN: 0-373-07495-6

First Silhouette Books printing May 1993

Printed in the U.S.A.

Books by Dee Holmes

Silhouette Intimate Moments

Black Horse Island #327
Maybe This Time #395
The Farrell Marriage #419
Without Price #465
Take Back the Night #495

Silhouette Special Edition

The Return of Slade Garner #660

DEE HOLMES

would love to tell her readers about exciting trips to Europe or that she has mastered a dozen languages. But the truth is that traveling isn't her thing, and she flunked French twice. Perhaps because of a military background where she got uprooted so much, she married a permanent civilian.

Dee is an obsessive reader who started writing casually, only to discover that "Writing is hard! Writing a publishable book is even harder." She has since become involved in her local RWA chapter, and says that she loves to write about "relationships between two people who are about to fall in love but don't know how exciting it is going to be for them."

To Kathleen Elizabeth Bulk,
with love for all that you can be.
To David and Ann,
with love for all that you are.

Chapter 1

Any hope Haley Stewart had that Cage Murdock would stay away dissolved twenty minutes after the meeting had begun.

Haley knew she had to stop him before he got too far into the room. She stepped away from the podium, where she'd been listening to the frustrated anger over the recent drive-by shooting that had killed Cage's brother. As she worked her way through the small group that surrounded him, she mentally cautioned herself against showing any hesitation.

After a perfunctory greeting, she took his arm and steered him back toward the door. He seemed pliant enough, which should have warned her. Pliancy, she had heard often from his brother, wasn't one of Cage's virtues.

She let go of him when they were some distance away, and slid her hands into her skirt pockets to hide a shivery sense of doom that she didn't want to feel. He simply waited, his expression calm and curiously expectant.

"I want you to leave," she said firmly.

"No."

"We don't need your kind of help."

"I don't recall offering *my kind of help,* whatever you think that is, but from glancing at your neighbors, it looks as if you're in the minority." He spoke in a low, husky, voice, not taunting or attempting to argue, but sounding very much as if he, and not she, were in charge.

She tried not to notice the wintry blue of his eyes as he glanced around the vacant store. Prior to the infestation of the drug dealers, the owner had sold used furniture. Just before the drive-by, Haley had made arrangements to use the store as a central meeting place. The sparse group who had greeted Cage made up the once-forty-strong Mayflower Heights Association. They were now gathered around the coffee urn, discussing, no doubt, the drive-by, which had been the main topic since it had happened. Haley hadn't missed the hopeful glances thrown in Cage's direction.

Nor, she realized, did she need to be too perceptive to know that the arrival of Matthew's brother had given a tremendous boost to their sagging spirits and discouraged outlook. They obviously viewed Cage as an unexpected but welcome help in their efforts to clean the streets of drug dealers. Under ordinary circumstances, Haley might have felt the same way, but now she feared that his unannounced and uninvited appearance would bring the simmering tension and street violence to a head.

She kept her voice soft so that the others wouldn't hear. "I know my feelings about you aren't shared, but someone here has to keep a clear head. All the progress of the past few months is gone. People are back to hiding behind locked doors and fearing even calling the police. Standish Street is once again a war zone, and those here tonight, despite their quietness, are furious. You could easily stir their anger into a vigilante mentality."

Any expectation that her words would make him cooperate and leave died when he walked over to one of the folding chairs. Pulling it around so that he faced her, he sat down and settled back with a kind of controlled ease that at least indicated he might be willing to listen. That should have made her feel better, but it didn't. Haley had dealt with plenty of men—including her ex-husband—who were skep-

tical of her abilities and wanted to take charge, but she knew
Cage's being here had nothing to do with either her ability
or male skepticism.

In fact, she decided ruefully, she doubted he even cared
if he had her cooperation. She noted that his black leather
boots were a dusty gray, and that his jeans were faded by age
and wear, rather than from any stonewash process. His body
was long, lean and muscled, as was evidenced by the snug
denim and the dark blue T-shirt that read ONLY THE STRONG
SURVIVE. She couldn't help but wonder if the strong sur-
viving meant physical or emotional survival.

She glanced up and was caught by his wintry blue eyes.

The room was fairly large, the members of the Association were only a few yards away, and she was in no way
trapped by him, yet she was aware of a tangible danger.

Watching her as if he could see clear to the edge of her
soul, he asked, "And just how am I stirring up a vigilante
mentality? You hustled me over here before I did much more
than enter the room."

If this were any other man, Haley thought, she wouldn't
have allowed the conversation to get this far. She would have
marched to the door, opened it and ordered him out.
Though she was fairly sure she'd hidden her sinking reaction when she'd seen him enter, she knew from what Matthew had told her that Cage always saw beyond the surface.
She had little doubt that his years with the Drug Enforcement Administration had honed and sharpened street-smart
skills that could assess, calculate and then make a decision
with flawless and unquestionable accuracy. The fact that he
might be using those same tactics on her flustered and distracted her.

"Don't tell me you don't have an answer?" he asked, as
if amazed she wasn't working from a prepared speech.
"You're the organizer of the Mayflower Heights Association and the female nemesis of the local drug dealers. I
would think a simple answer to an easy question wouldn't
be tough."

She made herself count to ten and not glare at him.
"What a quaint way of being sarcastic. I suppose you ex-

pect me to get huffy and defensive. The truth of the matter is that I don't care what you think of me, or what we're trying to do here. And as for your question, you know damn well what I mean. All these people, plus the ones who are afraid to be here, adored Matthew. And those present have guessed you're here to find the man who killed him."

"Which is exactly what they want. Three of them told me so before I cleared the doorway." He paused a moment, then asked, "How about you, Haley?"

She stepped closer to him. "How dare you insinuate that I don't care about what happened to Matthew? I'm angry and frustrated and outraged. I just don't happen to think using violence to fight violence is the answer."

He leaned back in the chair, his eyes hooded, his hands folded loosely above the buttoned placket of his jeans. Haley stared for all of a second, realizing she'd missed this particular detail earlier and at the same time damning her diverted attention. She immediately looked back at his face.

Contemplatively he said, "Ah, yes, the nonviolent approach. How could I have forgotten the bleeding-heart clamor for negotiation and peace without weapons. Just take down the bad guys with sensible, calm verbal precision. In this case, perhaps I could just approach the gentleman and ask him politely if he was the one who, two weeks ago, on August second—" Cage turned his wrist and glanced at his watch "—at precisely 11:04 at night, aimed his user-friendly assault weapon out of his vehicle and shot my brother. And when he answers yes, I could give him a card that says since violence is always in bad taste and a hindrance to world peace, would he mind turning himself in to the police at his earliest convenience?"

Haley folded her arms. "Very funny."

"And as ridiculous as you expecting me to leave, so let's cut the bull—and the fairy-tale approach. I don't want a hassle with you, Haley. I'm not here with any intent of wrecking what you and your neighbors have put together."

She took a deep breath. "But you *are* wrecking things. The focus will be diverted from a community effort to get rid of the scum to avenging Matthew. Their feelings are understandable, because they all loved your brother.''

''I loved him, too, but feelings, mine or theirs or even yours, didn't do a hell of a lot of good, did it?'' he muttered with a bitterness that made the emotion sound as senseless as Matthew's death.

Haley wanted Cage to leave, but she also wanted him to know she understood his coldness. ''Cage, your anger is more than justified. Matthew's death was a tragedy, but I can't let you use the Association as some sort of vehicle to carry out your personal vendetta.''

He dragged both hands through his thick black hair. Then he slowly straightened in the chair, hunched forward, and let his hands dangle between his thighs. He stared at the dust on his boots. For no reason she could think of, the move made her very uneasy. She noted, too, that he neither denied or argued with her accusation. A few tense moments beat between them.

Then his words came, soft and precise, as though he spoke from too much firsthand experience. ''Do you have any idea how many people die because some druggie wants money for a fix or a dealer stakes out new territory and doesn't want any interference?'' He glanced up, but didn't wait for her answer. ''Random shots fired in a drive-by aren't so selective. Kids playing on their front steps and old ladies in rocking chairs who happen to be near a window get killed, and now a young, idealistic lawyer who just happened to be in the wrong place at the wrong time. No warning, no chance to duck, just a car passing by and Matt is dead.''

Haley swallowed. The truth of his words made her recoil as the memory of seeing Matthew lying in his own blood moments after the shooting came vividly to her mind. She ignored her instinct to touch Cage, to offer a handful of comfort. She'd made that mistake at the funeral.

Cage had worn dark gray. His eyes had been shadowed from lack of sleep, his grief ragged, but his obvious fury had discouraged most from venturing too close. A final prayer, then murmurs of condolence were offered before the mourners returned to their cars. Haley, too, started to leave, but then she turned back, not quite able to just leave Cage alone. Perhaps she could take some of his burden, or share his pain; she wasn't even sure if words could convey her feelings, but she needed to reach out to him.

He stood with his head bowed, staring at the brass-and-mahogany casket that had been lowered into the ground. Baskets of flowers were wilting under the hot August sun. The cemetery workers stood off to the side, sweating and obviously impatient to finish their job, but none looked as if they wanted to tangle with Cage.

Haley approached him carefully. Whether it was his concentration, the total stillness of his body, or something Matthew had once said about Cage never leaving anything unfinished, Haley knew he'd made some decision.

She touched Cage's arm, and he turned as though she were a distraction. The raw chill in his eyes made her step away. Not from fear of him, but from fear for him. With insight culled from living in the eye-for-an-eye atmosphere of Mayflower Heights, Haley knew that Cage Murdock's fury had already plunged its roots deep into a need to avenge.

However he chose to carry it out, she had no doubt Cage could exact it in a way that would be swift, silent, and untraceable. In a disturbing way, she didn't blame him, and perhaps that was one reason she wanted him to leave. She knew that if she and the Association were ever going to restore their neighborhood to what it had once been, she couldn't allow violence to be the method.

When she'd seen no sign of Cage in the weeks following the funeral, she'd told herself that he'd come to his senses. Certainly, as one of the DEA's best agents, he knew better than most the difference between the law-abiders and the lawbreakers. She'd put herself firmly on the law-abiding side, but now she feared that what she'd sensed in Cage at the cemetery had only been reinforced. When it came to Matthew, the law didn't matter.

Now she realized that she was frightened not just by Cage, but by the danger his ruthlessness could create.

Cage was staring at her. "Did you hear what I said?"

"I'm sorry. I was just— Never mind. What were you saying?"

"That you want the drug dealers cleaned out so that you can live like human beings instead of cringing behind locked doors. That's understandable. I commend and support your efforts, and I'll be glad to help...."

She blinked. Had she missed something? He wanted to help, not hinder? Her own skepticism slipped into place. Just because he sounds as though he agrees, that doesn't mean anything, she reminded herself.

Haley was about to repeat what she'd said earlier about not wanting his help when he rose out of the chair and moved to a dirt-smeared window that looked out on boarded-up buildings, scattered trash and deserted streets.

He was standing with his back to her, and Haley was suddenly struck not only by the sheer physical impact of Cage, but by the guarded and insular demeanor that emanated from him. One that didn't invite advice, and discouraged interference. My God, she thought, no wonder Matthew had believed Cage hung the moon.

Then, in a voice so low she had to move closer to hear him, he said, "I had some loose ends that needed to be cleared up before I could take some time off from the agency, or I would have been here sooner. Now that I am, any delay is pointless." His tone sharpened to razor precision. "I want the son of a bitch who splattered my brother's blood all over Standish Street."

Haley shivered at the starkness of his words, and when he turned toward her, she was even more alarmed. If only she'd seen hot anger, if only he'd lashed out and pounded his fist against the wall, if only he'd done anything but stand so still, so alone, so resolute.

She whispered, "Cage, please, don't do this."

He ignored her plea as though she'd never spoken. Then, as if what he'd just said was now tucked in a locked place in his mind until he needed it, he added cordially, "Matt told me there were a lot of vacant apartments in the neighborhood. What about the building across the street from yours?''

Her mind leaped to fill in the blanks of what he was really saying. He intended to move here! "Matthew told you?''

"We talked the night he died. He mentioned his concern about you living down here, but he also said you weren't all by yourself. He said that your apartment building was about the only one with no vacancies.''

"I've been very fortunate to have good tenants who want the same things I want for the neighborhood.''

Cage continued, ignoring the underlying message in her words. "Matt worried about you and said he'd been urging you to move to a safer part of the city.'' He paused a moment, a muscle in his jaw tightening. "Rather ironic that his worry is what got him killed.''

Haley's eyes widened. "You're blaming me, aren't you? If Matthew hadn't come to see me that evening, then he'd be alive. That's what you're saying, isn't it?'' Admittedly, she'd made that very same accusation numerous times, but hearing it from Cage made it seem all the worse.

To her astonishment, Cage barely reacted. "No, Haley, that's what *you're* saying. It's too late to blame anyone, except whoever shot him.'' He started to walk away.

"Wait!'' She curled her fingers around his wrist to stop him. This wasn't like her touch at the funeral. This time there were no clothes, there was only the naked solidness of his warm flesh. "I can't let you do this, Cage,'' she said, surprised at the alarm in her voice. "It's not going to help Matthew, and it will destroy you.''

Instead of arguing or denying, he stared down at her hand. Haley couldn't help but notice the contrast of her lightly tanned fingers against his sun-darkened skin. His pulse beat thick and steady beneath her grip. Good sense told her to release her hold; she would have even welcomed him pulling away, but he didn't. Then she glanced up and met his eyes. Wintry blue, yes, but weary—and aware of her.

Intensely aware.

Not as someone who disagreed with her, not as Matthew's brother, not even in a superficial sexual way, but as if a quickening tension had bonded them.

Something had happened between them. Something not compatible with avenging Matthew's death, something magnetic and mystical. Haley felt light-headed, as though she'd drifted into some evocative moment never before experienced.

"This can't happen, Haley," he murmured darkly as he slowly loosened her fingers from his wrist.

She stiffened and broke the eye contact. My God, did he think she was coming on to him? She opened her mouth to deny his assumption, but before she could speak he pressed his finger against her lips.

The callused roughness felt erotically abrasive. "You don't know what I'm going to say," she finally whispered.

"I don't want to know."

"Cage, I can't let you think that by touching you I meant more than, uh . . . concern."

"This—" he pressed their wrists together so that their pulses pounded, rich and full, against one another "—isn't about concern, it's about you and me."

Haley was caught in his gaze and the sudden fire between their wrists, her thoughts jumbled wildly. When she realized the meaning in "you and me," she protested in a hushed voice, "No . . . that's not possible . . ."

He released her wrist and took a long breath. Relief, she was sure, and she felt a twinge of disappointment that was as strange as what had taken place in the past few seconds.

Her friend Alicia Brady called her name, and Haley jerked around, feeling awkward and disturbed. "We'll be right there," she answered, aware of the scratchiness in her voice.

When she looked back at him, the earlier sensations of magic and mystery were gone.

She pushed her hair back and sighed. Maybe she was just tired, or perhaps it was the heat and the general tension of the past weeks. Or she'd somehow momentarily lost her bearings.

As they walked toward the others, Cage asked, "What about the apartment building across from yours?"

She hesitated. She was supposed to be getting him to leave, not making it easier for him to stay. Yet it was obvious he wasn't going anywhere—except after Matthew's killer.

In a resigned voice, she said, "As a matter of fact, there are a number of vacancies. The landlord has been trying to sell, with no luck. I try to keep an eye on things for him, so I imagine he would be pleased to have you there."

"Sounds good. So where do I get in touch with this landlord?"

"Actually, I have keys. He left them with me while he went to visit his daughter in Michigan."

"In case the neighborhood turned into a garden district and everyone wanted to move into it, huh?" he said sagely.

Haley bristled. "Nothing quite so lofty, Cage. Like most neighborhoods, Mayflower Heights is like an extended family unit. And just as neighbors leave keys with other neighbors when they go away, he left his keys with me."

"How about the first floor that faces Standish Street?"

"That one is small, just three rooms and—"

He cut her off. "Just as long as the bed is comfortable, there's lots of hot water, and the kitchen has a microwave."

She was about to tell him the bed was a single, the water was hottest at 3:00 a.m. and the microwave had been stolen by the previous tenant, when she stopped. If he saw for himself that the apartment had none of what he wanted, he'd probably change his mind and decide to leave. And, given her evocative reaction to him, his leaving would definitely be for the best.

Fifteen minutes later, Cage was gone, and Haley was besieged with questions and opinions.

"Well, what did he say, Haley?"

"He's going to stay and help us, isn't he?"

"A man from the DEA will put the fear of God in those punks."

"Plus, he's Matt's brother. Sure don't look nothin' like him, but when I saw Cage at the funeral, I said to myself, this guy ain't gonna rest till that killer is dead or wishin' he were."

"Matthew talked about his brother a lot, but I had no idea he would have such a—oh, dear, I guess you would call it a kind of presence."

"Haley, does he have a plan? I mean, since he doesn't know who exactly shot the kid, then he's got to have some plan of attack."

"Say something, Haley. Good heavens, we've been waiting patiently. Cage is gone, and now we want to know."

Haley glanced at the crowd that had gathered around her so expectantly. She sighed deeply, but acknowledged to herself that she hadn't heard this much enthusiasm in weeks. "Why doesn't everyone get a cup of coffee and some of those terrific cookies Alicia brought, and then I'll fill you in on what Cage said?"

As they dispersed, Haley sagged down in one of the chairs, taking advantage of the few moments to collect her thoughts.

Cage had told her he had a few things to do, and that he'd be at her apartment in about an hour for the key. It was getting close to ten, and Haley didn't really want to answer everyone's questions, but she understood their curiosity and their anxiousness to find some new hope in Cage's unexpected appearance.

Haley's preference was to go home so that she could be alone to do some thought-sorting. Cage's presence, and his desire to avenge Matthew, were disturbing enough, but what had taken place on a personal level in those few seconds had managed to cause total disorder in her mind, as well as her emotions.

She kept trying to tell herself she'd overreacted or read more into that pressing together of their wrists than she should have—but Cage, too, had reacted.

She controlled an inner shudder. What had or hadn't taken place didn't matter. Since neither wanted anything to happen, then nothing could. The thought should have made her feel more confident, but it didn't.

Alicia Brady sat down beside her. Alicia and her teenage son, Kevin, were tenants of Haley's. Alicia, like Haley, was divorced, and the two women had often talked about the danger in trusting men who needed to control women.

Squeezing Haley's arm, Alicia asked, "Are you okay?"

Still distracted by Cage and wondering how to handle him, she muttered, "I don't know. Suddenly everything got complicated." Then, realizing how Alicia could take her response, she quickly managed a smile. "I'm just doing my usual worrying over things I can't control. I'll be all right."

"He's bad news," Alicia warned.

"I know. I told him the Association doesn't need his kind of help."

"I'm talking about bad news for you, Haley."

"Me? Don't be ridiculous."

"He's not the settling-down type. Probably great in bed, but I'll bet you if a woman mentioned commitment he'd be history before the sheets were cold."

Haley gave her friend an incredulous look. "Settling-down type? Great in bed? Commitment? What in the world are you talking about?"

"I don't want to see you get hurt," Alicia said vehemently. Since her divorce, Alicia's wariness of men tended to over-exaggerate every male motive. Haley didn't want to push her into an ongoing worry about something that would never happen.

"I don't even plan to get scratched, never mind hurt by him. Believe me, Cage Murdock isn't here with any intent to get involved with any woman."

Admittedly, since her own divorce, from Philip, Haley hadn't exactly encouraged male attention. Handling problems at the apartment house took up more than enough of her time. Her parents had owned the building since Haley's birth, and throughout their lives had been adamant about getting rid of crime. Haley had inherited the house, *and* her parents' tenacity.

Their death, when their van missed a turn and rolled over an embankment, had been difficult for Haley. At the time, she'd been living with Philip in a condo in Providence. When she'd decided to move into the apartment house instead of selling, Philip had been furious. That had been the beginning of the end for her marriage.

Now her involvement with the Association and her own personal mission to get Mayflower Heights drug-free required even more commitment. Besides being time-consuming and too often disappointing, romantic entanglements seemed frivolous. Or perhaps she'd seen too much crime and daily terrors and no longer believed in anything as sweetly innocent as falling in love. She sighed, wishing she could deny that she'd lost her idealism when it came to love.

Haley asked, "But I admit I'm curious about your concern. Why do you think I could be hurt by a man I hardly know?"

Alicia laced her hands together. "Promise not to lecture me about my overactive imagination."

Haley grinned. "Oh, no, not another the-plot-thickens theory."

"See, you're laughing already," Alicia said peevishly.

"I promise, no laughing." Haley pressed her fingers against her lips, but her eyes were filled with amusement.

Alicia gave Haley an intense look. "I watched the two of you while you were over there talking. Something happened."

Haley lowered her lashes. My God, had it been visible from across the room? Resolutely she said to Alicia, "The only thing that happened was that he refused to leave. Now I want you to quit worrying. Who he is or what type he is or how committed he is in his relationships with women doesn't matter to me at all."

"You sure?"

"I'm sure."

"Then why do I have this feeling he's not going to go away?"

Haley sighed. "Because he's not. He wants the man who killed Matthew, and—" Haley drew a deep breath "—he wants to rent an apartment in Earl's building."

"Oh God, you didn't."

"Don't look at me as if it was my suggestion. I don't like it, either, but he already knew there were a lot of empty apartment buildings. And you know Earl has been looking for reliable renters, since he can't get a buyer."

"A man bent on revenge is reliable?" Alicia asked, as if Haley had lost her mind.

"I'm hoping to change his mind."

"Uh-huh. Cage Murdock looks like the kind of man who listens to a woman about as often as he goes to those summer society balls down in Newport," Alicia said, with an easy sarcasm.

Haley grinned. A mental picture of Cage attending one of the elite society parties in Newport simply defied imagining. "Well, I intend to try to change his mind anyway."

Before Alicia had a chance to say any more, the rest of the group began to drag chairs over.

Including Haley and Alicia, there were twelve—the youngest sixteen-year-old Kevin, Alicia's son and a former drug user, the oldest Norman Polk, nearing sixty, who, despite a cigar-and-beer habit managed to have the energy of a forty-year-old.

They all settled in, waiting expectantly, as if their futures depended on how Haley answered their questions and comments.

She also saw in that expectation a renewal of the hope that had been missing for weeks. Despite wishing that Cage hadn't come, she couldn't deny that he had given her friends and neighbors their hope back, just by appearing.

"All of you had an opportunity to ask Cage questions. Why didn't you?"

They all glanced everywhere but at her.

"He didn't intimidate you, did he?" she asked.

Finally Norman Polk, puffing on his cigar, spoke, "Well, hell, Haley, we didn't know just what to say. He ain't exactly the approachable type, and anyone with a brain could tell the man is still ticked off but good about what happened to the kid.''

"I wish you wouldn't call Matthew a kid," Haley commented. "He was a successful attorney, and well beyond being a kid."

"Hey, when you're my age, anyone up to thirty is a kid. Including you, cupcake."

Haley winced at Norman's endearment, but didn't bother to say anything. He'd called her that for the past two years, ever since he'd bought and moved into a nearby duplex.

"So what's the deal? Is he hanging out, or is he gonna split?" Kevin asked as he lit a cigarette and ignored his mother's frown.

"He's here for a while," Haley answered. Then she explained that he'd be renting an apartment in Earl's building.

"That's cool."

"Yeah, that way he can really keep an eye on things."

Kevin grinned. "And he can park his bike in your hall, Haley."

Haley frowned. "What bike?"

"You didn't hear his cycle?" Astonishment filled his eyes. "Jeez, how could you miss that?"

"Probably because gunshots have become so commonplace I didn't pay any attention."

Kevin gave her his most superior look. "Anyone can tell the difference between a gun and a cycle."

"Unfortunately, Kevin, not all of us are blessed with such discerning hearing."

Kevin slouched in one of the chairs, cigarette dangling from the corner of his mouth, looking very James Dean. "Yeah, that's what I got, all right, discerning hearing." Giving Haley a quizzical study, he added, "So are you gonna let him park the cycle in the hall? If you don't, it'll get ripped off before the tires are cool."

She failed to see why the safety of Cage's motorcycle should have become the topic when the safety of the neighborhood was what really mattered. Then again, she supposed that for Kevin the cycle was a much more tangible object to focus his concern on.

Haley finally said okay, just because it would end the subject. She sighed, feeling punchy at the turn of events. Avenging Matthew, motorcycles in her hall, Cage living across the street, probing questions from Alicia, her own desire to make Mayflower Heights once again a safe neighborhood...

And then there was that strange, mystical wrist-to-wrist moment with Cage.

My God, she thought, no wonder she felt punchy.

Just hours ago she'd only had drug dealers to worry about. Her words to Alicia earlier had been right. Everything had suddenly gotten very complicated.

Chapter 2

The following morning, Haley told herself that she wasn't making the blueberry muffins as an excuse to pay him a visit. And that her restless night had not been caused by wondering if Cage was cursing the single bed. She had definitely expected to hear some swearing loud enough to carry across the street about the tepid water temperature in the apartment's shower. Yet she'd heard nothing.

Then again, she decided as she spooned batter into the paper muffin cups, if Cage was as determined as she'd sensed at the meeting, a few inconveniences weren't going to stop him.

She slid the pan into the oven and set the timer. She'd been up since six and had already dressed in a beige cotton blouse with tiny white buttons, darker beige slacks, and white sandals. She'd secured her shoulder-length dark blond hair in a loose twist that was up and off her neck. Deliberately she hadn't done anything with her appearance that she didn't do every morning. Because of the heat and humidity, she wore little makeup in the summer, and even though it was raining today and much cooler, she had no intention of primping as if she and Cage would be anything except temporary neighbors.

Haley assembled the coffeemaker, setting it for six cups rather than her usual four. She put mugs in a basket, added napkins, a carton of cream and then sugar, leaving room for the muffins on top. This is just being thoughtful, she reasoned to herself. After all, he probably hasn't bought any groceries. Anyway, taking coffee and muffins would give her a chance to see him in full daylight, and thereby dispel all those evocative sensations that had rocked through her at the meeting.

When he'd stopped to get the apartment key, the time they spent together had been brief. Little had been said beyond the necessary exchanges, but Haley had noted that he seemed remote and especially cool toward her. He'd taken the key, thanked her for the offer to park his cycle in her hall, but said the bike had been taken care of. He'd muttered a gruff good-night before retreating.

The oven timer rang. After she tested the muffins for doneness, she arranged them on a foil plate in the basket. As she poured the hot coffee into an insulated carafe, a thought struck her. Of course! Why hadn't she thought of it sooner? Besides being a good neighbor, she had a perfectly legitimate reason for a visit. The rent for Earl. She intended to call him later at his daughter's to tell him about Cage. Given Earl's penchant for frugality, the first thing he'd ask was if she'd gotten the rent and a damage deposit.

Outside, a light rain shower swept down the sidewalk. Dressed in a yellow slicker and carrying her basket, Haley crossed the street. As she approached his apartment, she felt a kind of anticipation that didn't bear close examination. Quickly she reminded herself that her response was only because he was different from the men she usually dealt with—self-contained, as if he needed no one, which he probably didn't. No doubt he could survive in an isolated environment with little difficulty. With that kind of disciplined mentality, he probably wouldn't get steamed because of a few missing niceties in an apartment.

Thoughts of what kind of woman would interest him drifted into her mind. From the few times she remembered Matthew's having spoken about Cage, she recalled that girlfriends were barely mentioned, although she'd known that he'd had a live-in relationship that hadn't lasted very long. Beyond that, Matthew had offered few details, only that the relationships hadn't worked out. At the time, Haley had thought that that generic explanation could very well have fit her own divorce.

Shaking off her musings about his personal likes and motives, she concentrated on the main reason she wanted to at least be neighborly. Cage was Matthew's brother.

Despite her disapproval of his determination to find the drive-by killer, given his work with the DEA—and what Matthew had told her about Cage's deep sense of responsibility toward his younger brother—Cage's fury and desire for revenge weren't surprising. His justified anger, shared by many in the neighborhood, was the reason she'd dreaded seeing him come into the Association meeting. But regardless of how understanding and sympathetic she was to Cage himself, Haley had no intention of endorsing his plan. In fact, she intended to continue to try to get him to change his mind. The Mayflower Heights Association had enough problems with the drug dealers. They didn't need to get caught up in Cage Murdock's personal vendetta.

Taking a deep breath and arranging her face into a friendly but neutral expression, she knocked on the door of his first floor apartment.

"Yeah, come on in."

She turned the knob and pushed the door open with her hip. When she turned around, she saw him sprawled in a gray recliner, wearing a pair of very old jeans. He wore no shirt, and Haley quickly averted her gaze from his thick black chest hair. Around his neck hung a silver chain that caught her attention because Cage wearing any kind of jewelry struck her as incongruous. His mussed hair looked as if he'd just dragged his hands through it, instead of a comb. His eyes were guarded, though the wintry blue warmed a fraction when he saw the coffee carafe.

Cage lowered his bare feet to the floor and swept a pile of papers off the coffee table and onto the the small couch. She noticed a large container of take-out coffee on a side table. He carefully rearranged a mass of newspaper clippings that he put on the floor beside the chair.

"If I'd known you were coming, I wouldn't have sent Kevin out for coffee."

After setting down her basket, she took off her slicker. Then she brought out the breakfast items, placing them on the coffee table. "Kevin was up this early? Alicia must be in shock," she said, keeping her eyes averted. She wasn't sure what she'd expected, but a shirtless Cage definitely wasn't it. Especially when the rainy morning had darkened the skies and given the softly lit room a drowsy intimacy. The combination did nothing to ease her nerves.

Cage watched her wordlessly, and she wondered if he sensed her nervousness. She told herself the reaction was silly and childish, but nevertheless she fussed with the mugs and tried to recall if she'd ever felt so strained around a man. Certainly she'd been in situations, after her divorce, when men had made raucous passes that she'd easily handled with a curt dismissal.

Cage had done nothing like that. Not even by the wildest stretch of her imagination could she add up those electric moments from the previous night and blame her present keyed-up unease on them. The quandary of emotions scurrying inside her now delved deep. The problem wasn't the intimacy of the room, or the morning darkness, or Cage without a shirt.

Cage, himself, unbalanced her.

Yet she'd known that the night before. But now, in these few beginning moments, a new concern emerged—the threat that his unbalancing her might complicate being around him.

The entire idea was ridiculous, out of any reasonable realm of possibility, and dumb, she admonished herself sternly.

And the last dumb thing she'd done had been to marry Philip and foolishly overlook his attempts to control her.

Thinking back, she could only blame the stars in her eyes. But she was older now, far more savvy about men's motives and a lot less willing to trust either them or those motives.

Realizing she'd been quiet too long, she seized upon the uncomplicated topic of Kevin. Briskly she said, "This morning he's bringing you coffee, and last night he was worried about your motorcycle. I think you have a permanent friend." She set the muffins close to Cage and poured the coffee.

"Yeah, I know. When I got back here, he was waiting for me, armed with horror stories about what would happen to my bike if I left it on the street. Just cream," he said when she reached for the sugar. He took the offered mug from her, and one of the warm muffins. Taking a bite, he closed his eyes as if savoring the taste, then took a swallow of coffee. He relaxed back in the chair and again propped his bare feet on the edge of the table. "These are great, Haley," he said, gesturing with a chunk of muffin.

For no reason that made sense, Haley felt as if she'd been complimented by a discerning food critic. Less tense now, she settled on the couch, crossed her legs and took a sip from her own mug. "So what did you do with your motorcycle?"

"Since I didn't want to fume up your hall, I took Kevin's other suggestion and parked it behind your apartment building."

She knew exactly where. There was a sheltered area that had been enclosed some years ago, when her parents had considered getting a dog. When they'd changed their mind, they'd used the area for storage. "To be honest, Cage, when Kevin said you had a motorcycle, I was surprised you would even consider bringing it here. Leaving anything that easy to steal on the street is an invitation to thieves. What had you planned if Kevin hadn't made the suggestion?"

"To park it in your storage area," he said matter-of-factly as he reached for another muffin. "Do you mind?"

"I brought them for you to eat." She watched him bite into the second one. "Then, Kevin telling you . . ."

"Just confirmed what I already knew."

"You allowed Kevin to think he knew more than you did?" she asked, knowing that that single acknowledgement to protect Kevin's ego would have the teenager championing Cage. But then, Kevin's admiration of Cage had already been obvious at the meeting.

Cage shrugged. "At the moment, he does know more. He knows Standish Street, who's on whose side, the kind of cash involved with the drug dealing, and how the local gangs and their weapons figure into the mix."

"Such as who owned the gun that killed Matthew."

"Exactly." He gave her a steady look, as if expecting another lecture on nonviolence.

Her earlier tension returned, as well as a solid reason why any feelings about Cage were ridiculous. She couldn't abide his mission for revenge. "I'm sure the police are doing all they can to find the killer."

"I'm sure they are," he murmured agreeably, as though he had no intention of getting into another argument over his reasons for being here. "A safe place for the bike was one of the considerations before I decided to rent an apartment. I don't ride often, because I'm away so much, but I always looked forward to it when I came back to see Matt. So, since I'd planned to spend some time in Mayflower Heights, I checked out places where the cycle would be safe before I saw you at the meeting."

Haley sipped her coffee. She'd assumed he'd made contact with her because she'd known Matthew better than the others. It was rather disconcerting to know that the chainlink fence to protect his motorcycle had been the reason. And on top of that, hearing that he'd been lurking around, checking out her and the neighborhood, unsettled her. She had a sense of playing catch-up, a sense of him only answering the questions she directly asked. "So last night wasn't your first visit since Matthew's death?"

"Third, actually. I was here the day before the funeral, and then again a few days ago."

Haley wasn't exactly sure why she wasn't surprised. If nothing else, his admission confirmed that Cage Murdock hadn't just wildly leaped into vengeance mode. He must have carefully planned and executed his arrival at the meeting. Nothing done by happenstance; he hadn't walked into the store out of curiosity, or to get a reaction from the Association. Nor, now that she thought about it, had he made mention of the motorcycle. Therefore, his timed arrival had been expressly to deal with her.

Damn. He was trying to unbalance her, to let her know that if she didn't cooperate, then he'd simply go around her. Or perhaps he was showing her how little he needed her help so that she *would* cooperate.

Haley's thoughts suddenly focused on those evocative sensations that had sprung up between them, sensations that still lingered, despite her resolve moments ago to ignore them. Those feelings hadn't been planned, at least not on her part. And, she'd assumed, not anticipated by him, either. Hadn't he said this can't happen? But if he did nothing by happenstance...

Her frown was troubled. Since she barely knew Cage, she couldn't possibly know his motives. No doubt Kevin had believed that he'd provided the answer to keeping the cycle safe, yet Cage had freely admitted to her that he'd already known about the chain-linked area. Had Cage used that same basic tactic with her? Had he simply allowed that awareness-exchange between them to go unchecked? Had he seen her confusion as a way of keeping her off guard?

Haley didn't want to believe she could be that easily duped, nor did she want to think he'd been deliberately manipulative. And yet...

You're allowing this to get ridiculously complex, she warned herself. In the first place, Cage hadn't had to make the admission about Kevin. And, in a broader sense, Cage was right—Kevin did know more about Standish Street and the goings-on than Cage did. As far as those seconds of sexual awareness the previous night were concerned, Haley decided, if seducing her to get her cooperation was part of his plan, he wouldn't have backed off.

When she glanced up, she had the distinct feeling he'd been studying her, as if taking a seat on the sidelines of her mind. Again she felt a subliminal swirl of tension between them.

"More coffee?" she asked in a raspy voice.

He shook his head. Staring at her as if he were carefully considering his next words, he said, "Your hair is different. Longer than when Matt introduced us last year."

Haley's eyes widened in astonishment, not at his recalling that rather strained introduction, but at his having taken note of a personal detail about her. "You're very observant," she said.

"Anything or anyone who influenced Matt got my attention," he said, continuing to study her, as if sorting out whether to abandon the topic or continue.

Haley waited for him to say more. The rain slashed down the window, and in the distance came the crack of thunder.

Better to take the initiative now, she thought, and not let the growing tension rattle her. She gripped her mug, trying to absorb its warmth into her cold fingers. "If I recall correctly, you were home for a few days to celebrate Matthew joining Donovan and Cross."

"One of the better law firms in Rhode Island," he added, his pride in his younger brother's accomplishments obvious.

"Yes, I believe it is considered to be so."

"You weren't particularly impressed, were you?"

"Matthew was a fine attorney and certainly deserved the invitation."

Cage said nothing, watching her with a steadiness that made her edgy. She sighed. Why was she parrying with him? No doubt Matthew had told his brother what she'd said. Yes, she'd been vocal about her concern when Matthew had said he was leaving his small practice a few blocks away from Mayflower Heights to join the Providence firm. But they'd been friends, and she'd given her personal opinion of the move as a friend. Besides, opinion and influencing weren't the same thing.

More than a little defensively, she said, "I just wasn't convinced that Matthew really wanted to practice law in such a high-pressure environment."

"In contrast to getting killed in this garden of low-pressure delights," he said sagely. "At least the high pressure didn't come equipped with an assault weapon."

Haley stiffened at the sarcasm. "Matthew asked my opinion, and I gave it. Since he went with Donovan and Cross, he obviously paid little attention to what I thought." Wincing inwardly, she realized that the more she said, the deeper she dug a hole she would eventually not be able to get out of. She knew that Cage laid some blame on her for Matthew's death, if only because he'd been such a frequent visitor to Mayflower Heights. And, from a wider perspective, she understood Cage's reasoning. If Matthew hadn't been here, he wouldn't be dead.

Then again, understanding Cage wasn't the same as just accepting his reasoning. She'd listened too many times herself to Matthew talk of wanting Cage's opinion, which Haley had interpreted as wanting his older brother's approval.

He got to his feet, and her mouth went just a little dry. He seemed taller, leaner and more muscled than last night. His jeans hung low, and her gaze dipped to the buttoned fly before moving quickly upward to concentrate on the silver chain around his neck. When she lifted her lashes and met his blue eyes, she made herself not look away.

He said nothing, which both relieved and worried her. Would this be another way he planned to unbalance her? Not likely, she reminded herself firmly. She cleared her throat. "As long as we're discussing opinions, did *you* ask Matthew what he wanted? Or even how he felt?"

Cage's expression was grim, and his eyes were hard. "Yeah, as a matter of fact I did. I threw out a few suggestions, but Matt wanted what I wanted him to do. Join Donovan and Cross."

Haley knew that if she was prudent she would simply nod and let this issue drop right here. Obviously Cage had regarded her as a stumbling block in his brother's life, or, more to the point, believed that she'd raised questions in Matthew's mind about how much Cage influenced him. But surely Cage had to know how much his opinion had affected Matthew.

Softly she said, "Matthew knew you wanted the best for him. It was evident in the way you made him stay in school, helped pay his way through college and then law school. He felt a huge gratitude toward you. He told me how, after your father died, you raised him and supported him on your own, how determined you were that he escape the poverty you both grew up in. It was certainly commendable—"

"Stop," he snapped. "You sound like you're about to pin some medal on me. No commendations. Getting him out of the hellhole where we lived was necessary to his survival."

She was startled by his sharpness. "And necessary for your survival, as well."

"I didn't matter. Matt did." Just the way Cage said it sent shivers down her spine.

She tried another avenue. "He also said you were determined he was going to have money and success."

"Yeah, but my motive was fairly clear-cut. I didn't want him to end up dead in the street like our old man did," he said succinctly, then swore under his breath, obviously annoyed that he'd said as much as he had. He walked over to the windows that faced Standish Street.

My God, she thought, Matthew's death had been history repeating itself. No wonder Cage had wanted Matthew to practice law far away from a high-crime area like Mayflower Heights. He'd wanted to lessen the chance of a tragedy like the one that had happened to their father. Certainly understandable, and yet, Cage hadn't taken his own advice and pursued some safe career. In fact, he'd done exactly the opposite. Why?

She wondered if his own career choice had been as deliberately planned as the one he'd laid out for Matthew. One thing, however, was clear to Haley. Cage's desire to avenge his brother went a lot deeper than any knee-jerk eye-for-an-eye angle.

Haley set her mug down and crossed to where he stood. Without pretense or excuse, she slipped her arms around him. He stiffened, but more in surprise than rejection, and

Haley tightened her arms before he could pull away. His warm skin, the solid feel of his back, the clean scent of him, all made him seem vulnerable. Holding this man was something she'd wanted to do at the funeral, if for no other reason than to show him that she, too, grieved for Matthew.

With her cheek against his back, she whispered, "I didn't know about your father, Cage."

"Now you do," he said bluntly. He gripped her wrists and tugged her hands loose from around him.

She didn't protest when he broke the contact between them. Trying to be agreeable, she said, "And you've answered some of my questions. At least now I understand why you're so angry."

This time he stepped around her, his movements as dismissive as the words that followed. "Just what I needed. An understanding woman."

He sat down again, and Haley felt the curtain of coldness drop between them. The silver chain glistened against the lawn of black chest hair.

"Sit down, Haley."

She sighed and did as he requested. Letting the issue of Matthew drop, she decided to get Earl's rent taken care of.

He glanced at the mugs, then at the almost empty basket, and finally at her. "Now that we've had coffee and muffins and you've discovered all these interesting tidbits about Matt and me, let's deal with the other reasons you're here."

His sudden agreeability sounded ominous. In an even voice, she said, "Besides the rent for Earl, there *are* other reasons."

"There always are," he muttered as he stretched his legs out and dipped his fingers in his jean pocket. He pulled out a folded-in-half wad of cash. Tossing it on the table, he said, "That should cover a month plus extra, in case I scratch anything."

Without counting it, she knew just by the hundreds that were visible that there was more than Earl usually got. Now she really felt guilty about the items he'd requested. "Uh, about the things that you wanted . . ."

"The bed, the microwave and the hot water?"

"Yes." Taking a deep breath, she plunged in before she had a chance to reconsider what she was doing. "I can switch beds with you. Mine is a queen-size. And since I'm sure Earl would want his tenant to be happy, an inexpensive microwave shouldn't be a problem. As for the hot water..." She hesitated, and then added quickly, "You're welcome to use the shower in my apartment."

He lifted his brows, and for the first time since he'd walked into the meeting the night before, she saw puzzlement. "First muffins, and now all this. Why?"

"I'm trying to be cooperative."

"Correct me if I'm wrong, but a few hours ago you distinctly told me you wanted me to leave."

"You're obviously not going to do that."

"And so you're going to be so generous, kind and neighborly that I'll feel guilty, reassess my vengeful motives and turn into a nice boy."

"Why do you assume *my* motives are ulterior?"

"Because most people's are."

"That's a cynical way of looking at things."

"Realistic."

"But, in this case, wrong." Haley picked up the folded cash and put it in the bottom of the carton. "How long do you plan to be here?"

"I took my vacation time, so about three weeks, give or take a few days."

Haley wondered how he could place a definite time limit on his revenge, as if it were a business venture. "How can you know you'll do what you said you're going to do in three weeks?"

"Don't couch your question in generalities, Haley. I'm not here on a goodwill tour. I'm here to get the son of a bitch who killed Matt."

"I know that, but how can you be so sure of how long it will take? I mean, even the police aren't able to predict when they can make an arrest."

"*I'm* sure. Let's leave it at that. I've already said a hell of a lot more to you than I intended," he said in a clipped voice.

"In other words, there's a lot of stuff you're never going to tell me." She couldn't suppress an inner worry about just exactly what might happen to Cage. Matthew's death might have been incidental, but should the people responsible learn that someone was after them, Cage could very well end up like his brother.

In a neutral tone, he said, "I'm renting an apartment, Haley, not asking you to be my confessor. Your disapproval of me is obvious but irrelevant." He once again propped his feet on the table.

Haley glared at him, that self-containment she'd noted about him earlier now very much back in place. If he wanted to be brutally frank, then she could be, too. "You know, it would take very little for me to dislike you."

For a moment, Haley thought she saw a tiny window of softness in his eyes, but then it was gone.

After a sigh, he said, "Haley, you're attractive, idealistic, and firmly dedicated to your efforts here. Matt praised you eloquently just about every time we talked." He hesitated, and Haley braced herself. His blue eyes met hers directly. He was plainly making no effort to hedge or apologize. "I'm nothing like Matt. I'm not here to become anyone's pal, leader, hero, good neighbor or lover. I'm here for one thing, and one thing only. When that's accomplished, I'll be gone. You don't have to understand me, worry about me, feed me or even notice me. And you sure as hell don't have to like me."

Haley sat speechless.

Cage stood and again walked to the window that looked out on a rainy Standish Street. When he didn't turn around or say anything further, Haley decided it was time for her to make her exit. She began to gather up their mugs and napkins.

Surprisingly, she hadn't take offense at his words, perhaps because they'd been unpretentious and left no room for debate or discussion, never mind argument. This is the way it is. "Like it or don't like it, but live with it" about summed up his feelings. Whether it was his straightforward, no-holds-barred approach or her own inner core of curiosity about him, Haley couldn't deny her fascination.

She wondered if her reaction was an innately female one, or something deeper. Challenge, perhaps—not taking no for an answer, and not accepting impossible odds as being impossible. Meeting challenges, such as remaining in Mayflower Heights, had spilled into a greater challenge, her desire to drive out the drug dealers.

Cage, however, would be more of an obstacle than a challenge. First she would have to cut through the hard veneer. She'd been lucky that he'd opened the door a little with the mention of his father, but she knew she couldn't count on such easily given revelations in the future. She didn't believe he was often careless with either his feelings or his thoughts.

She brushed up the crumbs. The carafe was still half-full, so she decided to leave that, along with the cream and the rest of the muffins.

Picking up her slicker where she'd left it, she pushed her arms into the garment. Just as she was about to tell him that as soon as the rain stopped they could switch beds, he turned around.

"I'm curious," he said thoughtfully.

"Oh? About what?"

"Why you haven't moved. I know you own the apartment house, but living in it in this neighborhood is risky as hell."

"This is my home. I grew up in this neighborhood, and besides, why *should* I move? For that matter, why should anyone who's lived here all their life? The drug dealers are the intruders. They're the ones who have to move."

"And just what are you using to convince them? I mean, since violence and weapons are out of the running."

She narrowed her eyes. "You're being deliberately sarcastic."

"I'm asking you a perfectly logical question. What's going to make them leave?"

"We are. We've used video cameras and recorded drug sales, then turned the tapes over to the police. Some arrests have been made. We've used bullhorns and walked in one big unit, telling them to leave and taking down license-plate numbers of cars that come from out of the area to buy drugs. The police have stopped a few of those. But our main goal is letting the dealers know we aren't going to put up with them anymore. We'd made good progress. Most of the violence we'd seen before Matthew was shot came from the gangs and the dealers themselves, but the drive-by has frightened many into going back behind locked doors."

"Not quite. You and the group I saw last night didn't seem to be intimidated."

"Mostly we're angry. The dealers want us frightened, and I'm sure they know that what happened to Matthew reduced our numbers. One thing I do know. They want us to stay silent and scared so that we'll leave them alone."

"I'm not the only one who's observant," he said, making no attempt to hide his admiration at her savvy. Strangely, Haley felt a tiny leap of pleasure. Cage asked, "Have you thought of the possibility that they shot Matt to warn the Association off?"

Haley couldn't believe how easily they were discussing this topic. Cage was talking and acting as if they had a common goal that could be reached on the same level. She slipped her hands into the slicker's slash pockets. "It occurred to me, but it seemed too much of a fluke. They would have had no way of knowing Matt, or anyone, for that matter, would be on the street that night. Around here, the only ones out after dark are the dealers and the buyers. What do you think?"

"It's just a question. Since most of the Association is back hiding in their homes—if that was the killer's objective in shooting Matt—then it worked."

"But Matthew didn't even live down here."

"But you do."

Her eyes widened. "You think they killed Matthew because he knew me? How would they have known he was going to be here that night?"

"They know about you, Haley. Matt wasn't their problem, nor is the Association itself. *You're* their problem. If you didn't exist, the Association wouldn't either. They know that. And, they're too smart to come after you directly, at least not yet. For the time being, they're going to send some warnings. Drug dealers don't like attention. They don't want to make the kind of trouble that could get them on the evening news, they just want to move their product from point of origin to destination. Money and territory are their objectives. Right now, you're a problem for them, but more on the hassle and bother level than anything else. They probably view you as just some do-gooder broad who, if not warned off, could become a real pain in the ass. They could have been sending a warning that they'd intended to be a strong scare tactic, but instead became a drive-by killing."

Haley crossed over to the window. The curb where Matthew had fallen after he'd been shot was just a few yards away. A cold shiver ran through her. Facing Cage once more, she asked warily, "You think they were firing at my apartment house?"

He lifted the newspaper clippings he'd put aside when she'd first come in. "From what I've read about the slime that hangs out around here, missing their objective doesn't happen often."

She almost didn't want to ask the question. "You think they'll try again?"

"Are you planning on moving to the mountains anytime soon?"

She shook her head.

"Then yeah, they'll be back."

"The police—"

"I know some of the cops in this area, and they do the best they can. They probably don't have enough manpower to patrol down here constantly. But none of that changes the fact that putting away Matt's killer could send a strong message."

"Are you asking me to help you play out this revenge scenario of yours?"

He shook his head. "I'm asking you to let me do what I came to do."

"The possibility of stopping you, Cage, seems more than remote." She walked past him, intent on leaving.

He caught her arm, turning her so that she had to face him. In a low voice, he said, "You already managed to get me to tell you more than I've ever told any woman." He cut off her protest by tucking a loose strand of hair behind her ear. "I never should have made the comment about your hair."

Haley knew she shouldn't ask, knew he would prefer that she just accept his explanation. "Why did you?"

He stared down into her eyes, and she felt the intensity clear to her soul. With clear reluctance, he said, "Because I remembered how it caught the sun at Matt's funeral. And when the preacher was saying the final prayers, I was thinking about the way your hair would feel in my hands."

Haley swallowed, trying to break the ringing in her ears.

He tipped her chin upward, holding it so that she couldn't look away. "I don't want those kind of thoughts about you," he said grimly, almost to himself. "I don't want to think anything about you. I told you last night . . ."

"This can't happen. . . ." she whispered, repeating his words so naturally that she knew they sounded as if they reflected her feelings, as well as his.

The intensity of his stare made her wonder suddenly if he would lower his head and kiss her. She should be pushing him away, protesting the callused feel of his thumbs against her chin. She shouldn't be standing here in some kind of breathless anticipation.

Cage scowled. "You're going to be a major headache if I'm not damn careful."

Haley bristled, his bluntness breaking the mystical spell. "You can relax, Cage Murdock. I have no desire to be yours or any man's headache."

She tried to back away, but he held her fast. Then, shaking her a little, he said, "Lay off the the huffy-outraged-female stuff. I'm not talking about some silly flirtation and you know it."

He slid his hands into her hair, destroying her pinned-up style. His mouth halted just a breath from hers, and Haley wondered briefly if his kiss would be some point of no return. She felt as if her pulse and heart were spinning in opposite directions. The warmth of his body offered nothing as simple as awareness—heat sizzled into an erotic flame, lapping and lingering and burning into her nerve endings.

She curled her fingers around his wrists. Licking the dry heat from her lips, she whispered, "Stop, please . . ."

He stared at her mouth for so long she was sure he'd memorized every line. In a low, precise voice, he murmured, "I want you out of here, Haley. Just get your stuff and go away."

She nodded mutely, and staggered a little when he released her. She fumbled, getting ahold of the carrier, and then quickly moved to the door. He held it open, but said nothing when she made her exit.

Back in her own apartment, she breathed deeply, waiting for the drenching relief at having escaped to wash over her.

Instead she realized, with a sinking heart, that if he hadn't sent her away, she might have allowed far more than just a kiss.

Chapter 3

Cage leaned against the door for a full five minutes after she left. His heart pounded, and to his disgust his blood hummed with a too-familiar energy. If he was about to lead a drug raid, then the building tension would be understandable. From his years with the DEA, he knew that the body reacted to the anticipation of a major drug bust the same way it did in anticipation of good sex.

Face facts, Murdock, it's been a while. Maybe that explained his internal havoc when it came to Haley Stewart. It wasn't focused on her specifically, but was just a gut-deep sexual response from weeks of celibacy.

He thought about that for a few seconds, then swore fluently. He'd had no such reaction to Brenda what's-her-name, that legal secretary from Matt's law firm. Just an hour before he'd arrived at the Association's meeting, Brenda had all but invited him to bed. He'd just come out of Matt's condo, preoccupied with folders of newspaper clippings about Mayflower Heights that he'd found among his brother's things. Brenda had stepped out of a red convertible. At first he'd paid no attention to her, but she'd hurried up to him as if they'd been ongoing lovers.

After a few words of greeting, she'd made a breathless declaration that she'd been so hoping to connect with him before he left town. She'd then pressed up against him, leaving no room for doubt as to what she meant by "connect." Whether it had been her lack of subtlety, or her bold comment that she just *adored* playing with "bad boys," Cage had disentangled himself, saying something about "another woman, another arrangement." Then he'd gotten on his cycle and left.

Cage grimaced now at the memory. Either he was getting too old, or Brenda had reinforced the fact that he'd never been turned on by overly aggressive women.

Odd, he thought now as he poured himself another mug of coffee. Brenda had been blatantly obvious, and he'd been turned off, but that didn't surprise him as much as his reaction to Haley. She hadn't done anything even remotely suggestive, and his insides were churning.

He lifted the mug and sipped, scowling as he noted that his hands still carried the scent of her hair. He could easily trace the shape of her mouth in his memory, could recall the rich green of her eyes, just as clearly as he could still feel the softness of her cheek against his back.

Her voice intrigued him. The slight huskiness sounded too innocent, too unaffected by the realities of having lived most of her life in the inner city. He would have expected crassness, not polish, a hardened edge that would be reflected in her eyes, not the idealism that already he found disturbing.

How could anyone live in this hellhole and be idealistic? he wondered. And yet he couldn't deny her intelligence or her courage. Videotaping drug deals and being so vocal she'd gotten the entire neighborhood involved had to be a boost to those who believed in a do-gooder philosophy.

Cage didn't deny his deliberate attempt to throw her off balance. He'd hoped that if she assumed he was trying to coerce her into cooperating with him she'd be so outraged she'd stalk out, and that would be that. He could do what he came to do, and she wouldn't be in the way. Instead, she'd stood her ground, and now he was the one flailing around wondering what in hell to do next.

"Damn," he murmured as he went into the small but functional and clean kitchen and put his mug in the sink. Finding Matt's killer was why he was here. Since that goal hadn't changed, why in hell did he feel gripped by thoughts of Haley Stewart?

He went back to the living room. Glaring at the food she'd left for him, he muttered in disgust, "And home-made muffins, for God's sake. Unaffected by a sexual come-on, but disarmed by hot muffins." At the low sound of his own voice, he clamped his lips together. Terrific, now he was babbling to himself. Keep this up and he'd be ready for a rubber room.

Wanting only to clear his mind of any thoughts of her, he swept up the remaining muffins and dumped them in the kitchen trash can. He rinsed out the carafe and the mug and put them aside to return to her. Better yet, he'd have Kevin return them. Cage knew he'd be better off if he kept his distance. No distractions. Not sexual ones, and not neighborly ones.

Back in the living room, he opened a window, ignoring the rain that splashed into the room. Amazingly, the neighborhood looked less dangerous under the overcast sky. Maybe it was because all the hoodlums were holed up where it was dry. He studied what he could see of Standish Street. The combat-zone raggedness permeated the area, the one bright spot of color a window box of flowers outside one of Haley's windows. A corner store at the far end, a trash-littered vacant lot, and then the abandoned store where the Association held their meetings. Dotting the street were rambling, elephant-size houses that had been built more than fifty years ago. Some were shabby, but a few, like Haley's, were well cared-for. All, again like Haley's, had been turned into apartment buildings. At one time, Cage realized, this had probably been a close-knit, ethnically diverse community that had been safe and clean. Obviously Haley's intent was to restore the streets to what they once had been—safe and friendly.

He folded his arms and listened to the rain, trying to ignore the fact that once again she was back in his mind. Despite her tenaciousness, Cage had no faith an inner-city miracle would occur, no matter how deep Haley's commitment. And the sooner he did what he came to do and got the hell away from here, the better.

He concentrated on his brother, on the sinking, dead feeling he'd felt when the police had called to tell him Matt had been killed. His fury at the murderer, Cage admitted, had been deep, cold and so focused that he knew if the bastard had stepped in front of him he would have killed him. No regret, no wishy-washy second thoughts, no worry that he would probably go to prison. For Cage, in those few days before and after the funeral, calculated revenge and the satisfaction that would follow had been something he'd feasted on with an anticipation that shocked even him.

Now he was just coldly resolute. And he knew that in some ways that was more dangerous and more deadly. Then he'd acquired this distraction in the form of one Haley Stewart. At first he'd planned to just ignore her, but her influence in the neighborhood was too deeply imbedded to do that. He'd decided he would face her—as he'd done at the meeting the night before—tell her what he planned to do and be done with it.

He shook his head derisively. In a neighborhood where guns and drugs were as common as comic books, Cage had to wonder if she was an aberration. He didn't even know a woman who cooked anything that required more than a microwave, never mind bringing him homemade muffins, in the rain, at seven in the morning. For that matter, why wasn't Haley married, with a couple of kids, and living in a suburb with a garden and a fence and running for president of the PTA?

He scowled at the realization that since the previous night she'd commanded more of his thoughts than avenging his brother had.

About to close the window, he noticed three scruffy teenage boys who sauntered up the street, oblivious to the rain. They wore jeans and denim jackets that looked as if they'd slept in them. One jacket had a skull and crossbones painted on the back. After glancing from one end of the street to the other, they huddled in the shelter of an abandoned store's doorway. The glow of their cigarettes was clearly visible. Then, with a stealthiness and swiftness that Cage had come to recognize as all too common, he saw the exchange of money for drugs. One boy flipped his cigarette onto the sidewalk, then turned away and tipped his head back. The other two didn't even try to block the view that displayed the teenager snorting his coke buy.

Cage noted a few salient details about the three and made a mental note to talk to Kevin. A too-visible doorway in the rain was an odd place to get high, Cage thought as he wondered if the drug buy was just part of the reason they were there. Maybe they weren't hanging out, but trying to look that way. It was possible, if they'd been sent by someone else to check things out visually. From Cage's own observation, his reading about the neighborhood's crime areas and Haley's comments, he knew the dealers and the buyers were bold from too much power and too few arrests.

He glanced at his watch. It was nearing nine, and he should get back to laying out exactly what he planned to do while he was here. Cage didn't like loose ends and indecision. Since he believed that life left no room for stupidity, lazy attitudes or irresponsibility, he made sure his life didn't get out of his control. He liked things self-contained and manageable.

He went back to the gray lounge chair and picked up the folder of newspaper clippings that he'd found at Matt's condo. They dated back to when Matt had met Haley, and they centered on the growing drug problem in Mayflower Heights. Matt had been concerned enough to collect clippings on drug arrests and other crimes in the area, but Cage had also found information on the Mayflower Heights Association. The clippings had been a godsend, in that they had let him get a good picture of what he would be dealing with, but Matt's reasons for the interest had disturbed Cage.

He settled back in the chair, the folder open on his lap, and stared at the ceiling. For the hundredth time, his last conversation with his brother rolled through his mind.

Cage had been in a Miami phone booth, tired, grimy-hot, and still shaken by the tragic sight of a nine-year-old dead from a drug overdose. He'd walked a while to clear his mind, to try and forget what he knew was becoming a too-familiar sight. Grammar school junkies.

From his pocket he'd extracted a four-day-old message from Matt that could have meant anything: "I've made some plans I want you to know about. Call me as soon as you can."

Cage had refused to speculate, but the wording had held enough holes to create concern. When he'd gotten Matt on the phone, the concern had rapidly changed to a chilled fear followed by anger.

"Are you out of your mind, Matt?"

Matt paused a few seconds, then answered in a resolute tone: "It's time I began making my own decisions."

"This isn't a decision, this is flat-out stupidity." Then, hearing how coldly furious he sounded, Cage took a deep breath and softened his next words. "There is no such thing as inner-city nostalgia, Matt. No one lives there by choice."

"Maybe not you, Cage, but I miss the neighborhood closeness. The condo is so sterile and..."

"Try safe."

"Okay, I agree, but, my God, safe housing can exist in the inner city, too. You and I had some good times when we were kids."

"Oh, yeah, they were just glorious," he said without tempering his sarcasm. "The old man coming home loaded and his wallet emptied. Then getting himself knifed in that alley. The street fights that were so common we wondered what was wrong when a night went by without one. The women who cruised the street, and the one who showed you more about sex than any thirteen-year-old had any business knowing. A hell of a lot of good times."

"Look, Cage, I know you think I'm nuts. And believe me, I appreciate all that you've done. I couldn't have asked for a better brother, but I have to decide for myself where I'm going to live and where I'm going to practice law."

He decided it was a good thing he was in Florida and Matt was in Rhode Island. If Matt were here, he'd take him down to the morgue and show him that nine-year-old, and a few of the other grisly horrors that had become commonplace in those old neighborhoods his younger brother was waxing nostalgic about.

Instead, he focused on what he was sure was the real reason. "Let's cut the bull. You're worried about Haley Stewart, and that's why you want to move down there. You handled her divorce and you became friends. Fine. But appointing yourself as her watchdog is insanity. She doesn't need you. She's got that Association and her tenants. The police probably recognize her voice when she calls."

"You're making her sound like a pest. She's not a hysterical woman, and she doesn't assume every stranger is up to no good. And not once has she said a word to me about needing help."

"Why in hell should she? You're offering it by the bucketful."

"I've tried to get her to move, Cage, but—"

"Since she won't, you're going to move down there. That's just dandy. Is this some white-knight-to-the-rescue syndrome? Or are you planning on buying a gun and becoming her protector?"

"Look, big brother, I know you're just worried that something will happen to me..."

"You're damned right I am," he said fiercely, feeling an uncharacteristic sting in his eyes. "I happen to love you, and, in case you've forgotten, you're the only relative I've got. I'm not too turned on by the idea of you offering yourself up as some sort of inner-city sacrifice."

"Just because I went to law school and my fingernails are clean, that doesn't mean I'm not street-smart. I grew up with you, remember?"

Cage ignored the question. He knew he was getting nowhere, and that scared him. "Matt, listen to me. I haven't asked much of you, but on this one I know what I'm talking about. Don't throw away everything you've accomplished for some altruistic pipe dream that isn't going to get you a damn thing but grief.''

A long silence stretched between them.

"Matt?"

"Damn it, Cage, I had this all settled in my mind. . . ."

At his brother's wavering words, Cage sank back against the side of the phone booth in relief. He immediately took advantage of the tiny crack in Matt's decision that the silence offered. In a warmer tone, he said, "Your hesitation tells me you're not totally sold on the idea."

"I was sold before you called," Matt said grimly.

Cage grinned. "I don't think so, kid. Maybe you were just looking for an excuse to change your mind. Look, I've got some vacation I gotta use, so how about the two of us take off to Maine for a few days? We can rent a cabin, do some fishing, maybe get a little drunk. What do you say?"

Another silence, and Cage had literally held his breath. He'd hoped that if he had a few days with Matt, he could find out exactly why his brother had such a tough time putting the inner city behind him and moving on.

They'd hung up, with Matt finally agreeing to Cage's plans of a few days in Maine. Plans that had never been realized, because hours later Matt had been killed.

Cage closed his eyes now and swore savagely.

Around noon Cage was on the phone with the police when he glanced out the window and saw a peach-colored mattress go by the window. Leading the way toward his front door was Haley.

He gripped the phone and let his head drop forward. Good God, he thought with no small amount of astonishment, she'd been serious about switching beds. "Yeah, I'm still here," he said to the cop as the knock came on the door. "I'll call back later, when Noah's in. Yeah, tell him I'm sorry I missed him. It's been a long time."

Dropping the receiver onto its cradle, he considered not answering the door and then decided she probably had a spare key. Any woman who gave away her bed probably wouldn't be stopped by a locked door. He began to regret ever asking her about empty apartments. He affixed a scowl on his face and made up his mind there would be no bed-switching.

He opened the door, only to be greeted by Haley's broad smile. Cage had pulled on an old T-shirt, but he was still barefoot, still in the worn jeans. Haley, however, had changed clothes. Dressed now in sandals, white shorts and a pink cotton knit top with tiny flowers embroidered on the scalloped neckline, she'd brushed her hair back so that it was held in place by a white band. A few strands had escaped, and her temples were damp from the heat. She looked to him as if she'd just stepped out of a magazine ad that was hyping summer picnics by peaceful streams. Cage knew he had stared a few seconds too long, and he deliberately shuttered his expression.

Behind her was the mattress, standing on its side and flanked by Kevin and Norman Polk, whom Cage remembered from the Association meeting.

"This isn't a bad time, is it?" Haley asked, coming inside the apartment and standing close to him so that the mattress and the movers could get by.

Cage tried to ignore her scent, which drifted along his nerve ends like dancing sparks. Things had gone far enough, and he intended to halt them right here. "A bad time for delivering a peach-colored mattress?" He glanced at his watch. "No, I usually expect them at this time of day at least once a month."

She grinned, but took his words as an "okay," rather than the way he'd intended them. To Kevin and Norman she said, "We'll have to get the single bed out first. Then you guys can go and get my box spring and the frame. Lean the mattress against that wall, " she directed, pointing to the gray-painted area next to the bedroom doorway.

"Haley, we're not going to do this," Cage began, but she took his arm and urged him out of the way.

"Of course we are. We settled it this morning. Kevin, don't knock the picture off the wall."

Kevin executed a quick swing and just missed the framed forest scene by a few inches. He and Norman settled the mattress against the wall and headed toward Cage's bedroom, obviously intent on dismantling the single bed. Cage moved instantly to block their way.

Haley sighed, coming forward. "Cage, please don't be difficult."

"I'm never difficult, but I tend to like being in charge of who goes into my bedroom." He gave her a direct look to let her knew that, despite the calmness in his voice, he was serious. To Kevin and Norman, Cage said, "Why don't you guys take a break and give us a few minutes to settle this?"

When both looked to Haley, as if they needed permission, Cage realized that the influence she had in Mayflower Heights was a lot deeper than he'd originally thought. Finally she nodded. At Kevin's grin, she warned, "No beer."

The grin collapsed. "Ah, hell, you read minds worse than my mother. Cage, tell her that guys my age drink beer all the time."

"Better do what she says, Kevin."

After a resigned grumble, he and Norman exited the apartment.

"Hey, no longer than ten minutes, you guys, and then I want you back here," Haley called after them, and received a nod of compliance.

When they stood alone and face-to-face, Cage propped his hands low on his hips. "Is that how long you think it will take to get your own way?"

"Cage, we settled this...."

"I didn't agree to anything except paying my rent. At the risk of sounding ungrateful, I don't want your bed."

"It has nothing to do with gratitude, it has to do with making sure a tenant is comfortable."

"I didn't come here to be comfortable, I came here—"

She touched her finger to his mouth in such an easy motion that Cage lost track of what he was going to say.

"There's no need for token protests. Everything has already been decided. I called an appliance store that Earl trades with, and they'll deliver a microwave this afternoon." She took her finger away, and he was sure it had left a permanent imprint. Scowling now, and peering out the door for any sign of Kevin and Norman, she added, "If you're not going to be here, I can send Norman over so they don't leave it on the doorstep."

"To be ripped off." He recalled Kevin's concern about his motorcycle.

"Yes."

"I'll be here," he said, thinking that he would just send the microwave back.

"Wonderful. So after we get the beds switched, the only other thing is the hot-water problem."

Somehow he'd lost control of this entire scene, he decided grimly. "It's August. I don't need hot water."

"You look like the type who would take very hot showers no matter what month it was."

He gave her an incredulous look. "I look like the type? Lady, you haven't got a clue as to what type I am."

Her eyes widened at the gruffness in his voice.

Cage dragged one hand through his hair, unable to recall when a woman had so caught him off guard. Maybe he should kiss her, maybe he should just flat-out haul her into his arms, plunge his tongue deep into her mouth and show her just what his "type" was capable of.

He was about to make a comment when another thought occurred to him. Damn it! She'd caught him off guard or off-balance, but she was definitely making him question whether her change in attitude was deliberate. Probably, he decided grimly. No doubt she was getting back at him for his trying the off-balance ploy with *her*. He folded his arms and gave her a direct look.

"Cage, I just meant that we decided earlier that you could use my shower and—"

"Correction. *You* decided."

He took a few steps toward her, but she didn't move.

"Please don't try and intimidate me. It won't work."

"Then let's try a little gut-deep honesty." They stood now with just a few inches were between them. In a low, precise voice, he said, "I don't want to use your shower, I'll survive without the microwave, and I sure as hell don't want to sleep in your bed."

She lowered her head, and then, just as quickly raised it. Cage saw the green in her eyes darken resolutely.

"Saying it that way is deliberately misleading, and you know it."

"And just how is it misleading?"

Cage had to give her credit. She didn't blush or flinch or act like some coquette. "You'll be sleeping in it alone."

He considered a totally inappropriate comeback and decided against it. Then, as if she'd suddenly recognized the volatility of her own comment, she let out a long slow breath.

For the briefest of seconds, he saw something he didn't want to see. Curiosity and a vulnerability that made him see why Matt had felt so compelled to keep an eye on her. He couldn't label it weakness, or some virginal female flutter of fear. Not when he knew that, as sharp as she was and as tenacious as he'd seen her, she really did believe that she could disarm and dissuade a bunch of nasty no-conscience gang members and drug dealers. On some level, Cage concluded, she saw him as just such a challenge, one she intended to meet and conquer, just as she intended to do with the dealers.

He cupped her chin. "Look at me."

"I've made this awkward, haven't I?"

"It's been awkward since last night. And you're being too considerate and too neighborly."

"That's the way most of us are down here. That's why we want our neighborhood back. You could help us, and if we worked together, then maybe we could all find Matt's killer. I want that, too, Cage, just as much as you do."

"This is a go-nowhere subject, Haley."

He didn't know whether it was deliberate or unconscious, but she curled her fingers around his wrist. "All right. I'll drop it for the time being, but I'm going to insist that you take the bed and the other two offers."

"So I'll eventually feel guilty and change my mind?"

"Actually, it has more to do with something you said this morning about you not mattering."

He frowned. "I don't know what you mean."

"When you were talking about getting Matthew out of the inner city, I said that it was a good move for you, too. You said you didn't matter."

"So?"

"But you *do* matter. You mattered more than anything to Matthew. And obviously you matter to the DEA, or you wouldn't be considered one of their best agents."

It took a few seconds for the impact of what she was saying to sink in. The simplicity of her effort to show him that he was important, that what he wanted *did* matter, would have amused him in any other situation. Yet from her he found it both sweetly naive and brilliantly done. In the next instant, though, his suspicious mind immediately leaped to the conclusion that this was yet another ploy to disarm him. Pointedly he said, "I'm not Matt, Haley. I don't have his polish, his ability to understand do-gooders like you, or his good intentions. I know exactly what I am and where I'm going. I've known it since I was ten years old. It makes life clear-cut and simple. No hassles, no involvements, and no worries about the future."

"But that's such a cold way to see things."

"Truthful. Expectation is a cruel game, and I don't play it."

"But you are hopeful. You're hoping to find Matthew's killer."

"That's not a hope, just a hard fact. As I said, when I've found him and dealt with him, then I'll be gone." Why in hell had all this seemed so uncomplicated just twenty-four hours ago? And now he felt as if each comment was like walking across a target range. "Let's back up to all your neighborly offers. For starters, let's just forget about the shower, okay?"

She considered that for a moment. "Only if you promise me that you won't be shy about asking if you change your mind."

"I'll definitely keep a tight rein on my shyness," he said sagely.

"Then you're not going to argue any more about taking the bed and the microwave."

Cage hated this. He hated obligations that required him to accept stuff and be grateful. Yet, despite an almost contrary reaction to someone wanting to do something for him, he found himself weakening. Due, no doubt, to liking the idea of sleeping in her bed. Maybe he was settling for crumbs because he knew the real thing was out of the question.

He peered at the peach-colored mattress languishing against the wall, waiting for its mate, the box spring. It looked fairly new, and he tried to tell himself that she was the only one who had ever slept on it. For reasons that annoyed him with their persistence, he didn't want to think any man had made love to her on it.

"Okay," he said finally. "I'll accept your offer."

She grinned with so much delight, he would have thought she'd just discovered a winning lottery ticket.

He gave her a hard scowl. "But that's it, Haley. I mean it. I don't want you knocking yourself out for me. You're supposed to be cleaning up the neighborhood, not worrying about someone who doesn't need worrying about."

She studied him as if trying to decide just how to respond. Cage raised an eyebrow. He could almost envision the direction her bleeding-heart attitude was going. The next thing she'd be here cooking for him, or checking to see if he had gotten home safe. Damn, he'd had enough. It was time to be decidedly blunt and make sure she knew exactly where he was coming from. Already his body stirred, too quickly, at the thought of her on that mattress, mussed and hot and tugging him down beside her.

Distractions were deadly in his business. His brother had been lulled and distracted by some nostalgic memory of the past, and he'd ended up dead. Cage didn't fear dying, mostly because he'd come close too many times. He *did* fear distractions that could be avoided. And Haley Stewart could too easily distract him.

He took her arm and stalked into the kitchen. Without apology or explanation, he snapped, "I threw the damn muffins out. The coffee stuff is there on the counter, all ready for you to take with you." He took hold of her shoulders and turned her so that she had to look at him. He ignored the hurt look in her eyes. "I'm not kidding, Haley. I don't want to be any more of a bastard than I already am, but I want you to stay away from me."

She pressed her lips together and blinked.

"Don't you dare cry," he warned her.

"No...I wouldn't do that...."

For seemingly endless seconds, they stood there, neither of them speaking. Cage fought the weaving of her scent into his senses, but knew that from that moment on, whenever he was near a woman, he would make the comparison to Haley. He loosened his fingers when he realized he was gripping her too hard and she wasn't trying to pull away.

She took a deep breath and whispered, "I wasn't trying to be a pest, Cage. I just wanted to show you that you matter to me." At what he knew was an obvious look of surprise, she quickly added, "Oh, not in a personal-relationship way, but just as one human being matters to another. Because Matthew was your brother, but also because I think—no, correction, I *know*—that the revenge you're planning is wrong. Wrong legally, but more important wrong for you."

"And just who in hell appointed you guardian of my thoughts and actions?"

"I just want you to rethink what you're doing."

"No, you want me to stop what I'm going to do." He hesitated only a few seconds before he dragged her closer, shoved his hands into her hair so that the white band fell to the floor. He tipped her chin upward. She moistened her lips, then rubbed them together nervously. "For example, I could stop wanting to kiss you. No question, if I did kiss you, it would be about the biggest mistake I could make."

She looked a little shaken by the sudden turn in the conversation. Cage had to credit her with gutsiness. She met his gaze without flinching. "We already agreed that nothing can happen between us."

"When I said that, I was talking about sex."

"Oh..."

He grinned, but just marginally. "Ah, do I detect that the all-together Haley Stewart is a little flustered?"

"Certainly not. I just wasn't expecting you to..." She touched her hands to his waist.

"To say what we've both been thinking about."

"I hardly know you."

"And I hardly know you, which has nothing to do with anything."

She closed her eyes briefly, as if acknowledging the truth of his statement. Again she rubbed her lips together. Cage murmured, "Maybe if I kissed you...just once. Maybe..."

The familiar hum deep in his body began to build, and Cage made himself stay perfectly still. The green of her eyes made him wonder just how deep the color became when she was aroused. And from that single thought others tumbled, one into another, as if this woman could provide something he'd never experienced.

The passing moments hung in soft breathing suspension. Their mouths were so close that just the tiniest motion would have given him a taste. Suddenly Cage knew he was about to step onto some slippery slope. He damned himself for refusing to take what he wanted, while at the same time reminding himself that involvement with a woman at this particular time would take his attention from the matter at hand. Namely finding his brother's killer.

He let go of her, and she stepped back immediately. Cage stared at her, at the warm slash of color on her cheeks that he was sure had nothing to do with the August heat. Her breasts rose and fell just a little more quickly than normal.

Finally, she whispered, "Now I really do feel awkward...."

"Better awkward now than later."

She blinked and glanced away. "Of course, you're right. It's probably a good thing that we had this, uh...well, moment of...uh..."

"Enlightenment?" he offered.

"Yes," she said, and smiled with the kind of relief that indicated the subject had been concluded. At the sound of approaching voices, she slipped out of his hold and gathered up the carafe. "Kevin and Norman are back, so we can get things finished up. I'll go and get the sheets and pillows for the bed."

Cage watched her leave the kitchen and wondered how all this had happened. Maybe he needed a vacation, or maybe he needed the mind-numbing feel of some woman who wouldn't argue with him or try to get into his head or, worse, make him too preoccupied with wanting her.

Maybe he'd give Brenda what's-her-name a call. He grimaced at the thought and knew that, Haley or no Haley, he wouldn't contact Brenda. Just as he knew that keeping his distance from Haley was going to be the test of a lifetime.

Moments later, Cage was in his bedroom, helping Kevin and Norman dismantle the single bed. Once they had the frame for the queen-size in place, the box spring was brought in, and then the mattress. The small room and the large bed made the room feel stuffy and hot. Besides the bed, there was a dresser and a small night table. The walls were a generic blue, and the last tenant had left a poster on the wall showing a composite of sights to be seen down in Newport.

Cage wiped the sweat off his face and decided he would buy either a fan or an air conditioner for the single window.

Cage thanked the two men for their help, and Norman left the apartment. Kevin was about to when Cage stopped him. "I wanted to ask you something."

"Sure."

"I saw three kids earlier, about your age." Cage went on to describe them. "You know any of them?"

"Yeah, I know the one doin' the coke. His older brother deals a few blocks away. Over where a few of the gangs hang out. There's a variety store on the next block. Most of the guys hang around there. The kid doin' the coke is a cycle freak."

Cage grinned. Maybe if he rode the bike and the kid was interested in it . . . "Sounds good. Thanks for the help."

By the time Cage closed the door, he felt good. He'd made progress, and the closer he got to finding the killer, the sooner he could get out of here.

It wasn't until he'd left the apartment and headed for the fenced-in storage area where his motorcycle was that he realized he'd told Haley he'd be home when they delivered the microwave. Shaking his head, he decided the hell with it. They'd probably take it back if no one was there to take it. If it got ripped off, he'd just pay for it.

A few minutes later, he'd just started the bike when Haley appeared with her arms filled with sheets and pillows.

He swore as he rode the bike the short distance to where she stood.

"You have a key to the place?" he shouted over the roar of the engine.

She nodded.

"Then just leave the stuff inside the door. I'll take care of it when I get back." Then, before she could argue with him, he roared off down the street.

Chapter 4

Haley saw the Venoms when she came out of the drugstore.

Swaggering, nasty and ominous, the five gang members fanned out so that they flanked her.

The first one smirked. "Hey, will you look at what we got here."

"She don't look happy that we're here greetin' her, does she?"

A tremor worked into a tight ache in the pit of her stomach, but Haley kept her eyes straight ahead, ignoring them. She'd encountered the kids on Standish Street who liked to intimidate and act tough, but usually it was more bravado than action. From the rumors she'd heard about the Venoms, though, she knew enough to be terrified.

Grinning and gesturing, two of them were suddenly in front of her, walking backward. Still wearing her white shorts and pink scalloped top, she felt leering gazes crawl up her legs and linger on her breasts.

One of them thrust his hips forward, then used his finger for emphasis. "A bitch in heat, and I got just the thing to take care of that."

All wore jeans, and some were shirtless. One carried a blackjack, and another had a switchblade that he opened and closed in such a way that Haley guessed it was an unconscious habit. Another carried a handgun blatantly tucked in the waistband of his jeans.

Haley clutched the plastic bag that held her purchases. She carried little money; it was a habit followed by most of the people in the neighborhood because of street shakedowns and all-out thievery. Now she almost wished they were after money. She knew better, though. Everyone in and around Mayflower Heights had heard the scary stories. Venom members had no conscience, no fear of being caught, and no motive for the mayhem they caused beyond the desire for some vicious thrill.

They circled and closed around her so that she had to stop or run right into them.

The leader—at least she assumed he was the leader, since the others all waited in deference to him—slung an arm around her neck. Big and dense, he looked as if he'd never outgrown a schoolboy-bully attitude. His fleshy arm squeezed her, feeling like a thick sausage, weighty and slick. She tried to fling it off, but he yanked so tight that she choked. Dangling from his other hand was the blackjack that he held with an ease that said he knew just how to use it. Haley tried without success to swallow the fear lodged in her throat.

Smugly, and with a biting smoothness, the leader said to the hip-thruster, "Whoa, cool it off, man. This here's the peace lady."

They all glanced from one to the other as if the words *peace lady* had been said in a foreign language.

"Huh? What's that?"

"You ain't never heard of the 'peace lady'? You been livin' off on some weird planet? Over on Standish Street there's only one broad called the peace lady."

"'Cause all the others make war?"

"Nah," said the one with the switchblade, "Ain't talkin' that kind of peace. Piece, man, you know? A piece of tail?"

Raucous laughter broke out, with all five howling and hooting as if a professional comic had just told his best joke. Haley decided that if she was going to get away, this was the time to do it.

"Now that you've all had your little joke, let me go." To her own amazement her voice didn't sound as shaky as she felt. Still, the sausage arm around her neck didn't ease up.

Instantly their laughter stopped.

"Hey, man, she thinks we're kiddin'."

"We oughta tell her how things are."

Nods all around.

"We oughta tell her what a smart broad does."

"Yeah, man," they all chorused.

"Take her on, Rattler. Do it, man...."

The hip-thruster gyrated obscenely, making Haley think she would have preferred to face down a real rattlesnake.

"Come on, Rattler, tell her how it's gonna be."

They all began to stamp their feet and hoot.

Rattler grinned lasciviously. "They do what a broad was made to do. She gets on her back, opens her legs and does her askin' nicely."

Haley knew the color had drained from her face, her cheek and jaw muscles felt slack and useless. Their elbow-jabbing hoots at Rattler's comments slid over her like thick sludge. She prayed someone, anyone, would suddenly appear out of nowhere and rescue her. Not a very independent concept, she decided grimly, but right now getting free was vastly more important.

Haley knew better than to take shortcuts down dangerous alleys. And she hadn't. This was three in the afternoon, just a few blocks out of her own neighborhood.

One of her tenants had wanted to use the Association's video camera to record his grandson's birthday and Haley had gone to get some new cassettes. She hadn't seen Cage since he'd roared off on the motorcycle, and despite the fact that she'd handled scary situations in the past, this one made scary seem like kids' stuff. The sheer boldness underlying their doing this in broad daylight, the brazenness of harassing her in the middle of the street with passersby giving them a wide berth, was frightening enough. But beneath her fear was the very real terror that no one was going to appear like magic and help her. Unless she got out of this herself, she might not get out at all.

One of them had a comic book rolled up in one hand. He kept tapping it on his open palm, as though it, too, were a weapon.

"Whatcha got in the bag, bitch?"

"Yeah. Empty it out here so we can see."

They had drawn so close around her that she could smell them. A muzzy, cloying odor that sucked at the oxygen in the air. Her mind struggled to find some means of escape. Screaming at the top of her lungs might just surprise them enough that they would back off, although she doubted it.

If Cage were here, he would handle this. He wouldn't spar with them, he'd— She closed her eyes briefly as her mind grasped for some way to deny the violence that now invaded her thoughts. Yet, for a few fantasy-ridden seconds, watching Cage take these guys on—and winning—held a great deal of appeal.

Sausage Arm shoved her, and she stumbled, only to be grabbed by the one with the nervous switchblade. He wrapped his hand in her hair and jerked her head back. He laid the blade against her throat and bent close to her ear. She could smell marijuana. He whispered something so crude and raw that Haley tasted nausea in her throat.

Someone snatched the plastic bag from her fingers and dumped the contents on the ground.

"Well, looky here." Half a dozen videocassettes lay at her feet.

"Hey, maybe she's one of those, you know, news hounds."

"I told you she was a bitch in heat. Hot for news that ain't none of her damn business."

"We oughta show her what happens to peace-lady news hounds."

"Hey, man, we gotta be fair. We gotta play by the rules. She might be seeing things our way. She might be seeing that we're givin' her a chance to show us her gratitude."

One hand passed across her breasts, and Haley shrank back. Her breathing rose and fell in tandem with the position of the switchblade.

Then he lowered the knife and loosened his hand from her hair. She staggered, the release of the grip on her scalp bringing a moment of sweet relief.

"Step on the tapes, bitch."

"Yeah, we wanna hear the crackin' sound."

"See if it sounds the way your head will."

"Man, we'll be rollin' in the grats over on Standish Street for gettin' you outta their face."

Haley obeyed, terrified that the alternative to her head being smashed might very well be her throat being slit. With great effort she positioned her foot over the first cassette. Her eyes were glazed and swimming with tears of pain and panic.

She stepped on the packaged black plastic, but even with the full weight of her hundred and ten pounds, it didn't break. She barely got her foot away in time before the blackjack came down and crushed the container and its contents.

"Oh, God," she whispered, unable to blank out the image of the blackjack crushing her head.

The leader grinned at her as if he'd used his blackjack to help her out. "Again, peace lady."

Sweat broke out beneath her arms, across her stomach and down her back. Her throat was parched, and her tongue was swollen. As she moved to step on the next cassette, her foot shook. Concentrating, she pushed down with all her might. The cassette cracked, the sound splitting through her as if it were one of her bones.

"Hey, the broad's got some muscle."

After four more attempts, the case lay in pieces.

"That's two, peace lady. Four more and then the real fun begins..." He allowed his voice to trail off menacingly.

Haley knew that something inside her had closed down. Her mind and emotions were shattered or overloaded. The air hung thick and stale. Sounds that she'd been aware of earlier from passersby had all disappeared. Was she alone?

Had everyone run into safe places, fearing that if they tried to help, the Venoms would turn on them?

By the time she got to the sixth cassette, something had changed. A restlessness permeated the small space, and Haley knew that whatever cruel fun she'd just been subjected to, it was all over. Now a new panic crawled over her.

Smirking grins turned to low, dangerous laughter.

The leader approached her and, before she could react, closed his hand around the neckline of her top and started to yank it down.

Haley cringed back, batting at his hands until someone grabbed her arms and held them behind her.

"Let her go."

Haley froze, and the five gang members abruptly became silent. Sausage Arm let go of her top. She wondered if the new voice was in her mind. Suddenly, for the first time in what felt like hours, she was no longer the center of attention.

The leader swung the blackjack up in a gesture to the others and then broke from the circle, turning toward the voice and snarling, "You gotta problem?"

Feet moved as the now-forgotten crushed cassettes were stepped over. Haley saw the open switchblade poised. Her hand immediately flew to protect her throat, but no one seemed to be paying attention to her.

"You've got the problem if you don't let her go."

Cage! Relief drenched Haley.

"Yeah?" The leader tossed his head back in a cock-of-the-walk manner. "And what are you gonna do? There's only one of you and five of us."

For a devastatingly long moment, Haley heard nothing. Had Cage looked things over and decided he needed some help? The practical side of her agreed he did, but the terrified side didn't want him to leave her.

The leader turned back to his friends and chuckled obviously confident that he had the upper hand.

Now even the silence chilled her. Haley peeked out and saw Cage, standing just a few feet away with an arrogance that stunned her. Behind him was his motorcycle, and behind that were clusters of people. Cage looked directly at the leader, as though he were considering a number of possibilities as to what he would do. Haley didn't know what they could be—she couldn't see a gun, and it didn't appear that anyone in the crowd was going to help him.

"Hey, man, you deaf or what? You want the broad, but you ain't saying just how you gonna take her from us."

"You're going to let her go."

"Screw you. Me and my friends—"

Cage shook his head. "Just you."

As if curious, the leader took a few steps toward Cage. Again he tossed his head back, cocky and cool. "And how you gonna make me do that?"

"Change the pitch of your voice." Cage said it so easily, and with such surety, that the four gang members still near Haley all gave each other confused glances.

The Venom leader stepped forward, egging Cage on to follow through on his threat. "Yeah? And what are you gonna use? Your smart mouth?"

"I had something messier in mind," Cage said flatly.

The leader glanced down at the blackjack, letting it idly swing, and then laughed. "Just one problem, man. See, I'm here and you're way over there, and you ain't got a chance to get close enough to take even this away from me."

Cage shifted slightly, then shrugged. "Hey, if you're scared and wanna back down right here in front of your pals, it's okay by me."

"You're livin' in la-la land, man. I got my friends here 'backin'' me up."

"Yeah, I noticed. Took five of you to deal with the lady, too. Lots of courage and guts. Real impressive," Cage said sarcastically.

"I don't need no help, man. I could wipe the ground with you."

"You're not big enough to wipe your nose."

The leader stiffened, and Haley shivered. Cage remained still, arrogance and bravado coming off him in rolling waves. The clusters of people behind him began to move away and look for cover.

Around her the five gang members murmured, and one talked about doing a "ribbon job on the bastard" in a gleeful chortle. Haley sucked in her breath, having no doubt that a ribbon job had nothing to do with pretty packages or bright colored spools. Then they began to fan out away from her. She knew that in a very few seconds she would be free, but Cage... Oh, God...

Cage straightened. "Just as I thought. You're nothing but a yellow-belly who can't handle himself. Hell, wait till word spreads that it took five Venoms to handle one woman."

"Shut up!"

"Hey," Cage yelled toward the other four. "If I were a Venom, I'd be checking out some new leadership."

The four began to move in, and Haley's fear instantly shifted from fear for herself to terror for Cage. The leader raised the blackjack. "I'll handle him alone."

"Hey, man, you don't need to," urged the one with the switchblade. "We can take this bastard in less than thirty seconds."

"I said I'd do it," he roared. The four halted, looking at one another and then glancing at their leader as if he'd gone crazy. Slowly he moved toward Cage.

Haley shivered, her eyes glued to the terrifying scene before her. How could Cage look so calm? Stand so unflinching?

Cage waited.

The leader closed in, the blackjack in his hand swinging wider and wider arcs until, like lightning, the weapon came at Cage.

Haley screamed.

Cage dived low, but went right for the leader, coming up hard and grabbing him, jerking him up close so that they were face-to-face. He wrapped his fist in the guy's shirt, jerking him even closer. To Haley's astonishment, Sausage Arm quit fighting.

She couldn't hear what Cage said, but after a few tense moments, the leader swung his head around to his friends. In a low croak, he ordered, "Get outta here."

They all looked at each other as if they hadn't heard right.

"Do it, God damn it!" he screamed.

They moved then, muttering and slinking away. Haley stood, mouth agape, while Cage slowly released the shirt, confiscated the blackjack and snarled, "Go near her again and I'll kill you."

The leader stumbled once and then turned and ran down the street, disappearing around the corner.

Cage stood for a long moment, staring at the blackjack he'd dropped to the ground. Then he slowly rubbed his hands down his jeaned thighs. His shirt was sweat-drenched, his bare arms rigid with tensed-up muscle. He glanced up, his mouth grim as he made his way toward Haley.

Her legs suddenly felt rubbery, and her own arms chilled and numb. The tightness in her throat released itself in a broken sob as she stumbled forward.

The moment he slipped his hand around her neck, the words tumbled forth in a rush. "Oh, God...they were going to... Cage, I thought..." She took a long gulping breath. "They were going to kill me, going to kill you..." She flung herself into his arms.

He caught her, holding her with a rugged fierceness. Then he lifted her into his arms, as if he couldn't get her close enough. Haley's feet left the ground, but she barely noticed. Her arms gripped his neck. His skin was hot and sweaty, and she buried her face in his neck, gulping in the scent as if it were ambrosia. His heart pounded, as did hers. When he shifted slightly, she thought he was going to release her.

"No, please don't let me go."

"Easy, baby, I'm not going to let go of you. Shh..."

She clung all the harder, as if she wanted to make sure. She swallowed, her gratitude toward him so immense that she couldn't speak. Cage rocked her against him. He slipped one hand into her hair and gently soothed her scalp where it ached from her hair being pulled. His other hand kept her anchored against him.

Around them pedestrians began to move, staring, shrugging, passing by, offering words of encouragement, words of praise.

A middle-aged man, walking with the aid of a single crutch, patted Cage on the back. "'Bout time someone dealt with them little creeps."

A shop owner squeezed Cage's shoulder. "Creep is too good a word for them. Bunch of slimy thugs. We sure could use more like you around here, mister."

A couple stopped. "She okay?" At Cage's nod, they added, "Touch and go there before you showed up."

"Sure was. I thought they were going to shred her like they'd pulled her across a cheese grater," said a heavyset woman wearing a turquoise apron.

More passed by, but Cage continued to hold her. Finally, after a few minutes, he spoke to her. "You ever ridden on a cycle?"

Haley blinked. The question was so normal compared to what had just taken place that she had to think for a few seconds. "Yes, a long time ago."

Cage eased her away and lowered her to the ground without completely letting go of her. His eyes absorbed her, seemingly intent on taking in the most miniscule detail of her face, then traveling to the streaks of dirt across the front of her cotton top, and to the wobbliness in her legs. Then his gaze returned to her throat. Her eyes widened as she watched a kind of lethal fury build in his expression.

"What?" she whispered as her fingers automatically went to the base of her neck, where the switchblade had been pressed. She touched the long scratch and winced. She felt dizzy, and she knew the color had drained from her face. She had been cut. Her throat being slit had been a very real possibility.

"That son of a bitch," he growled, then pulled her into his arms, swearing savagely. Again he held her, until they both stopped shaking. Still keeping her tight against him, he walked her to the cycle.

He lifted her onto the back of the bike, sliding his hands beneath her thighs and adjusting them so that her skin wouldn't touch the muffler. Haley got comfortable on the leather seat as Cage settled his helmet on her head. He hooked the chin strap. Her eyes never left him.

When finally he met her gaze, he said softly, "You have to hang on to me. Think you can do that?"

Her arms felt weak and numb, but she nodded. The alternative—walking home—was impossible. She felt empty and disoriented. She wanted to lock herself in her apartment, take a hot, hot shower and curl up to sleep away the nightmare.

Cage straddled the cycle, then started the engine. He reached back and again adjusted her thighs so that they were snug against his hips. She slipped her arms around him. He pulled her hands so that they met at his waist. Instead of just clasping her fingers together, she pushed herself against his back, hugged her legs to his hips, and locked her arms around him in a death grip.

"Good. Don't let go." He eased the bike off its stand and roared down the street. The sudden speed jarred Haley, but she held on. He drove the three blocks over to Standish Street, slowing as he approached her apartment house. Her tenants, including her friend Alicia, along with some of the older members of the Association, waited outside as though greeting a returning soldier. Cage slowed down, coming to a stop in front of the gathering crowd.

He touched Haley's hands, indicating that she was not to let go of him.

Alicia hurried forward. "A few people who saw the whole thing were just here and told us what happened. I just called the police. Haley, are you all right?"

She somehow managed to smile. "Cage took care of things. I'm shaky, but okay."

Alicia gave Cage a grateful look as she came forward to help Haley off the cycle.

From the distance came the whine of a police siren. Cage shook his head at Alicia. "We'll be back in a little while. Just wanted you all to know that she's safe."

"But the police will want to ask her questions," Alicia said, a worried expression coming over her face.

"Later," Cage replied. Before Alicia could object further, and before Haley had a chance to say anything, he sped off.

She had no idea where they were going or why, and she didn't care. How had he known that she didn't want to talk to the police, that she didn't want to even think about the horror of the past hour? Maybe he didn't know; maybe he just needed the head-clearing wind of the ride, wanted the fresh open space for himself.

Sighing now, and with a strangely profound content-ment, she snuggled in against him, laying her cheek against his back in much the same way she'd done early that morn-ing in his apartment. She watched the scenery speed by. From the congested city to the more open, wooded areas along the highway. They passed by small shopping plazas, houses that had been built before businesses came in and sucked up the open land. She registered a few scattered bill-boards advertising a local talk show and a popular beer, and one sign that urged support of a handgun bill that would be on the state ballot in the upcoming election.

As the cycle ate up the miles, putting distance between her and the city's terrors, Haley felt a measure of relief. She had no idea how long they rode or how fast they were going. She was conscious only of her body locked to his, the brisk, whipping wind against her arms and legs and an almost to-tal mindlessness that required nothing more of her than that she keep a tight grip on Cage.

Finally, when they turned onto an old stretch of highway mostly traveled by local traffic since the interstate's arrival, Cage slowed the bike to what felt like a crawl. He leaned back so that he could speak to her and at the same time watch the road. She raised herself up so she could hear him and worked her hands out of their death grip. Her fingers touched his belt buckle, and she quickly slid her hands to his waist.

"How are you doing?" he asked over the roar of the en-gine.

She let go of him with one hand and raised the face shield on the helmet. "Much better."

"Think you can get another good grip and not let go?"

She demonstrated just how tight she could hold.

"I'm glad you're holding my waist and not my throat," he said teasingly.

She grinned.

He slowed the cycle so that they were barely coasting along, turned just a fraction more toward her and, in a movement she knew must have been spur-of-the-moment, kissed her. There was nothing erotic, or hot, or even particularly intimate, about the kiss, and yet she returned it with a naturalness that amazed her.

By most standards it couldn't even have been called a *real* kiss, but after he turned away and she once again lowered the face shield, after she had braced herself against his back, after he had opened the engine's throttle so wide that they seemed to be flying, she could still taste him. She pressed her lips together and curled them inward to save his kiss as if it were the most precious of gifts.

More scenery blurred by her. The air, so hot and stifling when she'd been circled by the Venoms, now blew cool and refreshing. Cage felt warm and solid, and she gripped him against her as if he were a shield against everything that was nasty in the world. She had no idea of the distance traveled or the time that they rode after he touched his lips to hers. She knew only that the landscape rushed at them in country silence, filling her with the sight of two-story-high cornstalks and the dry, grainy scents of freshly baled hay.

They passed a vegetable stand and a field full of cows that raised their heads as Cage roared past. As he approached a small town, he slowed the bike to the speed limit. To Haley, it felt as if they were barely moving.

Cage stopped at an intersection, parking at a street corner, and lowered his booted feet to the ground. He dragged a hand through his hair. Haley started to loosen her grip.

"Not yet," he said. His fingers pressed hers against his flat stomach.

She resecured her grip, but lifted the face shield, and decided she could just stay in this cocoon of safety forever. She glanced around, not having any idea where they were. To her left, a general store that seemed to be the central hub of the town was doing swinging-door business. Kids tumbled out with frozen ice cream on a stick. Men lounged in sturdy barrel-back chairs, sipping from cans of beer or soda. A German shepherd lay in the coolness of a tree's shade, not even bothering to move when a cat meandered past him. The traffic moved at school-zone speeds, a few bikes wheeled past them, and a woman pushed a baby stroller. To Haley's right was a white steepled church with a framed-glass message board that announced the times for Sunday services. Next door to the church was the volunteer fire department, and beyond that the town hall.

It occurred to Haley as she looked around that what she wanted for Mayflower Heights was encapsulated at this intersection. Not the physical buildings themselves, but the essence of *neighborhood*: the freedom to leave a bike unchained, to walk around eating ice cream and not fear some bully would take it away, the excitement of meeting with friends to gossip about ordinary things instead of looking for solutions to street violence and drug crimes.

She realized that although the town looked like a fantasy, it wasn't. This was normal, this was how things should be. And if she believed that, and she did, then it was possible for this particular fantasy to exist somewhere else. Like in Mayflower Heights.

Cage shifted, and she gave him a fierce hug. Not for one moment did she think Cage had brought her here to shore up her idealism concerning Mayflower Heights. In fact, she was sure that once they began to talk about what had happened with the Venoms, he would reiterate in no uncertain terms that her life *and* her idealism had come close to being eliminated.

But for these few moments she intended to relax and enjoy. Later she'd deal with Cage and whatever he planned to say.

Cage pointed up the street a ways. "You thirsty?"

"Yes."

"Want some lemonade?"

Nothing had ever sounded so good.

Cage drove a few yards, bringing the bike to a stop in front of a lemonade stand. A child's picnic table had been covered with a flowered plastic cloth securely anchored at all four corners with rocks. An upside-down stack of paper cups stood beside a huge yellow-and-white cooler with a spigot. The handprinted sign read 25¢ a cup. Refills 10¢.

Cage chuckled. "Inflation has even hit the lemonade business."

At last Haley released her hold on him and lifted the helmet off her head. She shook her hair, and the breezy coolness after the hot confinement made her sigh with pleasure. Cage got off the cycle, and she did too, although she immediately grabbed his arm.

"Legs a little wobbly?" he slipped his arm around her to steady her.

She nodded. "They feel as if they're humming."

"Biker legs."

Her eyes skimmed down his jeans and when she glanced back up he winked.

Her eyes widened at the gesture. It gave her a sudden sense that he might not always be as grim as she'd thought. Intrigued, she asked, "Is there some private joke I missed?"

"Yeah, but you don't want to hear it."

Of course she wanted to hear it. "Tell me."

"Some other time."

"Really, Cage. I haven't been at the shockable age for a long time."

"I didn't say it would shock you. It would just get into areas that are best—" he paused, considering his next words "—left unexplored."

She opened her mouth, all set to tell him she was certainly old enough to explore most anything, but managed to stop the words just in time. She shouldn't want to explore those areas, either. Areas that she was now certain were sexual in nature. On the other hand, after what she'd just been through, she felt she could handle anything. No doubt he expected her to back off, yet he was the one who'd winked. And where she came from, that was a definite sign of flirting. The concept of Cage Murdock flirting boggled her mind. Then again, she'd expected him to take her home and leave her there, not come to this picturesque little town to drink roadside lemonade.

She tipped her head to the side, feeling just a bit reckless. In a low voice, she asked, "Is it sex that you're trying to duck talking about?"

He scowled, shaking his head, sorry he'd ever started the conversation. "Persistent aren't you?"

"About getting an answer? Yes."

He crossed his arms, watching her for so long that she felt suddenly flushed. Then she saw his expression change, and she was reminded of the Cage she'd confronted at the meeting when she'd asked him to leave. She wasn't sure whether it was his resistance to being pressured or a very real concern that he might have made a mistake and let his guard down with her, and her own thoughts were floundered between once again insisting and just letting the issue go. Finally she concluded he was right. Knowing would be more awkward than not knowing.

He lifted her hand from his arm and walked to the lemonade stand. Haley sighed. Just when she thought he'd become a little more relaxed and open with her, he pulled back. Maybe he'd realized how far he'd allowed himself to go with her and now regretted it.

She should be thanking him, she decided with a grimace. If she wasn't careful, she'd find herself forgetting the real reason he was here. And that she couldn't do.

Two little blond girls, with ribbons in their hair and wearing blue shorts and cartoon-printed tops, beamed with delight when Cage approached.

"We'll take two," he said as he dipped his fingers into the front pocket of his snug jeans and pulled out some change. Haley found herself staring at the leanness of his hips and the glovelike way his jeans conformed to his body. His back was damp, making the dark shirt he wore even darker. She glanced down at her own shirt and saw that it was damp from where she'd been pressed against him. Her lace bra wasn't visible, but her breasts were definitely outlined. Good heavens, Cage could very well have made some lascivious comment, and he hadn't. Her head came up suddenly.

Maybe his refusal to define biker legs had been more of an honorable one than an attempt to deflect any potential areas of sexual awkwardness.

Haley pushed her fingers through her hair and then pulled her shirt away from her breasts. Of one thing she had no doubts. He was totally different from any man she'd ever known.

Cage complimented the two girls on their entrepreneurial efforts and walked back to where Haley stood. His expression, while not totally open, was certainly less guarded.

She wished she had a camera. The aloofness, the careful watchfulness and the grim resolve that seemed, thus far, to be a permanent part of him, had softened.

He handed Haley the cup and glanced around as he sipped from his own.

"Nice town, huh? Quiet and friendly."

Haley drank. The cold, tangy sweetness tasted as good as anything she'd ever tasted. "And seemingly crime-free."

They were both silent, smiling occasionally as the two little girls discussed the profit they'd made that day and debated whether they should add cookies to boost sales.

"I'll make a prediction," Cage said with a grin. "In twenty years the two of them will be running a major corporation."

Haley laughed. "I think you're right."

He drained his cup and then asked, "Want to take a walk?"

"Yes, I'd like that."

"Let's get a refill first."

A few moments later they were walking down the sidewalk under a bower of maple and oak trees. A pretty lavender ground cover interspersed with ivy grew along the stone wall that divided the private property from the public. The sidewalk was old slate, cracked and broken in places. Haley found herself dodging the cracks, reminded of the childhood warning: Step on a crack, break your mother's back.

It wasn't until they started to turn a corner and she saw someone unlocking his car that she said, "Cage, your motorcycle! You didn't lock it to anything."

"It'll be fine."

"I know this isn't Standish Street, but still . . ."

"Justice Avenue."

"You're kidding."

"In a town called Paradise Falls. Corny, huh?"

"It's wonderful. Very Americana. I love it."

For the next few hours, the Venoms, the problems in Mayflower Heights, Cage's revenge, all seemed like yesterday's shadows. By unspoken agreement they talked only about pleasant things, like rooting for the Boston Red Sox, eating boiled lobster with their fingers and concentrating on the idyllic world they'd stepped into.

When they crossed a street and came to a park and playground, Haley spotted a tree swing. She grabbed Cage's wrist, pulling him along with her. "Come on, you can push me on the swing."

Cage did, indeed, push her—higher and higher until she felt as if she'd been transported back in time to when her father had pushed her on the swing set in their yard. The same yard she now wouldn't dare leave so much as a piece of lawn furniture on for fear it would be stolen.

Finally they left the swings, nodding a friendly greeting to a woman whose son was playing in a huge sandbox. They crossed to the far end of the park, where a baseball game was in progress. Cage bought hot dogs with relish and mustard piled on top, along with cans of soda and later Fudgesicles. Haley rooted for one team, while Cage cheered for the other. Haley's team won by two runs.

After the game was over, Cage laced his fingers through hers as they walked back to the motorcycle. The girls had sold out their lemonade and were counting their profits. Haley and Cage said goodbye as once again Haley climbed on the back of the cycle. She felt wonderful. Relaxed and rested and more than pleased that Cage hadn't just dropped her at the apartment house. The afternoon had been a much-needed diversion.

She started to put the helmet on, but he stopped her. Taking it from her, he hung it on the handlebars and then brought his hands up to cradle her face. In her position, she couldn't move, but then again, she didn't want to. He hesitated a few seconds as if unsure, but the need that had risen and fallen between them since that first meeting seemed to take away the will to resist. Her heart slammed as he lowered his mouth. At first he simply brushed his mouth across hers, and for an instant she thought he was going to draw back.

But then he angled her head, holding it securely as if to make sure he made this a real kiss, not just the soft, lingering promise of one. His mouth didn't hesitate, firmly capturing hers. Haley closed her eyes and her hands gripped his forearms. A sweep of passion rushed through her, but instead of a fleeting tingle or mere seconds of pleasure, it put her completely at his mercy. Cage groaned and tangled his hands in her hair, plunging his tongue deeper, opening his mouth wider.

Haley gasped at the fury, the possessiveness of the kiss, and she couldn't help but wonder if somehow he was reassuring himself that nothing would ever happen to her. She clung to the taste of him, gathering it all in while at the same time reminding herself where they were. Paradise Falls was a place of fantasies and dreams. Kissing her here wasn't the same as kissing her in Mayflower Heights. Then his mouth lifted, and he hesitated as if he wasn't sure he wanted to stop. Finally their eyes met and she saw desire edge out the wintry blue, and she had no doubt he saw the hazy luminous need in her own.

"Being here is just like stepping into and then out of a fantasy, isn't it?" she asked, licking her mouth to catch the last remnants of his taste.

Cage brushed his thumb across her mouth. "A sealed-with-a-kiss fantasy," he murmured as he touched her mouth once more with his own. This time Haley knew he wouldn't linger; knew he wouldn't dare. He pulled away and she watched him as he took the helmet and settled it on her head. He remained close enough to her that she couldn't miss his guarded expression. Their afternoon of leisure was definitely over.

"What is it?" she asked, already feeling the familiar weight of the problems in Mayflower Heights.

"When we get back, we have some things to talk about."

"What things?" She wondered if their shared kiss might be one of the things, but instinctively she knew differently.

"About what happened with the Venoms, and about a change in our relationship."

Chapter 5

Returning to Mayflower Heights, with its graffiti and its seemingly unending sense of hopelessness, seized Haley like cultural shell shock. The contrast between it and Paradise Falls could have been a century in time instead of a mere forty miles in distance. By the time she'd gotten off the motorcycle and entered her apartment, she felt drained instead of renewed.

Cage's attitude had changed, too. She'd noticed it in the level, guarded tone of his voice when he said he'd be over to see her in a little while. Gone now was the companionability of drinking lemonade at a roadside stand, of rooting for opposing teams in a kid's baseball game. But beyond his marked change in attitude, the most deeply disturbing thing about it all was her willingness to allow him to simply set the agenda. *He* wanted to talk about the Venoms. *He* wanted to talk about the change in their relationship. *He'd* be over in a little while to see her.

"Damn," she muttered as she switched on the ceiling fan in her living room. It was decorated in blue and green, the summer colors a comforting contrast to the old pine furnishings that had been in her family for years. A plump-cushioned new couch angled toward a bow window, where lace cream swag-style curtains added an airy and feminine touch.

Haley plucked at her cotton top as she adjusted the blinds to accommodate the setting sun. She glanced across the street toward Cage's apartment and shook her head at her own foolishness. Letting him set the agenda was no different from letting him run things, letting him control things, allowing him to control her. Hadn't she had to deal with that kind of superior attitude with her ex-husband? The I-know-what's-best-for-you-so-be-a-good-girl-and-don't-argue mentality that Philip had always tried to inject when he hadn't liked something she'd done.

In her bedroom, she scowled with disgust as she shed her clothes and tossed them into a barrel-shaped wicker basket. For a moment she stared at the single-size bed and wondered if she'd lost control of her good sense by insisting on the switched beds. Yet in those few moments she'd been undeterred and resolute, definitely in control. Somewhere between then and now, though, something had shifted.

Don't be taken in by his sexiness, or, worse, some need to understand him, she warned herself. She knew that at the root of her insistence that they switch beds had been her own desire to make things right for him, to show him that there was such a thing as one human being caring about another, to show him that even though he'd denied it, he did matter.

Haley sighed. Her father had told her that she'd inherited the Stewart social conscience. Bleeding-heart stuff was what Cage had called her hopes for Mayflower Heights. And yet his taking her away to Paradise Falls for those few hours had certainly revealed a tender side of him. Then again, she could be wrong. For all she knew, his motives might have been totally selfish. Just because she preferred to see things in the best light, that obviously didn't mean Cage did.

In her bathroom, she shut herself behind the opaque glass doors of the shower stall and stood immobile beneath the hottest water she could stand.

Closing her eyes, she acknowledged that in one sense the small town had been a boost of hope, for it had reaffirmed her belief that if safe, idyllic neighborhoods existed elsewhere, they could exist in Mayflower Heights. The hours spent there had convinced her that her neighborhood should be made safe to enjoy peaceful summer evenings when people could stay out after dark, instead of being terrified that some gang member would decide he wanted what didn't belong to him. And Cage's taking her there had greatly diffused the effects of her frightening experience with the Venoms.

But the afternoon of tranquility, she realized, had gone beyond a model for Mayflower Heights or blocking out those terrifying minutes with five gang members. The time they'd shared had seeped into and awakened other places in her mind. One of those places was the reality of what was happening with Cage. And right now that truth scared her more than never seeing Mayflower Heights as a safe neighborhood.

She tried to focus on her original reason for not wanting him here. His need for revenge still disturbed her, but on a different level. Her impressions of him, her inner feelings about him, were evolving. Certainly the fact that she'd thrown herself into his arms today was evidence of that....

She recalled the wonderful feel of his body, his arms gripping her, his words soothing and reassuring. Distracted by those thoughts, she squirted too much shampoo and soon was drowning in bubbles. Damn him, and her continual preoccupation with him! As she rinsed and rerinsed her hair, she tried to remember ever having thrown herself into a man's arms with such total abandon, with such unflinching confidence.

She couldn't.

Not even when the phone call had come that her parents had been killed. Philip had been there, but as grieved as she'd been, she hadn't let herself fall apart. Perhaps she'd feared never getting her emotions back under control. Perhaps, at some level, she'd known that her vulnerability would give Philip too much power over her. Whatever her

reasons, she'd held herself together until she had some private moments. But this afternoon ...

She'd simply dissolved in Cage's arms.

And the danger behind that trust now screamed through
her consciousness like the wail of a police siren.

Finally ridding her hair of the last of the shampoo, she
turned off the shower. Stepping onto the sea-foam-green
bath mat, she toweled herself dry. With a grim reluctance,
she admitted that whether she liked it or not, Cage had indeed gained some measure of control over her, making her
feel too young, too pliable, too impressionable. Thinking
through the past few hours, she realized they'd settled in her
mind like a staccato recitation from a first-grade reader.

See Haley surrounded by gang members—Cage to the
rescue.

See Haley desperately grateful—Cage holds and soothes
her.

See Haley telling Alicia that Cage took care of things—
Cage takes her away on his motorcycle.

See Haley enraptured by Paradise Falls—Cage kisses her
and then plays on that and milks it until he's ready to leave.

See Haley all pliable and relaxed—Cage tells her he wants
to discuss the Venoms and the change in their relationship.

She swiped the towel across the mirror to get rid of the
steam. Resolutely she stared at her reflection, voicing her
thoughts aloud. "The first way to break his attempt to control the agenda is to inform him that we have no relationship to change." With that seemingly simple decision made,
she felt better ... until her eyes drifted down to her throat.

And for the barest of moments she blinked, thinking she
must be seeing things. Then she clasped a hand over her
mouth to stop the yelp.

My God, she'd forgotten the switchblade cut. Forgotten!
How could any sane person forget a switchblade cut on her
neck? She leaned forward and examined it carefully. It was
actually more of a scratch than a cut. About an inch and a
half long, it resembled a thin, too-pink stripe and crossed
the point where her throat pulse hammered against her fin-

gers. Slowly she drew in a long, shuddering breath. She'd come very close to getting her throat slit.

She knew she owed more than a simple rescue to Cage.

She owed him her life.

With that realization came another one. If she owed him her life, then she'd handed him a powerful tool of control.

Gratitude.

Twenty minutes later, barefoot and wearing a hip-length red-and-white-striped terry cloth tunic over denim shorts, Haley was curled up in the corner of her pale green couch with a huge glass of iced tea.

Cage had arrived just moments before. When she'd opened the door, she'd arranged her face in a neutral expression, which he'd instantly destroyed by saying, "Doesn't look as if the cut on your throat will leave a scar."

His eyes told her nothing, and he didn't attempt to tip her head up to the light to examine the mark more closely. Haley had the strangest sensation that he wanted to separate himself from any assumption that he might be concerned. Perhaps this was the professional persona he adopted so that he stayed detached emotionally. Definitely the approach she should want him to take, and yet . . .

He glanced at the glass she held and asked, "You got anything stronger than iced tea?"

She stepped to the side so that he could come in. "I have a bottle of whiskey."

"Perfect."

"The cupboard beside the sink," she called as he went into the kitchen. Listening to him rummaging around, she sat down and made herself stay seated instead of going in and playing hostess. She winced now as she recalled this morning, when he'd pointed to her blueberry muffins that he'd dumped into his trash. So much for being a friendly neighbor, but then, he had warned her, hadn't he?

She glanced up, again noting his guarded manner as he stood in the doorway to her kitchen. She tried to predict how the next few moments would develop. If she didn't know better, she would question whether this was even the same man she'd just spent a most enjoyable afternoon with.

Suddenly the space between them crackled. His presence was a dangerous omen, even though Haley knew she had her own thoughts and emotions firmly in check.

He'd showered and changed into clean but old jeans, the fly more a strip of soft, whitened threads than rough denim. Despite a black leather belt, they hung on his hips with a sexy-casual grip. His shirt was a wrinkled white oxford that made his tanned skin seem darker, his face harder. A few shirt buttons weren't closed, giving her a peek at the silver chain around his neck. Leaning against the door, her only bottle of whiskey and a tumbler in his hand, she thought he looked like a gunslinger from another era. He lowered his head a moment, as if he had something he wanted to say and wasn't sure how to begin. Haley found her thoughts racing down paths they had no business taking—paths scattered with erotic possibilities, paths littered with warnings about getting involved with him, about wanting to feel his arms close around her.

She lowered her own head, grateful he couldn't read minds. In some compelling way, his presence summed up the loss of control she feared and the attraction that she didn't want to feel. And, worst of all, she didn't have the vaguest idea about how to deal with either.

She cleared her throat, took a bracing sip of her iced tea and tucked her legs snugly beneath her.

"Before we came home, you mentioned a couple things," she said as she watched him push away from the door, bottle and glass in hand, and come toward her.

"Yeah, the Venoms and our relationship."

"I'm afraid I don't quite correlate the two," she said crisply, hoping he wouldn't sit next to her. "Were you trying to make a point?"

He paused between the couch and a blue upholstered side chair. "No, but apparently you are. Do I detect the beginnings of an argument?"

"Certainly not, but I can't help but feel this is another of your attempts to throw me off balance. You did it this morning, and then again by taking us off to that lovely town. The entire time we were there, you never said one thing about what happened with the gang."

"I figured a few hours of not talking about that experience would be what you wanted."

"It was."

"Then what's the problem?"

"I don't like you running everything, Cage."

"Hmm, and I thought it was the other way around," he said pointedly as he did indeed choose the couch, sitting barely half a cushion away from her. "I agreed on the bed-switching and the microwave. You agreed on this. Perhaps we've reached a turning point."

He'd cuffed back the sleeves of his shirt, and for a moment her eyes lingered on the tight muscles in his wrists and forearms.

"Turning point to what?"

"To that change in our relationship that I mentioned earlier. I have a way to take care of our problem."

Haley blinked. Problem? What problem? Surely he didn't mean that erotic magic that they'd both emphatically declared would not go anywhere.

Cage leaned forward, knees apart, and slowly poured the whiskey into the glass. When it was about an inch full, he set the bottle down on the coffee table in front of the couch and leaned back, stretching his booted feet out beneath the table. Bringing the glass to his mouth, he took a swallow, then murmured, "Do I take your silence as agreement, or is that wishful thinking?"

She almost said it was wishful thinking, but then she changed her mind. Whatever he'd meant by "relationship," she would simply deal with it. She didn't need to be contrary or difficult. Just firm. Firm and resolute in *her* decision, not allowing herself to be directed by anyone else.

Feeling better, she said, "Let's talk about the Venoms first."

He shrugged. "Whatever."

To her astonishment, her heart sank. Obviously, any interest he had in this relationship "change" wasn't of drum-

ming importance. For no reason that was even remotely
plausible, she was disappointed.

Lifting her iced tea to her mouth, she sipped and then
asked, "How did you know that the Venoms had me
trapped?"

"I was talking to some kids a few blocks away, trying to
get some information on who might have shot Matt. Someone came running over to say the gang had a woman surrounded. If anyone was interested in seeing the fun, they
better hurry up."

Haley's eyes widened. "Fun? Being threatened by a gang
is fun?"

"The kid's words, Haley, not mine. No doubt he's caught
gang fever. Nicely put, that means women are easy targets
because of their sex and the fact that they're easily intimidated."

"Anyone would be intimidated when it's five against
one," she snapped, outraged, as she always was, at the cav-
alier attitude toward violence.

"Fairness isn't on their priority list. Besides, you held
your own. Some women would have fainted or collapsed in
hysteria."

She tipped her head to the side. "Don't tell me I just
heard a few seconds of admiration in your voice."

"I admire anyone who stays cool in a hot situation."

"Why, Cage Murdock, a compliment like that could very
well swell my head."

He went so totally still that Haley wished she could re-
tract her comment.

Then, as if warning her, he said, "Don't flirt with me,
Haley."

She took a deep breath. "I wasn't flirting. I was merely
pointing out my surprise that you thought I was capable of
handling a dangerous situation and not falling apart."

He stretched again and rested his head on the back of the
couch. Haley studied the sharp angles in his face. He hadn't
closed his eyes, but was staring at the revolving ceiling fan
as if framing some appropriate response.

In a voice that was almost a monotone, he said, "Matt thought you were gutsy. More times than I can count, he told me if more people were like you in their determination to hold on to their neighborhoods, drug dealers and gangs would never get so entrenched."

"I always appreciated your brother's confidence. However, Mayflower Heights is still riddled with problems."

Cage remained silent. As if the detour in the conversation had never taken place, he said, "When I got over there, I overheard a few in the crowd mention Haley Stewart. It seems that your efforts here are having a far-reaching effect."

She knew she had all she could handle in Mayflower Heights, but she hoped that those in other neighborhoods did draw some hope from what the Association wanted to accomplish.

She stared down at her nearly empty glass and thought about the word *gratitude*. It had the potential to give him a huge measure of control over her, simply because she now felt an obligation to him. Yet she couldn't just ignore what he'd done. "I'm glad you came, Cage. Despite you thinking I was cool in a hot situation, I was terrified."

He turned his head to the side and looked at her. His eyes were direct, unflinching, mesmerizing. Despite knowing that the longer they held eye contact, the more highly charged the tension would become, she couldn't look away.

"I was terrified for you," he murmured.

For a full five seconds, she stared at him. Nothing she had yet seen in Cage had ever made her think he could be terrified of anything. "But you were so cool and controlled. The leader acted like he'd come face-to-face with the devil himself."

"Maybe he did," he mused. Then he added, "Intimidation is often effective and useful."

Still a little amazed at the idea of Cage being terrified for her, she ventured another question. "What did you do to him?"

"You heard me. I told him I'd change the pitch of his voice."

"I didn't ask you what you *said,* Cage. I asked you what you *did.*"

"Ah, you mean when we were nose-to-nose and discussing serious matters?"

She nodded, telling herself she probably didn't want to know. Just the way he slowly rose to his feet and walked over to the bow window indicated to her that whatever he'd said hadn't been pretty.

"Cage, as I told you earlier today, I'm not shockable."

He pushed the cream lace sheers aside and stared out the window, as if he were looking for something, or watching for someone. A television program's laugh track echoed from a nearby apartment. She thought she heard him swear, but the word was so soft she wasn't sure.

She watched him take one last look down the street before coming back to the couch. She was starting to rephrase her question about what he'd done to the gang leader when he said, "Let's back up a little. What were you doing over there, anyway?"

She scowled. "What was I doing over there? What kind of question is that? What were they doing terrifying me?"

"You were on their turf."

"Me! Now you sound like they had a right to do what they did."

"Of course they didn't have a right to do anything, but street gangs aren't real concerned about anyone's rights but their own."

"And that's supposed to excuse what they did?"

Seated now, he picked up his glass by the rim and swirled the remaining contents. "Damn it, I'm not excusing anything. All I asked was a simple question. *Why were you over there?*"

Sighing, she decided that if she answered his questions, then she might get an answer to hers. "Mr. Isley, one of my tenants, wanted to borrow the video camera to tape his grandson's birthday party. I needed to get some tapes, anyway, so I told him I'd pick one up for him. The store I usually go to had sold out because of a sale, so I went the few blocks over to the drugstore."

''You tell anyone where you were going?''

She thought for a moment. ''That I was going to get the tapes, yes, but not where. Why would I?''

''Anyone follow you, or did you see anyone you knew before you went into the drugstore?''

''Not that I recall, but to be honest I wasn't paying any attention.''

''So you never noticed the Venoms?''

She shook her head and found that her hands were suddenly cold and clammy. She would have noticed them if they'd been there. Five gang members, especially from the notorious Venoms, would not have escaped anyone's notice. And she'd seen them the moment she stepped back outside.

''Then they weren't there,'' he muttered, making that sound even more ominous. ''Tell me what they said to you.''

Mostly she remembered fragments. But she did recall the term peace lady, and the way they'd taunted her with it. Her voice cracked a few times, and she tried desperately to keep her emotions under control.

When she'd finished, Cage set his glass down, then took hers and did the same with it. He then closed his fingers around her wrist. ''Come here, Haley.''

She didn't hesitate, but scooted across the couch and curled into his arms. The heat of his body felt soothing, and when his hand slid down her back to her bottom, she followed his urging and sank even deeper into his arms. Her throat felt raw and hot, and the tears that she'd held for so long slipped down her cheeks.

''Oh God, Cage, I . . . was so . . . scared.''

His hand curved around her thigh, positioning it close against his. The soft denim couldn't hide the tenseness she felt against her bare skin. ''Shh, baby, I know. Only a total fool wouldn't have been.''

He threaded his fingers into her hair, much as he'd done when he'd held her after the incident. She relaxed, opening her fingers and letting them press against his chest. His hands braced her head, tilting her face up so that he could see her eyes. Her heart tripped and sped up as she felt herself dissolve under the intensity of his stare.

"Do you know that I chewed Matt out for worrying about you? And now I'm doing the same thing."

She smiled. "Maybe it's a trait of the Murdock men."

"Matt worried about you as one friend worries about another. My concern isn't anywhere near that noble."

She swallowed, unable to break the tension that was tightening between them. "You said you didn't want to be friends or neighbors or a hero—"

"Or what?"

"Or... a, uh, lover."

He lowered his mouth, and when her lips parted he muttered, "Not a lover, Haley. They're available for the asking. What I want is you. Your legs wrapped around my hips. Your breasts in my hands, and your mouth open and hot."

Then, before she had a chance to agree, object or even question, he was kissing her. He settled back on the couch, pulling her across his lap so that her legs did in fact grip his hips. In her position she was just a little above him, which gave her every opportunity to pull away, but she didn't. She couldn't.

His hands slipped from her hair to her neck, his thumbs lightly brushing the switchblade cut, lingering for a meaningful second before his hands moved down across her shoulders, and then along the sides of her breasts, leaving a trail of sparks. His mouth pulled hers deeper. No coaxing here, nothing subtle, nothing that indicated anything but a fierce heat, burning blue-hot.

Her own hands slid inside the open buttons of his shirt to his skin, as if this were her private domain. His chest hair coaxed her fingers to swirl and luxuriate. She felt the heavy pumping of his heart and wondered if he could feel hers.

She pressed closer to him, until his hands bracketed her hips and stilled them. Haley lifted her mouth from his, her senses thick and confused, her tongue rich with the taste of him.

Cage's head fell back onto the couch, and he let out a long breath. "So much for self-imposed restraint."

Haley felt a wave of heat in her cheeks and tried to scramble off him, but when she tried to move, he held her fast.

"Let me go."

"That wasn't directed at you."

"But it applies to me. I should never have let you kiss me again. I hardly know you."

He stared at her. "Hardly know me? What in hell does that have to do with anything? This isn't some courtship that will progress from an attraction to a few kisses and on and on."

"I never said it was," she replied hotly. "But I'm not in the habit of being so intimate when—"

"When what? When you disapprove of everything I stand for? When all you really want is for me to leave here? Or perhaps you know just exactly where this could lead, and that's what scares you."

"I am *not* scared of you."

He slid his hand between her legs in a gesture so suddenly intimate that she froze. His palm cupped her, the heat from it burning through the denim of her shorts. Her own instant response of dampness shocked her when his thumb pressed high on her heated core. With his other hand, he grasped her chin, turning it until she looked at him. His eyes held no passion, only an intent probe of hers. "Don't deny what I feel against my hand, Haley. We want sex with each other. We want it at a level that has nothing to do with likes, dislikes, approval or promises. It has to do with primitive chemistry. Now that might be crude and raw and make you feel guilty as hell, but that's the way it is."

She pressed her lips together. She would not agree with him because it wasn't true. She'd been caught off guard, she'd been a little too vulnerable, a little too grateful for his help. But she would not allow herself to be controlled by her hormones any more than she would allow herself to be controlled by Cage.

He continued to cup her, and although she wanted desperately to move, she was determined to prove that his touching her meant nothing. In a stiff voice, she said, "Thank you for the lesson on sexuality."

Cage shook his head slowly and then pulled his hand away. In a continuous motion he lifted her off him and rose from the couch. Standing, he dragged his hands through his hair.

Haley's lower body was humming, and to her dismay, she realized that not only had the kiss they'd shared aroused her, but his blunt comments had been undeniably true, as well. She shivered as she considered the implications of what he'd said.

A few minutes of silence passed, and Haley realized she still didn't have an answer to her original question about what Cage had said to the gang leader. After what she'd just gone through, she was doubly sure she couldn't be shocked.

She stood up, straightened her tunic and bent to pick up the glasses on the table.

"By the way," she began, "You never did tell me what you did to scare off the gang leader."

"I sliced the denim on his fly."

Haley dropped both glasses on the table, where one bounced and the other broke.

Cage swung around at the sound. "I thought you said you weren't shockable."

"My God."

He caught her wrists when she tried to turn away. "Don't waste your pity on him. The worst he'll have to do is buy new jeans."

She twisted in an attempt to pull free, but his fingers were tight against her skin, his thumbs pressing into her pulse points. "You threatened to castrate him. That's barbaric."

The wintry blue of his eyes revealed for the first time the side of Cage that Matt had spoken of so often. When he'd lived in the inner city, he'd practically owned the street. And anyone who had so much as come close to Matt with any intent to hurt him had had to deal directly with Cage.

"Barbaric, perhaps, but effective." He carefully picked up the pieces of broken glass. Haley let him. Her fingers felt as numb as her thoughts.

"No wonder all his bravado collapsed," she said as Cage dumped the glass shards into the trash.

"Payback's a bitch. He wanted to play street-dirty, so I showed him he isn't the only one who knows how."

"How can you be so calm when you could have cut—" She couldn't say it.

"Nothing was going to get cut but the denim. As for the calm, that comes from practice."

She felt a little light-headed, and she rubbed at her arms to dispel the chill. Cage slipped his hand around the back of her neck. "Feeling sick?"

"Yes, I'm feeling sick. Sick that you can talk about doing something so horrible and so crude as if it were some everyday routine."

He gave her an incredulous look. "Don't tell me you feel sorry for that bastard and his pals. He—no, correction— *they*—could have raped you."

"I certainly don't feel sorry for him, but I don't see why you had to—" Her eyes widened as she pulled away from him. "My God!"

"What?"

"You said you cut the denim."

"Yeah."

"But I didn't see any knife."

"I carry a switchblade in my boot. Old street habit that often comes in handy." He stretched one leg out and worked the edge of the denim up from around his boot. From there he extracted a switchblade and flicked it open. Haley stared, too vividly recalling the way the other knife had felt against her throat.

"Threats and counterthreats are pretty routine. It's where I live and breathe and no doubt will die. It's how I learned to deal with things so Matt and I could survive. Matt was being a nice guy, and look where in hell it got him. I'm not nice, and when I see something like I saw today, I don't walk up and invite the bastard out for a beer so we can straighten matters out. He wanted to play hardball, he got it right back."

"I can't agree with your methods, Cage. Even though I can understand them, I can't—"

"And just when in hell did I ask you for approval or understanding?" Without waiting for her answer, which she doubted would have made any difference anyway, he added, "For the time being, the situation is under control. That particular Venom won't come near you again, so before we rehash my barbaric methods again, let's move on to the other topic. The change in our relationship."

Haley planted her hands on her hips. "We have no relationship, Cage, and after this *revealing* conversation, I certainly don't want to start one."

He folded his arms and looked at her. "Too late."

"Too late?"

"Sit down."

She narrowed her eyes. "Did Matt ever tell you why I divorced my husband?"

"No, but I can tell you're about to."

"He was a control freak, Cage. He liked to tell me what to do and when to do it, and usually had a lot of advice on how I should live my life."

"Sounds like someone who deserved to lose you."

"That's not the point. I'm not about to get into a relationship with another man who wants to control me."

"This is going to be a working relationship. You can give all the orders."

She glared at him, unable to imagine Cage Murdock taking orders from a woman. "And what do you get to give?"

"My cooperation."

Chapter 6

He had to get rid of Kevin.

Cage glanced out the window from the darkened kitchen of his apartment. A few feet behind him, the disgruntled teenager sat sprawled at the kitchen table, flicking crumbs into an empty pizza box.

"You better take off, Kevin."

"Ah, jeez, Cage, why can't I go with you?"

"You know why. You're not a cop, and you're a minor. Legally, I would be in big trouble if I involved you in this. Plus, Haley, as well as your mother, would kill me if anything happened to you."

Earlier in the evening, Cage had been on the phone with Noah Drake, his friend—and contact—at the local police station, detailing what he planned to do in the next few hours. Noah hadn't exactly approved of Cage hiding in a warehouse in the hope of overhearing something significant, but then, Cage hadn't exactly asked permission either.

The warehouse meeting had been just one in a number of fragmented pieces of information that Cage had picked up recently. He'd been in touch with Noah, at first just to say hello and let him know he was in the area. Noah had been more than pleased and had immediately asked Cage to help them out. Patrol cars did cruise the area, but the police didn't have the manpower to be there twenty-four hours a day. Cage understood Noah's frustration. God knows he and the DEA felt the same way whenever it seemed the dealers were winning. Yet Cage had no intention of revealing to Noah his real reason for being in Mayflower Heights. More hassles and lectures he didn't need, but he *had* volunteered to keep Noah updated on anything he saw that was suspicious.

Over the past few days, Cage had slowly been putting together bits of evidence. The talk that first morning with the kids that Kevin knew had gotten Cage the names of some of the major dealers in the area. Through the kids, he'd also "overheard" about the planned meeting in the warehouse. The first real progress, however, had come from Noah; two of the dealers had been caught in one of the Mayflower Heights Association's videos. Then the gang incident with Haley, which at first he'd thought was just an isolated case of gang-style intimidation, had taken on more significance.

Haley had mentioned the term "peace lady," and Cage had seen some graffiti on one of the buildings that read WAR ON THE PEACE LADY.

But just this afternoon he'd heard something even more unsettling. Through a recent contact, Cage had learned that the gang leader, known as Boa, was the son of one of the suppliers of drugs to Mayflower Heights' dealers.

That particular connection had unnerved him. Not the relationship of father/son or gang/drugs, but because his reaction had centered more on concern for Haley than on his original reason for being here.

As much as he wanted to deny it, he'd redesigned his thoughts about revenge. Initially he'd planned on finding Matt's killer and expending his rage. He grimaced now as he recalled how he'd so eloquently described that scenario to Haley. Something about splattered blood on Standish Street. On the dark side of his soul, the idea had pleased him immensely—until the Venoms had surrounded Haley.

Something inside him had shifted and taken on some vestige he hadn't recognized when he'd come upon Haley and those punks. Yet Cage wasn't quite ready to make the connection between the Venoms going after Haley and the drive-by killing of one of her friends—namely Matt.

Maybe he'd just reacted to the basic male-protecting-female instinct. He could live with that, just as he could handle the cooperative working relationship he'd suggested, although it was still in the fledgling stage.

No, it wasn't Haley Stewart the bleeding heart who was becoming a problem for him, but Haley Stewart the woman.

Just having sex with her would have been a hell of a lot simpler, he decided grimly as he tried without success to shake away his unwanted thoughts. He still hadn't sorted it all out in his mind, including the sexual angle. Bad enough he had to "feel" something for her, but now he also wanted to "feel" something *with* her.

A couple of kisses, at his age and with his experience with women, shouldn't have done more than mildly arouse him. Instead they had consumed him. Not only had he been unable to forget about her mouth, he couldn't let go of the feel of her legs and arms clutching him as if he represented the only safe haven in the world.

Not what he needed, and definitely not what he wanted, but she had already influenced him enough that he'd backed off on his original blood-and-guts-splattered-on-the-street fury. He still intended to find Matt's killer, but now he feared that the search would involve him deeply with Haley instead of focusing on his own need for justified revenge.

Cage dumped the pizza box into the trash, along with a few empty soda cans. All that needed to be done now was to get rid of Kevin. He liked the kid, but Cage worked alone, and even if he didn't, a sixteen-year-old—no matter how street-smart he was—couldn't be involved. No way would he put a kid into a potentially lethal situation.

"Time for you to split, kid," Cage said bluntly.

"No one has to know nothin' about me goin' with you. I could help. Didn't I help you when you wanted to know who those guys were the other day?"

"And I appreciate it," he said, but without any encouragement that his thanks were going to spill into tonight. Cage flipped off the lights in the apartment and opened the door, gesturing for Kevin to leave. It was close to midnight, and the street was fairly quiet. In an average neighborhood, that would have been normal; in Mayflower Heights, Cage wasn't so sure.

Kevin stood on the doorstep, a sullen look on his face. "Matt was my friend, too. Everyone else around here gets to do what the hell they want, and I get treated like some runny-nosed kid."

Cage's face was resolute. "Life's tough, kid."

"I bet you never got sent home when you were my age."

"Nope, at your age I found my old man knifed in an alley. After that I didn't have a home to go home to."

"You're just tryin' to scare me off. I mean, what could happen to me? I'll be with you. I'd stick so close I could be your shadow."

Cage sighed, thinking Kevin sounded so much like Matt at that age. Always wanting to be in the middle of things, always believing that since Cage was there he'd be safe. "Contrary to your unlimited faith in me, I wouldn't give you a guarantee on my own life. Certainly not yours."

"I bet if Haley wanted to go with you, you'd let her."

Cage gave him a direct look. "Kevin, let it go, huh? You're not invited. I'm not going to change my mind, no matter how many angles you try to twist into reasons."

Kevin swore, then kicked a soda can that bounced and pinged across the street. In the silent night, the noise was inordinately loud.

Keeping his voice low, Cage said, "And don't get any ideas about following me." With his head down, Kevin scuffed his feet. Cage waited a few seconds. "I want your word."

Still he said nothing, and Cage was beginning to regret ever asking about the teenagers he'd seen that rainy morning huddled in the doorway.

"Your word, Kevin."

"Ah, jeez..." He heaved an enormous sigh, but finally he nodded. "Yeah, okay."

Cage gave his shoulder a squeeze.

"Maybe my word don't mean nothin'" Kevin challenged in a sulking tone.

"I guess I'll find that out if I find you following me, won't I?" He paused a moment. "I wouldn't like to think that you're a liar. Not when I asked for your word and you gave it to me."

After a long pause, Kevin nodded. "You got my word."

Kevin shuffled off, and Cage couldn't help his small grin of amusement. Why in hell did danger appeal to kids? Must be that it-won't-happen-to-me confidence, Cage decided as he watched Kevin enter the apartment building.

Then his gaze shifted to the front windows of Haley's apartment. The lights were out. He heard her telephone ring and then stop after the fourth time. He knew she had an answering machine, and when no lights went on he assumed she hadn't bothered to get up and answer it.

He wondered how she was sleeping in the single bed. He'd been meaning to thank her directly not only for the bed, but also for the sheets and pillows, yet truthfully he'd wanted to avoid even mentioning the word *bed*. Bad enough he couldn't think the word without envisioning her naked, drawing him deep into her body, and crying his name when her pleasure reached out and clung to him.

Whether it was the fantasy or Haley herself, Cage had slept better the past few nights in her bed than he could ever remember. The significance of that jarred him, for he'd never been able to sleep deeply. Fear of not waking up, fear of having left something unfinished, fear that sleep would make him a vulnerable target, always kept him bare seconds from instant alertness.

He had no answer as to why sleeping in her bed had masked any of those things. Deliberately, he chalked it up to sheets that smelled like roses and dreams that had a lot to do with her curled around him.

He checked his watch. Fifteen minutes max should give the dealers time to get occupied with their meeting at the

warehouse. Earlier that day Cage had staked out a side door
that offered cover because it led to some stacks of old floor-
to-ceiling shelving. Perfect for hiding behind.

Dressed in black from boots to jeans to T-shirt, Cage
moved quickly down Standish Street, staying in the shadows. He hadn't gone more than a couple of blocks when he
thought he heard a sound behind him. He slowed his pace,
but didn't turn around. A vision of Kevin trailing after him
instantly sprang to mind, and Cage grimaced.

Looking in both directions and staying away from the
streetlights, Cage sprinted across an alley. If someone was
following him, they'd have to cross that alley, unless they
wanted to be in full sight.

He wasn't armed except for the switchblade he'd carried
since the old man had tossed it to him with a "Here, kid,
you probably gonna die on the streets anyway, this'll help
even up the odds." Cage had used the blade often, at times
to threaten—as he'd done with Boa—at other times to get
himself out of a few jams in South America.

Now he felt the smooth weapon in its familiar place in his
boot, wondering for a moment how he'd come to the place
in life where his most trusted ally was a switchblade.

The darkened buildings around him offered a variety of
doorways for hiding. From his vantage point, Cage checked
three more before he found one that would give him a view
of the warehouse. The recessed opening was shaped with the
door in the middle and the two sides of the building fanned
out at a narrow angle. The scarred door, bereft of paint, had
been bolted with a rusty padlock.

Cage glanced across the street toward the warehouse,
checked his watch again, and swore. He was running damn
short on time, and if this was Kevin...

He didn't hear footsteps, but instinctively he knew someone was approaching. Instinct, an edginess, an adrenaline
surge, all were more subliminal than vision, but often a
better gauge of impending trouble. Vision, he'd learned too
often, was the great deceiver, and could play the worst
tricks. Cage flattened himself against the blind side of the
doorway and waited.

A car careened around the corner, headlights off, stereo blasting, kids laughing. An empty six-pack carton was flipped from the vehicle's window and landed in the gutter. A few doors down from where Cage hid, a window was slammed down. Along the edge of the sidewalk, mere inches away, a rat scurried into the storm drain.

Beneath his feet he could feel the tiny vibrations of the steps nearing his hiding place. He relaxed, making his body totally motionless while his senses remained acutely attuned. The figure moved with the stealth of someone, Cage guessed, who knew he shouldn't be there.

Cage began to count.

One.

The steps drew closer.

Two.

The steps paused.

Three.

One more step, come on, he urged silently, just a few more inches...

Finally the form emerged, and Cage moved. In one lightning-quick motion he grabbed the figure and hauled it into the doorway. His fury firmly in check, he jerked the individual around. Small, soft, wiggly, and scented like roses. Definitely not Kevin.

"Oh, Christ."

Haley stared up at him, her rapid breathing causing her breasts to rise and fall. "Cage, what are you trying to do? Scare me to death?"

He shoved her against the wall and trapped her there, using his body to do so. Her eyes were wide, and her cheeks a little too pink. His gaze moved down her black-clad body. From the stretchy tights to the blousy black top, Haley Stewart looked like a dark elf. Her hair was caught up and covered with some sort of contraption that made her look as if she were about to burgle the local bank.

"What in hell do you think you're doing?" he snarled.

With her chin stubbornly set, she said, "I was following you."

"You better go back to your beginner's manual. I've known you were behind me for about three blocks."

"Well, I'm a little green at doing it so sneakily."

"Yeah, I guessed that."

"I know you're going to spy on that meeting in the warehouse, and I wanted to know what they're planning, too."

"How the hell did you know about the meeting?"

"I have my sources," she said, sounding like a newspaper reporter.

"You have your *sources?* He wouldn't by any chance be named Kevin, would he?"

She pulled the cap off her head and shook out the curls. "That's my business. Or I should say the Association's business."

Cage had had enough. He took her arm and started to drag her out of the doorway. "Come on, I'll take you home."

"Wait a minute—"

"No, *you* wait a minute. I just got finished telling Kevin he wasn't coming with me, and I sure as hell am not going to drag you along."

"You don't have to 'drag' me anywhere. Might I remind you that I did this sort of thing long before you arrived in the neighborhood?"

"And after I'm gone you can go back to playing Haley the Heroine, but tonight you're going home."

"No."

"Haley, I'm warning you."

"No, Cage. You can warn and threaten all you want, but I'm staying, and I'm going over to that warehouse, with or without you."

Cage lowered his head, shook it slowly and swore. There was no doubt in his mind that she would do just that. After her comments about her ex-husband being a control freak, the likelihood that she'd obey now was more of a wish than a reality.

She stood on tiptoe and brushed her mouth across his cheek. He reared back as if he'd been burned. "What was that for?"

"Just a thank-you for being so insistent about leaving Kevin behind. I knew he'd never talk you into taking him with you."

"And just how did you know that?"

"Because you're not very good about backing down when it comes to protecting someone who's important to you."

"Obviously you're confusing me with Matt." He scowled at being assigned idealistic motives when his own ass was the real reason. "The kid's sixteen. That's why."

"But I'm thirty, so you can't use being too young as a plausible reason to send me home."

He scowled, his mind racing to find a way he could get her home and be back in time to find out at least who was at the meeting. "I have other reasons for wanting to get rid of you."

"Well, right now, they don't matter," she said dismissively. "You wanted to have a working relationship, and that's what I'm trying to do here. You said you'd cooperate, so this is your chance to prove you meant what you said." She peered around him toward the warehouse. "We better hurry so we don't miss anything."

Cage didn't move. He lowered his head, shaking it slowly in disgust. What annoyed the hell out of him was that she was not only right, but was being damn logical. She'd obviously thought out what he'd said about cooperating the other day and had brilliantly applied it to this situation. Terrific. Just what he needed—a brilliant, logical female who made him far too preoccupied with anything but logic.

Cage dragged a hand down his face. No damn wonder she fascinated him; she was unlike any other woman he'd ever known. Then again, knowledge when it came to women and when it came to Haley were as diametrically opposed as having sex and making love. Oh, he knew the difference, he just avoided the emotion-laden latter. He had his reasons, not entirely selfish ones, either, but having more to do with his cynical and rather permanent suspicion that he might not see tomorrow. That too-entrenched belief didn't allow for enduring involvements.

Mentioning that conviction to Haley would no doubt get him either sympathy or a prettily packaged speech about the value of thinking positively and looking on the brighter side of things.

Letting her muck around in his private thoughts would be disastrous. God. And he'd thought his most difficult problem with Haley was sexual. Now he realized why those consuming moments when he'd kissed her a few days ago had been so profound. Her effect on him threatened to go way beyond sex.

Grimly he realized he had to figure out some way to deal with her, but now was not the time. Yet he had to come to some decision soon, or he was going to be in trouble, bigtime.

Gripping her arm, he muttered, "All right, you can come with me."

She grinned. "That was a big decision for you, wasn't it? I mean, not taking me home. It took you a long time to decide."

Cage leaned back so that what little light there was would reveal her face. "You're unsettling, Haley, and I don't like being unsettled."

She reached up and touched his cheek. "I don't want anything to happen to you."

He wrapped his fingers around her wrist, and when he spoke again, his voice was sharp. "Worry about yourself. I don't need anyone to worry about me."

"Matthew did." At his startled look, she continued, "He worried that you would get burned out or killed."

"Then no one would have been around to drag him out of some ghetto when he got gripped by some nostalgic memory of the good old days."

Her eyes widened, and Cage grimaced. Why in hell had he made such an asinine comment? It had to be the tension, and his own rawness of spirit.

Haley had already taken a step forward, attempting to go around Cage, when he glanced across the street and hauled her back.

"What's the—"

Instead of answering her he backed her against the wall once more and pressed his body against hers. Then he dipped his head and firmly closed his mouth over hers. For just a moment she squirmed, but he braced his legs on either side of her hips, shielding her from the street and curious eyes and effectively pinning her in place again.

He raised his mouth the space of a breath and murmured, "Open my jeans and slide your hands around my waist."

She stared up at him, her mouth just a little open, and he could tell by her expression that she thought he'd lost his mind.

"We're being watched."

Her eyes opened even wider. "By who? I didn't see anyone."

"Damn it, just do what I tell you."

Her fingers fumbled with his belt. "Why can't I just put my arms around you?"

"Because reality tends to be more convincing." Cage sucked in his breath when her fingers brushed his stomach. Finally the belt came open, and she went to work on the button above his fly. He considered sliding his hands to her breasts, but the way he had her shielded, no one would know if he was touching her or not. Plus, he didn't trust himself to touch her.

Cage knew, however, that her hands inside his waistband would definitely prove to whoever was observing them that more was going on than a little necking.

Finally she got the button open, and her fingers dipped to the zipper.

"Are they still there?" she asked, and he heard the grating hiss as she worked the metal tab.

Biting back a curse, he gripped her wrist to stop her.

"I thought—"

"That's far enough. Slide your hands around inside so that they can see what you're doing."

"I feel like we're giving some Peeping Tom a free show." Her hands didn't exactly slide, they sort of crept, as if she weren't at all sure what she would encounter.

"Relax, Haley, the dangerous stuff is in front."

She lifted her lashes, her face so close in the darkness that he couldn't see her so much as he could smell her. Her hands flattened against the small of his back, but instead of just staying still, her fingers began a kind of slow massage.

Cage repositioned his legs, so that he more or less fit into the niche of her thighs. He waited a second for her to relax. He was hard, not powerfully so, but enough that she would have no doubt that this wasn't completely faked.

He stared down at her. "You don't have to rub your fingers that much."

"You don't like it?"

"I like it too much."

She swallowed, and Cage began to feel the reasons why they were doing this blur. He wished they were sprawled naked on her peach-colored mattress.

"Aren't you going to touch me?" she whispered.

"Not necessary."

"Oh."

"They see your hands and assume that I am."

Their eyes seemed to draw sustenance from one another. Even through the darkness he could see the pools of desire in her eyes. He knew his own gaze reflected the same wants. He wanted more from her as clearly as he knew that asking for it would mean trouble later. Yet the closeness of her, the sweet rose scent that had now melded with the hot fragrance of eager flesh and the possibility of earthy sex, was driving him crazy.

Cage knew he need do nothing more. Whoever was across the street could see enough just with her hands inside the back of his jeans. All they had to do was stand here, he reminded himself. Yet he couldn't resist. Call it temptation or foolishness, but having her this close made him too willing to push at his own self-imposed restraints.

"Touch your tongue to your lips," he murmured, cursing himself for his growing weakness for her.

Cage could tell she was as surprised by his words as he was in saying them. After a moment's hesitation she obeyed, wetting them, her eyes never leaving his.

He brushed his mouth across hers, taking up her moisture and leaving his behind.

Haley relaxed, and Cage wondered if the darkness and their situation had made her more than willing. Or perhaps simply knowing this was all an act was enough to lessen her tension.

She touched her tongue to his throat. "Why do you wear the silver chain?" she asked, soft and husky.

"Matt gave it to me a few years ago for luck." He threaded his fingers into her hair, slowly guiding her mouth across his throat.

She willingly complied, and he guessed that she was caught up in both the urgency of their game and their valid excuse to touch each other. Her hands moved over him, drawing him in close to her, matching their bodies intimately. "You don't seem like a man who believes in luck."

Cage easily ignored the small voice of reason that said he'd gone far enough. He easily ignored his usual coolness, which had worked so well in the past. What he couldn't easily ignore was how this had happened to him, how he could allow this kind of need, the kind that threatened to be permanent.

From some dark abyss in his soul the whisper urged, Don't chance this, Murdock. Don't...don't...*don't*...

Ignoring his own warning, he palmed her cheeks, and brushed her lips. They were hot, and he heard her catch her breath. Slowly he lowered his mouth, whispering, "Never believed in luck. I don't believe in much of anything except the power of this."

He kissed her then, his tongue tangling with hers, his mouth pleasuring, absorbing, drinking and going back for more. She didn't object, but became a willing participant. Cage slid his hands down to her hips and tipped her body forward. She came against him and he felt her fingers grip the tight flesh just below his spine. Her breasts pushed into his chest, and he swore he could feel her heart pounding. Bracing himself snugly between her legs, he moved his hands beneath her blouse.

Her breasts were enclosed in lace, but the fabric was little barrier against skin that was burning hot.

Cage again tried to remind himself he didn't have to do any of this for the benefit of the two men standing across the street watching them. His position, straddled in front of her, and her hands, said everything that needed to be said, and yet...

He wanted more. Hell, he wanted inside her. Not just in her mouth and between her breasts, but in the hot, hot sweetness of intimate joining.

As though keying into his thoughts, her hands moved, coming back around and now working at his zipper. Whether it was deliberate or just a slip of her hand, she covered him.

"God, baby..."

Knowing he'd be calling himself ten kinds of a fool for stopping what they both wanted, he reached between them and grabbed her wrist.

"No, I want to touch you."

"Not half as much as I want you to."

"No one can see."

"Thank God." Cage took deep breaths, gathered some control and then muttered, "We better stop before I can't."

"I didn't mean..."

"Shh, it's okay. This just got a little out of hand."

She stood very still, her hands not moving.

Cage turned enough to check the street. The two figures who'd been observing them had gone, and Cage hoped that he and Haley had convinced them the only goings-on in the recessed doorway were some super-heavy petting.

He turned back to find her still staring at him.

"How can you stop just like that? Most men would simply take what they could get."

"I don't take from women, Haley." He had to quell any belief she might have that this meant anything beyond what it was. Then again, she probably wouldn't. Any woman who dressed in black and followed him would know enough to play the cards that had been dealt. In this case, two men watching them. Taking advantage of the few moments of awkward silence, he smoothed things over. "Besides, this is supposed to be a working relationship. What just happened between us was part of working together. Whoever was watching us could have thought we were just what we are—a couple of spies. This way we allayed their fears. Just a pair of horny adults gettin' it on in the dark. It's a good ploy that works."

Her hands dropped away from him, and she sighed. "I guess I got a little too involved."

It was what he wanted to hear, wasn't it? Then why did he feel as if he'd been deserted? His body, too, seemed oddly disconnected from the rest of him, floundering for the intimacy it had expected.

Cage rebuckled his belt, not following up on her comment. He turned so that some light fell on his watch. If he was to have any hope of learning anything at that meeting, he'd have to take her with him. There simply wasn't enough time to take her home and come back. "You ready to go?"

She managed to push herself away from the wall. "I'm ready."

He gripped her arm, keeping her behind him as they moved along, almost hugging the building. Two women came out of one door. They were dressed in high-heeled boots and short, tight dresses with low-cut necklines, and both looked Cage over with a greediness that had Haley gripping his arm possessively.

One of the women said, "Keep him happy, honey, or someone will steal him for sure."

Haley moved closer, and Cage found himself intrigued that she hadn't reacted angrily to the women or denied their assumption.

"I prefer my women a little less obvious," he muttered in a low voice, not even bothering to stop and figure out why he was reassuring her.

"Well, they certainly didn't hide the fact that they wanted to eat you up." She peered behind her as the two women went on down the street.

"I'm saving myself for you, Haley," he said teasingly. "No one's ever undone my jeans with such innocence."

She stopped, glaring at him. "Innocence? I was married, you know."

"So you told me. The control freak."

"Then, obviously, I'm not innocent."

"Not a virgin, but definitely innocent." He dropped a quick kiss on her mouth. "No more talking."

Maintaining a firm grip on her arm, he crossed the street with her. The warehouse had once belonged to a small lumber company, and when Cage opened the small side door, the faint smell of sawdust and wood shavings drifted over them.

Haley whispered, "There's a light over in that far corner."

"Stay close."

The floor-to-ceiling shelving that he'd found earlier gave them an eerie but effective cover. Small scratching noises had Haley walking with great deliberation. The floor was covered with dirty sawdust, obvious remnants of drug parties, empty beer cans, liquor bottles. Old mattresses were flung about. The men in the warehouse were still too far away to be heard distinctly.

Cage wrapped one arm around her neck, hauling her close against him. She curled in, but he sensed it was more a case of staying close so that she could hear him than from fear. Any woman who held her own with the Venoms could handle this.

The voices became more distinct. "So what about that whore on Fuller Street? She gonna cooperate?"

"All set. Keep her supplied with crack and she'll let us use her place to cook the coke. Hell, she even gave us keys to the dump."

"Too bad we can't do the same to the Stewart broad. Get her the hell off our backs."

"Get her happy and flying? Not a chance. She's too busy trying to save the world. Probably doesn't drink or screw, either."

"Hey, the Venoms scared her. She's probably still quakin' in her shoes."

"No one told you what happened?"

"What are you talking about?"

"Some cowboy on a cycle pulled a knife on Boa and cut his fly clear to his underwear."

Laughter erupted. "Man, I would've liked to have seen that. Bet the bastard is still having nightmares about singing soprano."

"Yeah, I hear there's a shake-up in the gang. Bad stuff going down. They were supposed to scare that bitch so bad she'd head for another state, and what happens? Poor Boa gets wasted big-time."

"Then we've still got our problem. That group she formed all look to her for advice, so once we get rid of her we'll be rid of the rest of them."

"We could make life easy on ourselves and just dump Standish Street."

After a long-drawn-out silence the last speaker said, "Hell, it was only a suggestion. You don't have to look at me as if I was a traitor."

"Get it straight, man. No way in hell are we gonna get put down by some woman. We're gonna take her out. It's just a matter of when."

Suddenly the door that Cage and Haley had come in flew open and two men stood there.

At first Cage thought, *cops,* but they would never have come through a door that way. Then he saw enough to know who they were.

"Son of a bitch," Cage murmured as he grabbed Haley and dived for the nearest mattress. Shoving her beneath him, he sprawled on top of her and clamped his hand across her mouth. "Don't move, don't even breathe."

The men walked toward them, their feet heavy on the wooden floor. The smell of cigar smoke drifted toward them.

"So how's the kid doin'?"

"Not good. Word is spreading, and he's scared."

"Yeah, cavin' in when your manhood is threatened might be natural, but doin' it in front of gang friends strips the gears pretty clean."

Cage stayed still, with Haley molded under him as if it were the safest place in the world. He'd taken his hand away and buried her face in his neck. His heart galloped, and for the first time since he'd hauled Matthew out of a bar brawl Cage tasted the acrid tang of fear.

The two new arrivals were now just a few feet from the edge of the mattress. Cage slowly began to move in a simulated lovemaking motion. Haley slipped her arms around his neck and then, to his astonishment, she wrapped her legs around his hips. With both wearing black and the added dark shadows in the warehouse, Cage hoped they could pull this off.

The two men had almost moved past the mattress when one stopped and poked the other. "Hey, will you look what we got here."

Cage knew they couldn't see more than the back of him. God, he hoped they made the connection. He heard steps, and then one of them kicked Cage's boot. "Hey, lover boy, how did you get in here?"

Haley gulped, her hands tightening around Cage. Cage damned himself for not taking her home.

"Hey! You hear me, buddy? I asked you a question."

"Cool your jets, man," Cage said, in a deliberately petulant voice. "You're embarrassing the lady."

"I don't give a flying—" He drew closer. "Hey, didn't I just see you two humpin' in the doorway across the street?"

Haley's breath whispered across his cheek. He had to give her credit, she was playing this like a pro. Cage muttered, "Come on, man, give us a break. This has been a rough night."

The two men chuckled, obviously enjoying catching two lovers in the middle of a tryst. "Tryin' to find some place private, huh?"

"Yeah, her old man's been givin' us some kind of grief."

"Well, I'm gonna give you even more if you don't get the hell out of here."

Cage didn't move.

"You hear me, pal? I want you and your broad outta here!"

"Could you give us a few minutes? You know, sorta step over to the side? Hell, man, the lady is kinda exposed."

They looked at one another, the chuckles turning to a roll of laughter. But then one said, "Why not? Never let it be said that old Morey came between two lovebirds." He nudged his friend. "Must be pretty bad when you gotta use a crack-house mattress to get it on." Then, to Cage, he added, "You got three minutes to get yourselves out of here."

Cage watched them turn away. To Haley, he whispered, "Okay?"

"Okay."

He mussed her hair and opened the top buttons of her blouse. "They won't see anything, but I don't want you to look too well put together. Remind me later to tell you what a pro you are."

Swiftly he got to his feet and hauled her up beside him. Keeping her close, he started for the door.

"Hey!"

"Oh, no," Haley murmured.

"Take it easy. We got this far." He called back. "Yeah?"

"Have fun and, remember, the best sex is safe sex." Then the man who'd spoken broke into laughter as did his friend. Cage and Haley moved quickly, slipping out the door and into the fresh night air.

Not until they were almost to Haley's apartment did Cage realize that if she hadn't been with him he might very well be dead. And for the first time in his thirty-seven years, being alive felt wonderful.

Chapter 7

Late Saturday morning Haley opened her apartment door to find Norman Polk, Alicia and others who were members of the Association. Their eager eyes and curiosity more than told her that they wanted all the details of the previous night.

"We have a meeting scheduled for tonight. I could have answered your questions then," she said, inviting them inside. She wore white shorts and a loose pink candy-striped cotton top, and she'd skewered her hair up with a pink clip. She'd just begun watering her plants.

It had been nearly midnight when she and Cage returned, but Alicia and Norman had been seated on the front steps like chaperones awaiting the return of an errant daughter. Haley had convinced them she was all right until Alicia had peered at her mussed hair and wrinkled blouse.

She'd dismissed her friend's speculative look and said something vague about walking too close to dark and musty walls and shelves. She'd said nothing about the recessed door or the mattress.

Actually, the condition of her clothes and hair had been the last thing on her mind. The overheard warehouse conversation had merged in her mind with the comments of the two men who'd thought she and Cage were lovers.

Threats had been made against her before Matthew's death, but they'd been mostly a few threatening phone calls or gossip-type warnings. But last night's threats were different. To dismiss the words she had overheard would be totally foolish, but more frightening to Haley was the hate and the anger underlying how they felt about her, the determination of those dealers to prove their power. She had no doubt that if they got rid of her they would go on to destroy anything and anyone who got in their way.

Throughout the night and again this morning, as she'd replayed exactly what had happened, she'd become annoyed with the direction her mind insisted upon taking.

It wasn't the angry threats in the thugs' conversation, which was what she should be worried about. No, the details that occupied her thoughts this morning were the moments in that recessed doorway, when Cage had kissed her and she'd opened his jeans.

And then there was his incredibly quick thinking in the warehouse. My God, she knew she'd never forget how scared she'd been and how cool Cage had been. And he'd said *she'd* acted like a pro. Even now, she realized, the entire episode seemed more like fiction than real life.

Haley quickly gave Norman, Alicia and the others a condensed version of what had happened.

"Haley, we should consider getting you some protection," Alicia said worriedly.

"Like a bodyguard? Don't be silly. I'm perfectly safe here. Last night in the warehouse was a different situation."

Norman stared at Haley as if she'd forgotten to tell him something. "How come Cage isn't here? Hell, he'd make a better bodyguard than someone hired to come in from the outside."

"Now, wait a minute. Cage isn't in Mayflower Heights as my private protector." However, she, too, wondered where he was. She'd expected him to appear this morning so that they could hash out what they'd heard at the warehouse. As to a full-time bodyguard, that was ridiculous.

True, the overheard threats had intensified her need to be extra cautious, and she did want Cage's opinion as to what he thought the dealers or gangs might do. But, at the same time, she had no intention of hiding in her apartment. She felt that would be the worst move she could possibly make. It would indicate she was intimidated, plus it might make the dealers wonder why she'd suddenly become a recluse. A woman who'd faced five Venoms and come out of it relatively unscathed, even considering her "cowboy-on-a-cycle's" help, wouldn't go into hiding for no reason. After all, they didn't know she'd heard their plans for her.

"I haven't seen Cage this morning." She went to the kitchen, refilled her watering can and returned. She felt the dirt in the window box outside the bow window in the living room for dryness. The geraniums she'd planted in early June had flourished and now spilled over the wooden edge in a pretty profusion. She glanced across the street toward Cage's apartment, but there was no sign of him.

Casually she said to Norman, "Maybe he's still asleep."

Norman and one of the other men shook their heads.

Haley looked from one to the other. "I assume I'm supposed to ask how you know."

Norman frowned. "To be honest, cupcake, I'm a little worried."

Haley's heart sped up, and she felt a *swoosh* of uneasiness settle in her stomach. Norman rarely admitted to being concerned unless it was about her.

She pinched off some yellowing leaves and finished her watering, while at the same time telling herself she was overreacting. Cage had no doubt been in more scrapes and dangerous situations than she could imagine and had obviously gotten out of them without a hassle. She paled a little, however, when she recalled his cynical not-believing-in-a-tomorrow philosophy, and his comment that first morning about how he didn't matter, how only Matthew had mattered.

Oh, God, she thought suddenly. Had he learned something about Matthew's killer and gone after him? That had been one of her main fears last night when Kevin had told her Cage planned to listen in on the warehouse meeting. Following him, she knew, would infuriate him, as would her insistence that she intended to go to the warehouse, with or without his company. Especially since, if his original intent had been some sort of revenge, her presence would obviously change his plans.

Certainly he'd given no indication the past few days that he'd backed away from his intent of avenging Matthew's death. She'd honestly expected, even in the warehouse, that Cage would go after anyone who even uttered a word that could be connected to Matthew's death. Yet the conversation had been more about her and the Venoms. Maybe Cage had heard something she hadn't? He *was* with the DEA, and dealt with drug dealers all the time. That had to be it. No doubt he'd read more meaning into their words than she had.

Long after Cage had gone home last night, Haley had tossed in the single bed, remembering those disturbing moments of hot passion. All staged, she told herself as she returned the watering can to the kitchen.

And yet he'd been aroused, and so had she. And what was even worse was that her edginess hadn't subsided. Remember what you don't like about him, she reminded herself. Maybe he wasn't as obvious at Philip, but she knew Cage liked to run things, to be in control. That had been as evident the few times they'd agreed on something as when they'd disagreed.

Now, as she walked back to the living room, her mind scrambled for some reason other than Cage following through on some kind of revenge. "Maybe he just went out for breakfast."

"Musta gone a long way, that or he has a big appetite. Saw him leave around six this morning." Norman said.

Haley frowned. It was nearly ten now. Where would he be for that long a time? Of course, it was none of her business, and she should be pleased that while he was off doing whatever he was doing he wasn't trying to tell her what to do. Yet she was worried.

"Well, I'm sure he'll show up in a little while. Meantime, I want to visit some of the Association members who haven't been coming to meetings. We need everyone's support."

"Forget Al Pedenazzi," Norman said flatly. "He's stubborn, and the last time I talked to him he said the Association was a waste of time."

"Al stays on my list," Haley said staunchly. "Once I explain to him that we've missed him and that we all have to pull together—"

Alicia interrupted her. "Norman's right, Haley. I saw his wife, Lena, yesterday, and she would love to come back, but Al is adamant."

Haley sighed. Maybe she was expecting too much, but she had to at least try.

A half hour later, Haley stood outside her apartment, saying goodbye. The August morning was warm, but as Haley glanced around, she wished that the summer sun would make grass grow on the small areas that should have been lawn. Instead, the heat baked the dirt and revealed the struggle of a few scraggly bushes. This was definitely nothing close to Paradise Falls.

Haley hugged two women who'd given her comments about how grateful she must have been to have Cage with her when the gang had harassed her. Norman, too, said his goodbyes, remarking that he had to unplug a neighbor's sink. All assured her they'd be at the meeting tonight.

Only Alicia remained. Mostly, Haley soon realized, to talk about how she now admired Cage.

"This is quite a reverse from when he first arrived," Haley said matter-of-factly.

"Well, after watching him and seeing how much you need him—"

"Alicia, I don't need him. I thought I needed Philip and all he ever did was tell me what to do, or expect to have a say in even the smallest things I did. You remember how angry he got when I made the decision to move back here." She took a deep breath. "Damn, I don't want to talk about Philip. He's in the past, where, incidentally, Cage will be once he leaves here."

Alicia paused and then nodded, obviously getting Haley's point that the discussion was ended. "Actually, I had another suggestion."

Haley smiled. "I apologize for being short with you. Maybe I'm just tired. What's your suggestion?"

"I think you should ask Cage to come and address the Association. He certainly could give us a needed boost."

For reasons she didn't want to examine too closely, she agreed with Alicia. "Hmm, maybe you're right. Why don't you say something to him?"

"Me? He wouldn't listen to me. You're the one he's interested in." Alicia grinned. "In fact, I was sure he'd be here with you this morning, Haley."

"Here as in protecting me, or as in sleeping with me?" she asked, not about to pretend she didn't know what Alicia was implying.

"Okay, I'll admit that I thought you two would be heavily involved by now."

"I told you the night Cage arrived that he isn't interested in getting involved with any woman."

"You're wrong. He's already involved with you. I saw his face when he stopped here after your encounter with the Venoms. His eyes were so cold with fury, I was very glad he's on our side. Then, last night, even though he didn't say very much, his face was sort of set and he kept looking at you as if he wanted to pack you up and move you out of here."

Stunned at Alicia's assumption, she asked, "How could you see all that? I thought Cage just looked exhausted."

"I'm very observant."

"Or stirring up another one of your the-plot-thickens theories."

"Seriously, Haley, please be careful."

Haley shivered as she recalled how Cage had terrified Boa, hearing, once again, the comment at the warehouse that the knife had cut the denim clean to Boa's underwear. She knew that only a totally controlled grip on his emotions could account for Cage keeping the cut just a horrifying threat.

The two women chatted until Haley directed the conversation toward the upcoming meeting of the Association. She found discussing Cage awkward, mostly because of her rapidly changing feelings. She'd been quite content with her life before his arrival, but now she found herself more and more restless. Whether her attraction to him was a result of curiosity, or sympathy because of his loss, or was simply due to a sexual reaction to a very sexy man, she felt caught between wanting him and knowing she shouldn't. Her response to him the past few times, she realized grimly, had been neither sympathetic nor curious in nature.

Alicia sighed. "Guess I better get going. There's a back-to-school sale over at the mall, and Kevin needs just about everything."

Her friend had just turned to go when a little girl neither Haley or Alicia had ever seen hurried toward them.

Haley smiled. "Hello. Are you new in Mayflower Heights?"

"I live a few blocks away." She pointed in a vague direction that could have been any number of different streets. She looked about ten years old, and was nicely dressed, with pigtails that had red barrettes on their ends. In her arms was a huge stack of comic books.

"Those look brand new," Haley said, not at all sure what the child wanted.

"They are. I brought them for your kids."

"Are you selling them?" Alicia asked.

The little girl shook her head. "A man asked me to give them away. He said it's a new pro—" She frowned.

"Product?" Alicia asked, but the little girl shook her head.

Haley said, "How about promotion?"

"Yes! That's it! He said if he gave these away for free, then the kids would want to buy the next issue."

Haley glanced at Alicia. "Makes sense. Marketing is becoming an art form." She took one of the comics and thumbed through it quickly. It was a fantasy/adventure type similar to what she knew most of the kids between eight and sixteen watched on television and read these days. "Okay, I'll take a few to pass around."

"Take a lot. I get fifty cents for every one."

Haley shook her head in amazement. "I can't see how the owner is going to make any money if he's paying someone to give them away."

"That's what someone else said." She shrugged, then gave Haley ten of the comic books. "Bye, and thanks."

Haley offered one to Alicia, who took it reluctantly. "I keep telling myself that reading comics leads to reading books, but with Kevin it isn't working." She glanced at her watch. "I better go."

Haley said, "Oh, Alicia, would you get some videotapes? The ones I bought got broken."

"So I heard. Sure. And when you see Cage, tell him I'm very grateful he refused to take Kevin last night."

"Grateful," Haley muttered. "It seems everyone is grateful to Cage for something."

"What did you say?"

"Nothing. Just talking to myself. I'll tell him what you said."

Alicia said goodbye, and Haley glanced down at the armful of comic books. Just what she needed, she thought grimly, being the distributor for a line of funny books. She was just about to go back into the apartment building when she heard the motorcycle.

Cage came around the corner, bringing the bike to a stop a few inches from the curb. His worn jeans had a long horizontal tear in one thigh, and he was wearing his ONLY THE STRONG SURVIVE T-shirt. Dark glasses covered his eyes and his hair was windblown.

She was so glad to see him, she knew her eyes lit up with pleasure. Walking toward him, she wondered if the other women he'd known had thought him as incredibly sexy as she did. Then again, after the way her thoughts had been more preoccupied with Cage than with her own safety, this was a good time to take charge of her emotions. Perhaps a cool, detached attitude would help to get her growing—and scary—feelings about Cage in perspective.

He turned the bike off and Haley said, "I should give you a lecture on the safety of helmets."

"Don't. I just heard one, and two in one day is two too many." He got off the bike. "I was hoping to catch you."

"Actually, I have a bunch of things to do, so perhaps another time."

"What things?"

"Things." She hadn't meant to sound so abrupt, but she resented being expected to lay out her day for his approval. Why did he have to act as if he had a right to know?

"Well, while you're trying to remember what things, we can have some coffee. How about my place? I even have some jelly doughnuts."

He removed a flat brown box tied with string from a carrier on the back of the bike.

Then he took her arm, and he was already propelling her across the street when she balked. "You are *not* in charge of me, Cage Murdock."

He wasn't fazed by her bluntness or her resistance. "Working relationships come with certain rules. One is that each person knows what the other person is doing. Makes for less stress and fewer arguments."

"Wait a minute. You haven't told me everything *you're* doing."

"What do you want to know?"

His forthrightness threw her, and she scrambled to come up with any one of the dozen questions she'd had about him since he arrived in Mayflower Heights. Not a one came to mind. Determined not to let the opportunity go by, though, she asked, "Where were you this morning?"

For a fraction of a second, she saw amusement in his eyes. "Being a good citizen and talking to the police." He unlocked the door to his apartment and ushered her inside. "I'll get the coffee started."

She touched his arm. "You really did go to the police?"

"I can tell that makes an impression."

"I'm just surprised, given your reason for coming here."

"Just what a good working relationship needs. Lots of surprises," he said as he went into the kitchen.

Haley glanced around. The apartment was remarkably tidy, but stark, as well. No beer cans or newspapers, no clothes tossed over chairs. The room had an empty feel, as if Cage passed through it rather than lived in it. She wondered if his objections to switching the beds had had more to do with personal distaste for anything that had the power to bind him. In this case, perhaps, a link to her. To accept anything from her would put him in a position of either gratitude or obligation.

With a flash of insight, she realized that Cage was as frightened of anyone exerting control over him as she was of men who were control freaks.

Haley sighed. Never had she met such a difficult man. Just when she thought she had him figured out, he threw her a curve. His having gone to the police pleased her, of course, but she had a sense of the Association being pushed aside as if its influence no longer mattered. Certainly the police would rather deal with a DEA agent, and one with Cage's reputation would carry a lot of weight when it came to police response. But what about after Cage was gone? He'd told her explicitly that he was only here to find Matthew's killer.

Haley knew that Mayflower Heights had a long way to go to become like Paradise Falls. But she also knew that the neighborhood's greatest source of cohesion and strength was the Association.

What she had to do was make sure the Association benefited from Cage and became stronger. The alternative, depending on Cage for direct help, would leave too huge a gap after he was gone.

Perhaps having him speak to the group would be a good idea. And if the reaction to Cage that she'd seen that first night was any indication, the turnout would be excellent. What she needed to do this afternoon was to convince those who hadn't been coming to return. Cage as the speaker might just be the ultimate incentive. A grin tugged at her mouth. Al Pedenazzi would be a great place to start.

She set the comic books down on a table. A promo of a free issue wasn't a new concept in marketing to get customers. If she could get Cage to agree to come to tonight's meeting, she knew many would turn out, if only out of interest and respect for Matthew. In an odd way, she realized, she would be using Cage as a draw, just as the free comic book would get a lot of customers.

In the kitchen, Cage poured freshly made coffee into mugs. The microwave sat on the counter, and Haley had the oddest urge to go into his bedroom to see how her bed looked after he'd slept in it.

He glanced up when she slid into one of the chairs.

"I thought you got lost or decided to leave."

She raised her eyes. "Maybe I was in there going through all your things to find out more about you."

Totally nonplussed, he said, "Now that would be quite a feat. I don't have any things for you to go through." He put the box of jelly doughnuts on the table. "What kind do you like?"

"Apple."

He placed an apple-filled, sugary one on a napkin and slid it across the table. Taking a chair beside her, he lifted his mug and stretched his legs out. Haley was surprised at the sudden soft nostalgia in his eyes.

"Matt and I used to eat jelly doughnuts when we were kids. There was this bakery a few blocks from where we lived, and we'd go over early, while Louie was still making them. He always gave us a couple of extras." He lifted his mug from where he'd rested it, just below his belt buckle. Taking a sip, he added, "Doughnuts on Saturday got to be a kind of tradition, even after he went to law school and I joined the DEA. When we got together, we always made sure we got doughnuts on Saturday."

Haley broke the sugary pastry in half. Jelly oozed onto her hand, and she licked her fingers. "Did you get together a lot?"

"As often as we could. Sometimes we went up to Maine, rented a cabin and got drunk. A couple times I just came up here to his condo, and we'd visit, get caught up. The semesters that I took college courses I stayed with Matt."

Haley bit into her doughnut, chewing thoughtfully. "I never had any brothers or sisters, but in many ways Matthew was like a brother to me." She paused a moment and wiped her mouth. "I just realized something. You and I have something else in common, besides a mutual love for Matthew."

"Yeah, what's that?"

"Neither of us have any family left. My parents were killed two years ago, when their van rolled over an embankment. It was a foggy night, and I guess Dad missed the curve." She felt a sudden dampness in her eyes. "They'd gone on vacation, the first one they'd had since the drug dealers moved into Mayflower Heights. They were so involved here that they were afraid if they were gone for an extended time the dealers would just take over."

Cage nodded. "Sounds like your folks knew what they were doing. Drug dealing depends on apathy from a neighborhood. A kind of looking in the opposite direction, or a way of seeing occasional crime as an aberration rather than a prediction of more to come."

"That's exactly what happened here. We all had the NIMBY attitude."

"Not in my backyard?"

"Hmm…" She took a swallow of coffee and touched one finger to the sugar on the napkin. "Maybe if the dealers had come en masse it might have been different, but it was just one or two at first and they were quickly arrested. Most everyone saw them as nothing more than an occasional problem that happens in the best of neighborhoods. But more and more dealers came as the demand for drugs grew. Not just to Mayflower Heights, but all over the area. The dealers were as prevalent as the buyers. Pretty soon the police didn't come as quickly as they should have, or the dealers knew the patrol times so well that they just made themselves scarce. After a patrol car left the neighborhood, the dealers would pour back out on the street and set up business. Fridays were the worst. From about noon on, it was like walking through a flea market, except the only thing selling was drugs."

"Must have been frustrating as hell for your parents."

"It was. A lot of people saw the drugs as just recreational fun. I knew a couple who used coke just on weekends. She told me once that since they both worked, the weekends were when they had sex and got high. But then on Mondays they went back to work and didn't do either again until the following weekend. I even found myself thinking that if that couple were the average, then maybe the whole drug thing was overblown."

Cage pushed his chair back and propped one foot on the opposite knee. Haley found her gaze drawn to the tear in the denim. Grimly he said, "That's the insidiousness of drugs. There are people who use only occasionally for years and never do more. Then there's the other extreme. The individual who takes one snort or one pipeful of crack and they're instant junkies." Cage got up to get more coffee. "You mentioned frustration with the dealers. Was this mostly your parents, or was it everyone?"

"Everyone, but my parents were the most realistic in that they knew it would get worse before it got better. My father had read news stories of the streets being sucked into a drug network, and he feared it would happen here if something wasn't done, and done quickly."

"Did he form the Association?"

"The beginnings of it, but ironically, it wasn't until after my parents were killed that the neighbors really came together."

"Nothing like a tragedy to get people involved."

She nodded, thinking that the tragedy of Matthew's death had involved Cage and her, and not just at the grief level. "By the time I'd moved back here and gotten my divorce, the dealers were like locusts."

"But your work with the Association has made progress, Haley. You have a lot of the dealers looking over their shoulders or scanning the area for a video camera. And then there was that mention of you last night.''

"You mean that comment about me never doing drugs because I wanted to save the world?"

"I thought it was insightful.''

"You would. You think I'm just a bleeding heart."

"True, but a lot of times bleeding hearts make enough of a ruckus that the rest of us have to take notice."

Haley shook her head at his offer of more coffee. "I don't know what you mean."

"They know you can't be corrupted."

"Like you."

He chuckled. "I don't know about me. Maybe I haven't been offered the right incentive yet. So far, money, sex and part ownership in a small country haven't appealed to me, but who knows? Maybe someday someone will come up with a deal too good to pass up."

"Ownership in a small country? Good grief, if that didn't appeal to you, I'd say nothing would."

He shrugged. "Material stuff. I've never had it, and never wanted it. It just clutters things up and makes you get attached to things that have no meaning."

"Your only attachment was to Matthew, wasn't it?"

"And he's gone."

With those words, the conversation slipped into an uneasy silence. Haley kept thinking of things that Cage had said about himself. He didn't matter. He didn't believe in anything. Then there was the starkness of the apartment, and his attitude toward her. A working relationship in which he would cooperate; but why? If he was that much of a loner, why would he even bother? Surely he didn't need her or the Association to find Matthew's killer. He'd even admitted to going to the police.

Then there was the sexual attraction that she was finding more and more difficult to fight. And if those moments last night were any indication, he was, too. But again, why? He certainly could find sex if he wanted it. The innovative, exciting stuff that most likely would make kissing her seem like kissing a warm doorknob.

Maybe he saw her as some innocent thing to toy with. Or maybe he wanted to use her to get whatever he needed to find Matthew's killer. Then again, maybe neither of those ideas was true. Both presumed some measure of attachment. Maybe she was just an object to be passed by, touched when necessary and forgotten moments later. Haley didn't know if she should be insulted or pleased, but the disappointment she felt was real and painful.

She sighed, deciding that if disappointment was the worst thing she felt from contact with Cage, then she would survive.

"So did you get hit with questions this morning?"

"As a matter of fact, I did." She scowled. "You knew I would, and that's why you weren't around."

"I don't like to answer questions."

"I know, you prefer to ask them."

His face was impassive. "Which brings us back to what you have planned today. I know the Association meets tonight, but that's all. And since you surprised me last night with that unexpected appearance, I'd like not to be surprised again today."

She put her elbow on the table and rested her chin on her open palm. "You know what I'd like to know?"

He raised an eyebrow. "What?"

"How you can simply ignore everything I've said about preferring to run my own life."

"Haley, running your own life is what I want you to do. All I'm doing is making sure you have one to run. After what we heard in the warehouse last night, plus what Noah gave me this morning . . ."

"Who's Noah?"

"He's a cop I've known for years. I got in touch with him shortly after I got here."

Haley's eyes widened. "You mean you've been working with the police all this time?"

"More like keeping them informed."

"Why didn't you tell me that before?"

Cage got up and crossed over to her, leaning down and planting his hands on the table. "Because I didn't want you to know before."

"Oh."

"That's all you're going to say? No lecture about controlling things? No attempt to find out if I have an ulterior motive?"

"Do you?"

"Always, and lately it has too damn much to do with making love with you."

She started to say she'd been thinking about that, too, but she stopped herself in time. Cool and detached, she reminded herself. "Okay, why didn't you tell me about going to the police?" she repeated.

"I wanted to see what you were capable of. If you'd known I had a link to the cops, you might have gotten careless or lazy and assumed that nothing could happen to you."

He was probably right. Oh, not about getting careless with the crime element the Association was trying to get rid of. She was too concerned with bringing the community back to what it once was, and too aware of the dangers involved, for that ever to happen. But, Cage was becoming very easy for her, personally, to depend on. Easy to trust, easy to make her forget that he liked to run things, that he liked to be in control. "Tell me, did your friend Noah know about what you did to Boa?"

"Yeah, he knows."

"And he wasn't angry?"

"On the record, he was furious. Off the record, he said he would have done the same thing if anyone came near Pamela—that's his wife. But Noah called me this morning with a break in the investigation into Matt's murder."

"Really? You mean they know something?"

"They know there was a witness to the drive-by."

"Who?"

"That they don't know yet. Just that someone called the station and said they'd seen a car drive away. They got part of a licence number and the color of the vehicle. It will take a while, but once they narrow it down to this area, we could be close."

Haley stood, feeling a sense of loss. She'd known Cage would be leaving, but if they were this close to finding the killer, then he would be leaving even sooner than she'd thought. But she couldn't be disappointed about the news. "That's wonderful, Cage. I know you're going to be very relieved when this is all over and the killer is caught." Carefully she set her mug in the sink and said, "I better go, but I wanted to ask you if you'd do something for me."

"A leading question if I ever heard one," he muttered.

She frowned at him. "You have a dirty mind, Cage Murdock."

"Just too many unsettling thoughts about you." He gave her a direct look that said, "this is dangerous territory." "Last night, you were, how should I say this . . . Hot? Wet? Or both?"

She knew her cheeks were slashed with color. "You weren't exactly turned off yourself."

"And in the warehouse—your legs around my hips was a nice touch."

"It convinced them, didn't it?" she asked crisply.

"Hell, it convinced me."

She marched over to him. He didn't move, and she stopped close enough to touch him. She knew her eyes were bright and her rapid breathing betrayed what she was feeling. She wanted to kiss him, but most of all she wanted him to kiss her as he had in the recessed doorway. Deep and hot and wet.

She was trying to frame exactly what she wanted to say, holding her emotions closely in check, when the phone rang in the bedroom.

Cage cupped her chin, then, as if unable to resist, he dropped a kiss on her mouth, and murmured, "I should get that. It might be Noah." Before she'd had a chance to object, he'd walked out of the kitchen and into the bedroom.

Haley licked her lips, surprised that she could still feel his mouth. She wasn't sure if she was thankful for the ringing phone or annoyed at the interruption.

Be thankful, she told herself staunchly. She rinsed their coffee mugs, closed up the box of doughnuts and turned off the coffeemaker.

"Haley, you still here?"

"Yes," she called back.

"Come in here. Noah wants to talk to you."

She scowled. Why would he want to talk to me? she wondered as she crossed the living room.

Cage was seated on the edge of her unmade, thoroughly rumpled queen-size bed. The pillows were bunched up as if he'd been reading in bed. The room was dim, because the window faced the shadowed side of the house next door. A small fan whirled atop a wooden box. On the table beside the phone was the folder of newspaper clippings that Cage had been sorting through that first morning. She hesitated in the doorway, feeling gauche and self-conscious.

"It's about an arrest they made, Haley."

He was trying to ease her awkwardness, and for that she could have kissed him. She walked into the room and, since there was no place else to sit, sat down beside him.

"Relax," he murmured when her bare thigh brushed his jeaned one. "Nothing's going to happen."

"I feel so dumb," she whispered, disgusted at her prim behavior. However, she was more than pleased that he hadn't made fun of her or, worse, made some off-color remark.

Cage squeezed her arm reassuringly. "Here, talk to Noah. He'll make you glad you came in here."

She took the phone, and Cage moved so that he could stretch out on the bed behind her. Perched on the edge, she made herself not move. Cage jammed the pillows beneath his head, and she caught just a quick glance of his muscled arm. Good heavens, she thought, she was as nervous as some trapped virgin on the verge of being seduced.

To Noah, she said, "Yes, Cage has told me about you. What were their names again?" Her eyes widened in recognition. When she turned and glanced at Cage, her smile was broad. "I can't believe our video led to the arrest of two major drug dealers. Yes, they've been two of the worst.

That's just terrific. I can't wait to tell the Association. Thanks for letting me know. Thank you for telling me." She hung up the phone and started to get to her feet.

Cage snagged her wrist. "Congratulations. Noah was very impressed with the stuff you got on tape. Arresting the Frazer brothers is a real dent in the drug network."

She grinned, unable to keep her excitement in check. Now she felt twice as silly about her hesitation in coming to his bedroom. She giggled, her eyes animated.

Cage chuckled. "I don't think I've ever heard you giggle," he said as he brushed his finger down her arm.

Then, in one of the most spontaneous things she'd ever done, she threw herself in Cage's arms, hugging him with bursting enthusiasm. He caught her, sliding his hands down her back to her bottom and anchoring her solidly against him.

"Oh, Cage, this is so wonderful, so fantastic. Do you know what this means?" But without waiting for an answer, she said, "Our efforts are working! We're winning!"

"Three cheers for whoever invented the video camera," he said huskily.

Then she looked full into his eyes, those wintry blue eyes that were now intensely dark. She went very still, swallowing, suddenly aware of her position. Sprawled across him, abandon welling up in her body, desire coming up and through her as if she'd released a pressure valve that she'd held tightly closed and hidden.

Haley felt the rough denim of his jeans against her bare thighs, the slight abrasion of his T-shirt against her cotton top as her breasts cushioned pleasurably against his muscled chest. Her nipples hurt, and she longed to be rid of her bra, her top, his shirt. Her arousal had come quickly, yet it had done so naturally, not really sneaking up on her so that she was shocked by it. Almost as if this moment, this place, had been tucked away like an interlude awaiting their arrival.

Cage saw the moment differently. If he'd planned it, or sought it out or even just coaxed her into his arms, he would have felt more in control. As it was, the suddenness of her sprawling across him had left his thoughts floundering. He wasn't accustomed to women flinging themselves at him with such enthusiasm, such trust, such certainty that he would interpret their gesture in the innocent way in which it was offered. And with Haley, he knew the gesture hadn't been intended as a sexual one, a come-on, or, for that matter, as a teasing flirtation carefully hidden under the guise of enthusiasm. No, he knew without a doubt that the gesture had been as natural and fresh and innocent as her giggle.

Yet she hadn't pulled back, which both delighted and scared him. A part of him wanted to tuck her beneath him and kiss her thoroughly. But the cool objective side knew that would be fatal to everything he'd told her about not getting involved. But who was he kidding? Hell, he'd found out already just how involved he was. That night in the doorway had proved with sumptuous accuracy just how deliciously she could tempt him. Faced now with a choice, he should be smart and lift her away, thereby avoiding any further complications. He would be heeding the ever-present restrictions—don't touch her, don't kiss her, and don't make love to her.

"I should move," she said softly, but stayed perfectly still.

He didn't want her to move. Not now, not ever. "Yeah, my thoughts about you on this mattress haven't exactly been about sleeping."

"Well, I'm not really on the mattress."

Cage shuddered. No, she was on him. "A definite technicality, Haley." But he didn't push her away. Instead he tucked the pillow higher beneath his head, not yet touching her intimately, not yet really holding her down, giving her plenty of space if she wanted to move. Or leave.

But she still showed no inclination to pull away. Against him she felt like a long-sought missing piece to a puzzle. Maybe that was why he'd been basking in the feel of her. Maybe she was exactly what he needed for this exact moment. Not so much in what she could give to him, but in what *he* could give to *her*. She had spread languidly across him and deliciously surrounded him with such natural pro-

vocativeness that he was sure if she glanced in the mirror she
would not recognize herself. Then again, Cage realized, he
wouldn't know his own reflection, either.

She was having a profound influence on him, and he was
fast losing the will to fight her.

"Cage," Haley whispered as she tried to find her breath
and get a grip on her emotions. Her will to resist the longing for him, the need to let go with him, the compulsion to
experience making love with a man she truly desired
drummed through her with unrelenting persistence. Where
would he take her? What would she like? What could she
give back to him?

His voice got softer, huskier, mesmerizing her. "Know
what I like?"

With that question she knew he'd turned some crucial
corner. Still, beyond a lazy clasp of his hands on her hips,
he wasn't really holding her. She could still pull away, still
leave, but she, too, had turned a corner. "Tell me what you
like."

His hands slid up her body in a profoundly sensual motion as though to seal in his mind the exact feel of her shape.
At the same time he settled their bodies together so that the
fit was erotically timeless, a promise of forever.

He tangled his fingers in her hair as he eased her mouth
down closer to his. "You against me, heating me." He
brushed her mouth. "On top of me." Again he caught a
taste of her. "Wanting me . . ." And this time he kissed her
fully, drawing her tongue against his that sent sweet shim-
mers of arousal through her.

Haley gathered in the kiss as if her mouth against his were
as precious as jewels. His hands slipped under her top and
unhooked her bra. With a catch to his breathing that Haley
adored, he gently and exquisitely freed her breasts.

He lifted her then, but only enough to help her to pull off
her top and discard it with her bra. Even in this, the awkward shedding of clothes, he went slowly, as if determined
not to push her beyond where she wanted to go. But she
knew what she wanted, she wanted to ease this ache that was

quickly moving from pleasurable to a sweetly throbbing pain.

She straddled him, her head tossed back, her breathing getting more erratic, coming in hot pants. Cage cupped her breasts, thumbing her nipples, drawing one breast and then the other to his mouth.

"You taste so sweet," he murmured, drawing her nipple deeper into his mouth, the tugging motion making Haley gasp. Despite his jeans and her shorts, she could feel him nestled snugly against her own softness.

She wiggled a little, and he immediately gripped her hips to still her. She could feel the tension in his fingers. Her eyes found his in the dim room. Her heart speeded up with a sudden wariness. Why was he stopping? Didn't he want her? Had he changed his mind? She swallowed, and when she spoke, her question was hesitant. "Am I doing something wrong?"

"No, you're doing everything exactly right."

"I don't understand."

Cage took a deep breath, damning himself for not just taking her hug of enthusiasm and then doing something noble like springing off the bed and getting them out of the bedroom. Then he damned himself for wanting her and wished he didn't give a hoot in hell about birth control. But he did. And since he didn't believe in any kind of permanency in his own life, he had no intention of having to wonder, for the rest of his life, if he'd fathered a child. No way in the world would he walk away from here not knowing whether he'd left her pregnant.

In a gesture that was almost unconscious, he rested his hand on her stomach. In a low voice, he said, "I haven't got anything, baby. Nothing to protect you."

She ducked her head, knowing her cheeks were slashed with hot color. She folded her hands across her breasts. "I'm sorry. I mean. Oh, God..."

Cage closed his eyes, damning himself for not being prepared. But then he hadn't planned on ever going even this far with her. Furious with himself for leading her on, he debated making love to her and using withdrawal... Too dangerous, he immediately told himself. Mostly because he doubted he'd be able to pull back in time. It had nothing to do with the way his need for her was scorching all his good intentions.

Cage tried to draw her hands away from her face, but she resisted, and he cupped her chin instead. "Look at me."

"I can't. Never in my life have I done anything so..."

Cage drew in a long breath and let it out. His words slipped between them like a swish of insight. "So out of control?"

She nodded, scrambling off him to perch on the edge of the bed. She grabbed her bra and shirt. Again Cage cursed himself for the mess he'd provoked. He should never have kissed her. He watched as she fumbled with her clothes, coming to a decision.

He sat up, moved behind her and slid his legs around her hips so that he enclosed her in his thighs. She clutched her clothes to her breasts and tried to ignore the heat of him fitted so snugly to her back. He kissed her shoulders, her back, and finally nuzzled his mouth into the back of her neck.

"Remember your biker legs?" he asked, tightening his own.

She nodded, for her legs were indeed humming, just as they had when she'd gotten off his cycle in Paradise Falls. "Like they feel before making love."

"Yeah," he whispered, then moved his hands over her bare legs. "Ease the zipper down on your shorts, Haley."

"Cage, no..." but her protest fell away, forgotten. His hands were touching her breasts, and the clothes she was holding fell to the floor. She whimpered when he brushed his fingers across her bare stomach. How he managed she didn't know, but her zipper hissed down, and her heart skittered in anticipation.

"Lift your hips, just a little," he murmured as he continued to kiss her. She moved automatically to let him push her shorts down. She should stop this. She should pull away from his mouth... his fingers...

Then he slid his hand full onto her, and Haley felt as if every nerve in her body had burst to life in that one place.

When his finger slipped into the warm cove of her intimacy, Haley jumped.

"Easy, easy..." he murmured soothingly.

She closed her eyes, letting her head fall back, and she knew her body was wantonly reaching for his fingers. Her body pressed upward, and the resulting rush of sensation began in her toes, curling and winding its way up her thighs in dizzying spirals.

Cage's thighs braced her, and his mouth was still against her neck, sipping, tasting, knowing that no woman had ever felt so good, knowing that he'd never wanted so badly to see a woman's pleasure be so complete. His fingers slid deep.

"Ah, Haley... It's okay. Just let go, baby, let it happen."

She wasn't sure if she groaned or moaned, but Cage urged her on, whispering about her softness, her richness, how special she was. She arched high, turning to allow him to capture her mouth. She felt as if she were hanging in a glorious suspension that stretched and reached higher and higher. Then, with a breathless swirl, she tumbled down into a sea of languid softness.

Moments slipped by as she tried to find the will to move.

Cage held her, kissing her neck, and once more on her mouth, murmuring something about the magic and mystery of feeling and watching her come apart in his arms. Then, very slowly, he eased away.

She glanced at him. His hair was mussed, his shirt was wrinkled, and his jeans were unable to hide a very definite arousal. She reached for her clothes and concentrated on getting her bra and shirt on. Quickly she adjusted her shorts and got to her feet. She didn't know what to say, but the most damning reaction wasn't anger or even embarrassment, just a bleak sense of having allowed herself to go that far with him. Not even with Philip, at the happiest moments of their marriage, had she been that out of control.

Cage's silence was as loud as her uneasiness.

She took a breath and then said softly, "I guess we didn't do too good a job of not letting anything happen between us, did we?"

The second the words were out of her mouth she realized the stupidity of them. Nothing had happened *between* them. It had only happened to her.

Chapter 8

Hell.

Cage muttered a few additional expletives as he stood beneath the shower spray that was cool when he wanted cold. Ice water, he knew, would freeze out the unrelenting thoughts about Haley that he didn't want to have. His unsatisfied sexual longing didn't disturb him nearly as much as the other longing.

The one he didn't want to think about.

The one he didn't believe in.

The one that, if he didn't scrape it loose, would be a disaster.

The hell of it was, he had no defined name to pin on it beyond the need for it. He knew instinctively, though, that the emotion—whatever it was—ran counter to his purpose in Mayflower Heights, to the revenge he wanted for Matt. He could blame her bleeding-heart nonsense, her generosity when he'd wanted only to be left alone, even his own curious attraction to her. Yet in reality, Cage knew, those weren't at the soul of his churning feelings.

Since the incident with the Venoms, his distraction had become calcified, as much by Haley herself as by what that

gang could have done to her. If he could have kept his mind
on the protective, very professional area of things, then he
wouldn't now be that concerned. But the trip to Paradise
Falls, the warehouse scramble and her reaction to the news
that the Frazer brothers had been arrested had begun to peel
away a veneer that Cage had layered and depended upon for
most of his life.

And, he decided, facing another grimly realized truth,
concern for her safety had become more important than the
other news from Noah's phone call. The identity of Matt's
killer.

Cage stepped out of the shower and toweled himself dry.
A member of the Venoms, Noah had told him. The car used
in the drive-by had been stolen; the thieves had been identified as members of that gang. Now, it seemed, all that was
necessary was to identify the particular gang member who
had shot Matt.

Not a major problem, and Cage had confidence that
Noah would be ready to make an arrest in a few days. So
why wasn't he champing at the bit to get the bastard? He
had even more reason to want him now, because, as Cage
had suspected from the beginning, the final target was
Haley. Confirmed by the conversation at the warehouse and
supported by a comment Noah had told him the Frazer
brothers had made: "That Stewart bitch is gonna lose, she's
gonna be finished big-time."

Cage pulled on clean jeans and a blue oxford. He stuffed
the tails into his pants and then carelessly ran a comb
through his hair. He glared at his reflection in the bathroom mirror. "You're worried about her, that's why. You're
scared right down to your socks that someone will take her
out. You're furious that anyone would destroy a woman
who still believes in honor and goodness and making a difference."

Cage lowered his head and shook it slowly. How in hell
had he gotten embroiled in all this? Then again, if there was
an easy answer, he wouldn't be asking the damn question.

He flipped off the bathroom light and stalked out to the living room. Do what you gotta do, Murdock, just don't screw yourself up in the process.

With that core thought, he knew he had to convince Haley that their working relationship was going to become even closer than it had been.

Dropping that fact on her, he mused, would not please her. Therefore, he knew, the first step on his part was cooperation. A visit to some old geezer Haley viewed as cantankerous but necessary to lead other fearful members back into the Association, and then, later, speaking to the Association.

Cage was on his way out the door when Kevin stopped him. The teenager's face was pale, and he clutched a comic book in his hand.

"Oh, jeez, Cage, I gotta talk to you."

Cage narrowed his eyes. "What happened? It's not Haley, is it?" His heart raced.

Kevin shook his head. "A bad scene, man. A bad scene about drugs and kids."

"Why were you so late?" Haley asked fifteen minutes later, after she and Cage had left her apartment.

"I'll tell you later."

"Is it about what happened?"

"Now, why would I scowl about that? That was personal and special. Just between you and me." He took her arm as they stepped off the curb and crossed Standish Street.

Haley told herself that embarrassment was silly. Yet she knew that the one-sided lovemaking had taken them steps into a relationship that had little to do with working and everything to do with involvement. She took a breath, reminding herself that she should have known better than to allow Cage that kind of control.

Odd, she realized as they approached the Pedenazzis' small house, that control, her best reason for not getting involved with Cage, had more than marginally weakened. She felt the need to shore up that control, to find reasons to apply it to every situation. The difficulty for her was that she was finding the inability to fight her attraction itself scary. And even if she did want to give in to her growing feelings for Cage, she couldn't. Instinctively she knew she'd never be satisfied with anything less than all of him. And it was clear he would never accept anything traditional, like commitment or marriage. He'd been unwilling to handle a simple live-in relationship. So where exactly did that leave her? Nowhere, she decided grimly.

Keep your feelings in check, she told herself. And if you have to wring more mileage out of your hatred of being controlled, then, damn it, do it.

"Awfully quiet, aren't you?" Cage asked as they stepped up on the small porch. The house was small and boxy, sandwiched in between a trash-littered vacant lot and an apartment house.

"I was thinking about the best way to avoid you," she said evenly.

"Really? You could go with something simple, like telling me to get out of your life."

She tipped her head to one side, not trying to hide her amusement. "And would you?"

"No."

She grinned as she knocked on the newly varnished wooden door. A hand-lettered sign read The Pedenazzis. "That's what I like about you, Cage. Blunt and to the point."

Al Pedenazzi, a retired factory worker, peered through the small opening in the chained door. Looking a little suspicious, he glanced at Haley and then at Cage for long seconds before he released the chain lock and opened the door.

"Al, this is Cage Murdock. Matthew's brother. Cage is going to speak to the Association tonight, and we wanted to invite you to come."

Pedenazzi scowled, but gestured for them to come in. The interior was filled with religious symbols, dozens of framed family photos on doily-covered tables, and the scent of lemon oil and spice cookies. When Lena Pedenazzi wasn't dusting and polishing, she was cooking for her grandchildren.

Although he'd acquired a small paunch, Pedenazzi still carried the burliness of a factory worker. His eyes were alert and probing, missing nothing. He directed Cage and Haley to an overstuffed sofa with freshly ironed lace covers on the arms.

Al studied Cage. "My Lena has heard stories about you."

Cage raised an eyebrow. "I think I'm in trouble."

Haley patted his arm, murmuring. "No doubt it's the one about your expertise with that switchblade. That seems to fascinate everyone."

"Except you."

"Me, most of all. I owe you my life, or being spared rape, or both."

Lena bustled in. She was small, round and dark-haired, and Haley was sure she had some gypsy blood in her. Lena pressed her hands together. "Oh, we have company. Haley, my dear, you look wonderful. Doesn't she, Al?"

"Huh?" Al gave Haley a quick glance. "Too skinny. Why don't you get some of them spice cookies you made, Lena?"

"Oh, dear, of course. Where are my manners? I'll bring lemonade, too." Lena rushed out, returning moments later with tall glasses of iced lemonade and a plate of frosted spice cookies.

After everyone was served and compliments had been exchanged, Haley put her glass down on a coaster and got to the point of their visit.

"I'm contacting all the Association members who haven't been to a meeting since Matthew was shot. I've talked to some, and they plan to come, but I'd especially like to see you there, Al. Your support has always been seen by the others as a sign we're going in the right direction."

Lena shifted in her chair, lacing and unlacing her fingers. Pedenazzi leaned back, but not for a moment did Haley think he was relaxed and receptive. He'd always been contrary and suspicious, and while she knew Cage's appearance with her might allay some of that, she also knew she would have to present her side forcefully.

Cage had reminded her that she shouldn't give any impression that he was actively involved for more than the few weeks he planned to be here. False hope, he'd warned, was worse than no hope.

Haley began by choosing her words carefully. "I know you and many of the members are wary and afraid. I understand that, because I'm afraid, too. But we can't let the drug dealers win."

Cage said, "Haley's right. The best help you can give the dealers is to let them think they've scared you off. No one is advocating violence or telling you that you have to go on one of Haley's video jaunts, but a united front shows confidence and support."

Al leaned forward, and when he spoke his words were low and directed at Cage. "Is it true what my Lena said? You that good with a knife?"

"Sometimes a threat is better than the actual act. Boa wasn't hurt, but the possibility of the blade cutting just a little deeper scared the hell out of him."

Al sat back, gave Cage a long look, and finally grinned. "Scared him, huh? Didn't think them punks were scared of nothin'."

"That's what they want you to think. Actually, many are more afraid than you are. They have a lot to lose. Power, respect, money, territory—and there's the ever-present possibility of dying."

Haley leaned forward. "Al, if you could just come to the meeting ... Cage is going to speak, and he has some wonderful ideas for getting the Association back to what it was. He's had a lot of experience with drug dealers."

He scowled. "I got my grandkids to think about, you know. Even been thinkin' about movin' down by the shore. Enjoy my retirement instead of havin' to check the street before I let my Lena go outside."

"But you have to admit that things have been quieter," Haley said forcefully.

"Just since this boy got handy with his knife. So what happens when he leaves? You ain't stayin' here forever, are you?"

"'Fraid not."

"So, Haley, what happens when he leaves?"

As much as Haley wanted to offer full assurance that the neighborhood would be pristine and peaceful, she couldn't. "We keep fighting, because we can't quit."

"So then nothing changes."

Cage gave Al a direct look. "The change has to come from good people like you getting involved, Al. Haley needs the whole neighborhood to cooperate."

"They're gonna win. I watch the news. I see the riots and the killing. Pretty soon it will happen here. Just a matter of time."

Haley shook her head all the time he was talking. She understood his reluctance and his cynicism and, most of all, his fear, but she had another fear. Apathy.

Since Matthew's death, she'd sensed a growing feeling that, no matter how much they tried to combat the dealers, their efforts were no more than a temporary barrier. Cage's arrival had injected a huge dose of confidence, but if that confidence didn't show itself at the meeting tonight, she feared, the Association would lose even more credibility. For the sake of all that was at stake, Haley didn't want to appear to the drug dealers as wishy-washy.

Taking a breath, she chose her words carefully. "No, it won't happen here. We're not going to let it. My parents worked hard to keep this a safe neighborhood, and I won't let punks and gangs like the Venoms invade our streets and push us all out."

Cage touched her arm. "She's right. I've talked to the police, and they have nothing but praise for Haley and the Association. The cops can't be everywhere, and if citizens don't take an active role in their own neighborhoods, soon there won't be any neighborhoods left."

"Your kid brother got shot. If you're any kind of man, you gotta be here to hunt down the bastards. That true?"

Haley went still.

"Yeah, it's true."

"And when you got 'em and they're taken care of, then you're leavin'."

"That's right."

"Kinda selfish, ain't it? I mean, you come in here and get everyone all fired up, make them hang their mugs out there on the street for one of them Uzis to use for target practice and when you finish your business you say, 'see you later.' You're off in some resort with some lady friend, makin' whoopie, while the rest of us are back to dyin' in the streets."

"Al, Cage works for the DEA. He can't just not go back to work."

"And what in hell is the DEA? Drug Enforcement Administration, right? Well, ain't we got the required product that the DEA is supposed to be enforcing against? It's stupid. Why ain't the DEA's enforcement against drug use important in Mayflower Heights? Especially now that one of their own men has been touched by it. My tax dollars are doing a goddamned lousy job of protectin' me and my Lena if our street ain't even safe."

"Oh, Al, please don't swear, and don't get yourself so excited," Lena said, embarrassment and concern in her voice.

He reached over and patted Lena's hand. "See what them bastards have done? My wife is afraid I'm gonna have a heart attack. Ain't because of hard work or cholesterol, it's the stress of livin' here. Never knowing if, when I open the door, I'm gonna be lookin' at and livin' the last minutes of my life."

Cage got to his feet. "I can't argue with a lot of what you say. And I do understand your anger and frustration."

Haley got up, too. She couldn't believe that Cage was just taking this. She didn't totally disagree with a lot of what Al said, but his lashing out at Cage as if it were his fault annoyed her. "I think the problem is that you don't really know enough about Cage. He grew up in a gang-infested neighborhood, and his father—"

Cage squeezed her arm and interrupted her. "We'd like you to come to the meeting tonight. You don't have to commit to anything, but your support will help the others. I'd also appreciate it if you didn't say anything about me 'hunting' down Matt's killers. I certainly don't want what I have to do to become an excuse for vigilante violence."

Al narrowed his eyes. "Ain't a damn thing wrong with a little eye-for-an-eye stuff. The pretty words and dancin' around is for the politicians. What you did with that knife is what needs to be done to all them punks. Ain't never done anyone harm to know God is shakin' His fist and makin' things right again. Makin' life safe again."

He sagged back in his chair, and Cage murmured to Haley, "We better go."

They both said goodbye to Lena, who took Cage's hand. "Don't be mad at my Al, Mr. Murdock. He would like to be you, but all he can be is angry and scared."

Cage squeezed her fingers. "You don't have to apologize for your husband, Mrs. Pedenazzi. He's right on target. Mayflower Heights needs more like him."

When they were outside and once again alone, Haley said, "You should have let me tell him about your father."

"Why?"

"Because then he would have seen that you're not just talking. That you know what life in the inner city is like."

"Al's too smart to fall for that. It would have made him twice as angry. His assumption would be that since I knew the violence not once but twice, then I should be willing to move in here and become some kind of crusader for justice."

"And would that be so bad?"

"Look, I fought to get Matt out of the inner city. And all that went for nothing, because where does he get killed? Right here in another godforsaken neighborhood with drive-by killers. A real step up," he said sarcastically. "That kind of failure on my part isn't the beginning of idealistic endeavors."

"I don't think you failed, but I do think you feel terribly guilty."

"Damn right I'm guilty. Guilty as hell. Matt and I argued about this very thing a few hours before he was shot. I hung that phone up thinking I'd bought some time to change his mind before he did something incredibly stupid.

The next thing I get is a call that he's dead." He hesitated, his scowl deepening. "At first they didn't say exactly where he was killed. You know what went through my mind?"

"What?"

"Relief that the shooting had happened in front of his condo. Then I could at least excuse it as a fluke. I could tell myself that violence happens in nice neighborhoods and that I'd done the best job I could by getting him out of the ghetto, into law school and living in a place where guns and drugs and gangs are in the newspapers, not right outside the bedroom window."

"You mean if Matthew had been killed in front of his condo, instead of here, you wouldn't have wanted revenge?"

The possibility that the revenge was more focused on the *where* of the tragic incident indicated to Haley that Cage's anger was far more inner-directed than she'd thought. More of an anger at a failure on his part, an anger that the idealistic life he'd mapped out for Matthew had no substance, because it hadn't given Matthew the one thing Cage had wanted to provide. Security and a future untouched by crime and hopelessness.

He turned away from her and swore, obviously not pleased by her question.

Haley folded and refolded her hands. "If you want to talk about it..."

Bluntly he said, "Matt's dead. Dealing with my own guilt over that is going to take a hell of a lot more than a few heart-to-heart talks. Once I face the bastard who did it..."

"And splatter his blood all over Standish Street," she finished for him.

When he didn't come back with some kind of agreeing word or gesture, Haley's eyes widened.

He stared off into the distance, as if everything he'd ever wanted was out of reach. Either something had changed, or Cage himself had changed. Gone was the deep, revenge-filled fury. Had he decided against such a vicious revenge? She shivered. God, she couldn't believe she was viewing revenge as coming in degrees.

Suddenly she felt as if she were treading on shaky ground. If he *had* rethought why he was here and changed his mind, she didn't want to inject any opinion of her own. She knew he had to conclude in his own mind that killing whoever had shot Matthew would accomplish nothing. Most of all, it wouldn't relieve his guilt.

As they walked back to her apartment building, she kept thinking about his words. His guilt did seem greater because of where his brother had died. Saving Matthew from the inner city, pouring all his energy into making sure his brother would be a success, had been as idealistic as any parents' wanting only the best for their child.

My God, Haley thought as she realized just what she'd uncovered. As cynical and cold and unattached as Cage could be, beneath all that lay a fierce need to believe, to hope. He had longed for answers that would counteract all the terrible things he and his brother had grown up with. Matthew's death had not only proved to Cage that idealism was a pipe dream, but had convinced him that his own efforts to keep his brother safe had proven to be of little use in the end.

Haley wanted to curl around him and somehow infuse some new beginning, a renewed hope, into him; somehow give him a chance to see that he had done all he could do. Sadly she realized that one of the tragedies of this entire mess was that Cage had never really allowed Matthew to take responsibility on his own for building on the security Cage had provided.

By the time they got back to her apartment, Cage's temper was short and his scowl deep.

"The meeting is about an hour from now. We can go over together and—"

He slid his hand around her neck and into her hair. Haley reacted instantly and, to her shame, with an inner eagerness that made her wonder if Cage's effect on her was making her sex drive function on overload.

"I don't like this clawing need for you, Haley. It's eating up my guts."

She glanced around. They stood outside her apartment door. She could invite him inside, where it would be more private, but she didn't dare. After what had happened just hours ago, she didn't think it prudent to be alone with him, at least not until she got her thoughts in better perspective.

She tipped her head back as he eased her against the wall by her door. His voice was a self-annoyed mutter, "I'm not sure if you're in more danger from me or the drug dealers."

"Not from the drug dealers."

"From me, then."

"You're very persuasive, and you like to handle things your way."

He grinned, but just briefly. Then she realized how easily her words could be applied to their one-sided lovemaking, and she ducked her head self-consciously. As if he, too, preferred not to comment, he said easily, "Ah, that old fear that I'll control you."

She narrowed her eyes, glad for the shift in topic and tension. Being peevish was much easier to deal with than being aroused. "I won't allow you to control me."

"Always alert to every one of my motives, aren't you?"

"I don't trust you."

That seemed to startle him, and he scowled again as he searched her face. "I see I'm not the only one who's blunt and to the point."

"I don't mean not trust you *generally*. I trust you with my life, but my heart isn't ready...."

To her astonishment, he looked immensely relieved. He brushed his mouth across hers in the softest of kisses. "Then we're on safe ground. I can't give your heart anything. All those ideals like love and permanency and happiness forever are just not possible for me to give you. But your body..." His hand skimmed down her throat to her breasts, and then to her stomach and her thighs, touching her and drawing her near. She felt more than a little dizzy. He murmured against her cheek, "Giving you pleasure. Sharing a bed. None of those have to involve your heart."

She stared up at him, trying to figure out how she could be so caught up with and attracted to a man who had just told her all he wanted from her was sex. "I don't think I can do that, Cage." She swallowed quickly, speaking before she lost her nerve. "I mean, to sleep with you and only care about what our bodies feel and not care for you as a person."

Her honesty seemed to startle him, and he released her. "Maybe I should get the hell out of Mayflower Heights."

Suddenly she realized the enormous hole his words created. No doubt he wanted to leave because the attraction between them had already escalated out of control once too often. Had he realized that he'd given her a too-carnal glimpse of his intentions, and he didn't like her response? She wasn't sure, but if he left, she knew, she'd never find out.

She touched her fingers to his waist. "I need you to stay." Then, in case he misunderstood her motive, she added, "We have this working relationship, remember? And you don't know who shot Matthew yet. Plus you said you'd speak at the Association."

"I think this is called reminding me of my obligations."

"Well, they were important to you a few hours ago. Certainly the visit to the Pedenazzis hasn't changed that."

"No, baby, the one who's causing all these changes in me is you."

Haley couldn't contain her excitement as she glanced around the rapidly filling room. She and Norman had set up enough chairs for thirty, and it looked as if they were going to top that number.

Cage stood surrounded by a dozen people. Haley had no doubt they were quizzing him on everything from his work with the DEA to what he'd done to Boa. Having Cage here to speak had been a brilliant idea, she decided, and she wished now that she'd steered him to the front that first night. She'd known then that everyone was curious and fascinated. That had been more than evident in all the questions she'd been asked.

Haley had dressed in jeans and her old college sweat-shirt. Her hair was swept up into a high ponytail, and she wore small gold hoop earrings. Cage had glanced at her once, longer than necessary. The distance between them prevented her from making any judgment, but she'd liked the sense of intimacy that had come with the look.

"Think we should get started, cupcake?" Norman asked.

"In a few minutes."

"Haley, you're not waiting for Al Pedenazzi?" Norman gave her a skeptical look. "Cage said that you two visited him, but he wasn't exactly won over about coming back."

"Cage is right, but I'm hoping that Al's curiosity might get the better of him." They waited about five more minutes, but when it was evident that all who were coming had arrived, Haley went up to the front of the room.

Cage stood with his arms folded, leaning against one of the building's support beams. The relaxed stance, the neutral facial expression, even just the hint of the silver chain, along with the oxford tucked into snug worn jeans and the dusty boots he wore, all gave him a presence that had Haley's mind rushing back to those moments in his bedroom. His thighs around her hips, his mouth at her neck, his fingers...

How was it possible that just a glance from him was enough to make her wonder if perhaps she could just give her body and not her heart? The difficulty with that question was why she even had to ask it in the first place. It didn't square at all with her belief that making love involved more than just great sex, yet the longer she was around him, the more she was thinking that, with a man like Cage, great sex just might be enough.

She dragged her eyes away, but not before she saw Cage grin. My God, could he read her rambling thoughts? Of course not, she decided, and turned her concentration to the now-seated crowd.

"I can't tell you all how pleased I am that you're here. As most of you know, Cage Murdock is going to be saying a few words, but before he comes up here, I want to reiterate my own thanks to him for getting me out of two very tight situations. Most of you know of the incident with the five gang members."

Half a dozen people shouted their approval.

"Right on, Cage!"

"We knew you'd shake things up."

"Hell of a skill with that knife."

"Heard from my kid that Boa's still got the shakes."

Haley glanced over at Cage, but his expression was still neutral. She turned back to the crowd. "And then the other incident—"

"Haley?" Cage interrupted.

"Yes."

"Why don't we save the old business until later?"

She frowned, but nodded. "All right. And since you're the new business, why don't you come up here? I know everyone wants to hear your views and your suggestions."

The applause was so enthusiastic that Haley felt a lump in her throat. How ironic that this man who didn't believe in anything had simply, by his presence in the neighborhood, created new hope and energy, even in people who'd never met him.

Cage got a chair, turned it around and straddled it. In a low voice that had everyone leaning forward, he said, "I have to add something to your comments about Boa and the gang that surrounded Haley. From most of the talk that I've heard all the credit is going to me for rescuing her, or to my ability with the switchblade.

"The credit really goes to Haley. Standing her ground in that kind of terrifying situation takes more courage than I've seen in a long, long time. She was being harassed and threatened for a good fifteen to twenty minutes before I got there. I'm telling you this because she is the strength of your Association, not me. I'm just here for a short while, and then I'll be gone. And while muscle and a deft hand with a switchblade looks cool and tough, being cool and tough *without* a switchblade, as Haley was for those minutes, takes a depth of courage and fortitude you'd all be wise to emulate."

Haley stared at Cage through eyes that were suddenly blurry with tears. Not for the praise itself, but because the praise came from him. She rubbed her knuckle across her cheek to catch a tear. Then someone began clapping, and someone else followed suit, then another and another, until pretty soon they were all on their feet, giving her a standing ovation.

She had no idea what to say or whether saying anything was even necessary. "Thank you" seemed shallow and frivolous, for she felt awed and honored and embarrassed and more than a little astonished. Except for the conversation at her apartment after they'd returned from the motorcycle ride, Cage had said so little about the incident. Yes, he had complimented her then, too, but to present what had happened that day as if he'd been secondary...

She swallowed. His praise for her was just so extraordinary that she didn't know what it meant, but it said a great deal about Cage, and about why Matthew had so admired and loved his brother.

Finally they all took their seats and Cage began. He praised the Association and the work they'd already accomplished. He singled out the use of the video camera as one of the most feared by anyone who was breaking the law. He mentioned Noah Drake and the appreciation that the police had for neighborhood groups that got involved and worked toward a common goal.

Then he cited some of their failings. A few coughs were heard, and there was some shuffling of feet, and squeaking of chairs as they were moved back.

Cage waited until everyone was quiet again. "There are two things I want to focus on. And both involve perception." He got up and walked over to a table, picking up one of the comic books that Haley had left in his apartment.

"How many of you have seen these?"

A few hands went up.

One of the members called out, "My kid was reading one this afternoon."

"Yeah, mine, too."

Cage asked, "Have you looked at them? I mean, more than just the cover or a quick thumb through?"

The members all glanced at each other, scowling, shrugging or shaking their heads. Haley, too, wondered what Cage was getting at. She'd forgotten about the funny books that she'd left at his apartment.

Cage reached for the pile on the table and passed out the bright books.

"Hey, Cage, come on, a comic book? Let's not get paranoid here."

"Bear with me, okay?"

Walking back to the front of the room, he said, "I want you to turn to the page I've marked and tell me what you see."

Pages were shuffled, and Haley walked over to Cage. "Cage, what is it?" she whispered.

He shook his head, indicating she should wait until everyone had had a chance to look at the page.

Norman Polk who came to his feet. "It's a damn instruction manual on how to snort coke and smoke crack! In a comic book, for God's sake!"

One by one the members saw what Norman had seen. Anger began to spread through the room, with questions about where the comics had come from and how anyone could be so horrible as to use the innocent vehicle of a child's comic book to promote illegal drugs.

Cage waited for them all to express their outrage, and when they were all quiet once again, he said, "There is no limit to the inventiveness of people who want to hook your kids on drugs. They've used space-gun toys packaged with instructions on blasting marijuana into the lungs, cans that look like soda with secret places to hide pills and small quantities of crack. The worst mistake you can make is to underestimate the enemy."

Norman asked, "You mean we got to expect drugs to show up in the places we don't expect them?"

"Yes. The more you fight against them, the more they will try to come at you from different angles. You've all got to be alert and shrewd and aware. A drug dealer's worst fear is an educated, aware and involved public.''

Low murmurs of "Yes" and "That makes sense" moved through the group.

Cage continued. "Now, as long as we're on the subject of perception, we need to show off Mayflower Heights the way you want it to be." He paused a few seconds, then added, "I can see by your confusion that I've lost you. For example, Haley has a window box outside her apartment building, and it's filled with flowers. I noticed it because it's an oddity against the trash, the boarded-up buildings and all the graffiti. However, all of you would feel better about the progress you're making against the dealers *and* make more progress, if your neighborhood reflected it. So I suggest that first thing in the morning we begin to get rid of the combat-zone look. We'll need brooms, some plastic bags for trash, some paint to get rid of the graffiti."

"Make Standish Street look the way it did before the drug dealers started messing up our neighborhood, huh?" asked someone in the front row. Nods and agreeing smiles appeared on many faces. After a few questions, the meeting was ended. Many of the members came up to Cage to thank him.

Norman asked in a low voice, "Where did you get the comic books, Cage?"

Haley stepped forward, her face pale, her hands in her pockets to stop them from shaking. "They were given to me, Norman. Of course, I had no idea of the contents. I just assumed..."

Cage dropped his arm around her and tugged her against him. In an easy voice, he said, "Actually, Kevin spotted the drugs and told me. Norman, could you finish up here? I have something I need to check out with Haley."

He steered her across the room and into a deserted corner.

She buried her face in her hands.

"Sweetheart, you couldn't have known."

She took deep breaths before speaking. "Kevin knew."

"And Kevin had a drug problem, which gives him an edge when it comes to spotting this kind of stuff." At her look of surprise, he added, "He told me about it, that it was last year and that he'd been in rehab and had beaten it. As to the comics, my point in showing them was not to make you or anyone else feel as if you'd failed in some way. I just wanted the members to know what extremes the drug networks will go to."

"Thank you for trying to make me feel better, but I could have passed those out!" she said in disgust at her carelessness in just taking the comic books. "That's what I was going to do, and if I hadn't left them in your living room, I would have."

"But you didn't," he said reassuringly. "And from the reaction and comments from those here tonight, the comics have already gotten into the hands of kids. You can't save the world, Haley. You do what you can and you don't dump on yourself for what you can't or couldn't do."

She sniffled. "Do you know how guilty I would feel if one child—"

He touched his finger to her mouth. "Don't. Don't do that to yourself."

"Oh, God, Cage." She put her arms around him and let him hold her. He rubbed his hands down her back in a soothing motion. She lay against him, soaking up all that he offered in strength and support and comfort.

Moments later, when they were walking back to join the others, it occurred to Haley that keeping her heart closed off from Cage was no longer possible.

He had already captured it.

Chapter 9

For the next two days, Haley and Cage and the other residents of Mayflower Heights worked on giving an overall face-lift to the streets. Bags of trash were collected and hauled away to the city dump. Repairs were made to broken steps, windows replaced, fresh coats of paint used to cover up the graffiti.

Barbecue grills were brought out, and community meals were served, with Norman Polk remarking that the get-togethers reminded him of the old block parties that had been held every Saturday night before the drug dealers had moved in. Residents who hadn't spent any more time on the street than it took to go from one place to the next now lingered to talk. Bicycles and skateboards swerved along the swept asphalt. The sounds of hammers and hope and enthusiasm rang down Standish Street.

Positivity such as hadn't been heard since the Association had originally been formed rejuvenated even the most jaded cynic. Haley was now more certain than ever that what she'd seen in Paradise Falls that afternoon was indeed possible here in Mayflower Heights.

She'd seen Cage only in snatches. He'd taken part in the early cleanup, but then had organized a crew to work in the vacant lot next door to the Pedenazzis' house. Haley had been centering her own concentration on getting the Association's meeting place in inviting shape. With some of the old members now returning, she wanted them to feel welcome, as well as safe.

She'd just finished overseeing the placement of a new white sign with blue letters that read The Mayflower Heights Association. She stood back to admire it, her grin growing.

"Very impressive," Cage said from behind her.

She whirled around, smiling broadly, and then spontaneously threw herself into his arms. He caught her in a fierce grip. "Oh, Cage, doesn't everything look wonderful?"

"Terrific. The neighborhood's done a great job."

"Thanks to you."

He set her away from him, and she caught a flash of resistance in his expression. He probably didn't want any credit at all, especially when it involved a neighborhood so much like the one he'd so eagerly put behind him.

"You have a few minutes?" he asked. "I want to show you something."

"Sure." She walked with him across the street, saying hello to a woman pushing a baby stroller. Two kids whizzed past them on Rollerblades. Flower boxes now hung from many of the windows, an offshoot of Cage's citing Haley's geraniums as one of the bright points on an otherwise dismal street.

"Where are we going?" she asked.

They passed the Pedenazzis' house, and Cage came to a stop in front of a repaired chain-link fence. "Right here."

Haley stared at the once trash-littered vacant lot in amazement. The area had been raked clean of trash. Two men were working at putting up a swing set, and park benches had been brought in. Already trying out one of the seats was Al Pedenazzi.

"Cage, how did you ever get him out here?" Haley stared in astonishment.

"I didn't do anything. He told me he'd been watching the 'goin's-on', and although he thought it was a wasted effort, he had to give credit where credit was due. Mainly to you. His exact words were 'she's a do-gooder, and my Lena says there ain't enough of those in the world. Guess we're lucky to have a homegrown one.'"

"Good heavens, he makes me sound like a tomato," Haley said, not in the least offended.

"A cupcake, I believe, according to Norman."

She groaned. "Please. Norman's called me that ever since I can remember, but anyone else isn't allowed." Her eyes took in all the work and the potential hope for a safer neighborhood that the cleaned-out lot represented. However, Haley reminded herself that the dealers wouldn't just disappear the way the graffiti and the trash had. Vigilance and tenaciousness would still be needed, but they had made progress.

Her eyes smarted as she watched Al. He'd been so adamant, so pessimistic, and yet here he was, inspecting the benches and nodding in approval at the swing set.

Lena came toward them, wiping her hands on her apron.

"Oh, Mr. Murdock, how can I ever thank you? Ever since you left the other day, Al's been talking about you. He couldn't get over you agreeing with him about the drug problems."

"He made some valid points. In fact, I intend to pass them on to my superior." Cage gestured toward Al. "I'm glad he's over there helping. After the meeting the other night, a number of your neighbors remarked how much they missed both of you being involved."

"Cage is right," Haley added. "We need you and Al."

Lena grinned, but then a worried look passed over her face. "I just hope this lasts."

Haley pressed her hands around Lena's. "We're going to keep working to see that it does."

They said goodbye and walked back to the Association's building.

Inside, a newly installed ceiling fan—donated by a local hardware store—hummed softly. Haley went over to the large cooler that had been filled with beer and soda. Cage paused to glance out the now-sparkling window where he'd stood the night he'd come to see Haley. She shivered as she recalled his words about splattering the blood of Matthew's killer.

"Beer or soda?"

He shook his head. Haley opened a can of soda and took a long swallow. She walked over to the window, stopping just close enough to stare out the window with him.

Wondering if Cage had decided he'd spent far too much time on her idealistic dreams and not enough on why he was here, she asked, "I haven't had a chance to talk to you. Any progress on the license plate number the police were going to check?"

"I haven't heard from Noah, but then I haven't been at the apartment much, either, so I could have missed his call. I did take the comic books down, though, and Noah admitted he thought he'd seen everything, but that the books were a new one."

"When I think of how close I came to passing them out to the neighborhood children, I get a little sick to my stomach."

Cage touched his finger to her lips. "Stop beating yourself up. People moving drugs spend a lot of their time looking for angles and approaches that don't raise suspicion. Unfortunately, there's a lot more of them than there are of us. Or perhaps I should say there are less of you who are willing to get involved."

"Including you. You're very much involved."

"It's my job, Haley, not my mission."

She sipped the chilled soda. "Why did you ever go into the DEA? You've made it clear you want nothing to do with the inner city, with any reminders of where you used to live. And you certainly worked hard enough to get Matthew into a successful career and away from living in any crime area."

"Actually, it was Noah who set up a meeting for me with some representatives of the DEA in Washington. At the time, I knew I needed to get into something where I could use my street skills and make some steady money. They wanted to use me undercover to infiltrate the drug networks. Matt had gotten a scholarship into law school, and I had no ties here beyond some college courses I was taking. I ended up squeezing the courses in throughout the past eight years whenever I had some lag time."

"What about time for you? Time to be happy, time to fall in love?"

Cage stared at her. "There were women. In fact, I even lived with one for a while, down in Florida. She was beautiful, terrific in bed, but also fixated on the hope that I would agree to marry her."

"What happened?"

"Nothing happened. I didn't marry her, and she found someone else."

"I didn't mean *her.* I meant *you.*" At his frown, she added, "You had a chance to be happy, and you allowed it to slip away."

"Don't you think you're making a major leap in reasoning? Just because we lived together and had great sex didn't mean it was destined to last forever."

"But you lived with her, Cage.... That says a lot. I mean, you don't want attachments, you don't want anyone obligated to you, and you've been very clear about how you feel about any kind of idealism, yet you actually lived with a woman."

"For a few months. And it was a big mistake."

"Why did it end?"

"I told you. She wanted to get married." The wintry blue of his eyes chilled her. "What in hell is this? An inquisition?"

Haley continued, undaunted. "I just find it odd that you would walk away from a relationship that you obviously enjoyed, based on the sole fact that you didn't want to get married. The worst thing that could have happened was a divorce. I've been through one, and they aren't pleasant, but they do prove there is a way out of a bad relationship."

"Thanks for the insight," Cage muttered. "I'm always on the lookout for ways out of a relationship. Now, can we drop the subject?"

"There *is* a reason, isn't there? A reason that no one knows but you."

"Cut the soap-opera stuff." Then he narrowed his eyes and gave her a penetrating look. "Let me see if I can figure you out. You resent anyone trying to control you, but you, in turn, want to control everyone else. You just can't stand it when you don't know every facet of someone's life. And not only *know* it, but either try to change it or, if that doesn't work, try to rearrange it. You've been doing that to me since I walked into that first meeting. Switching beds, following me to the warehouse meeting and using me in the hope of dragging Pedenazzi into your Association." He backed away from her, and suddenly she sensed he was disengaging himself in more than just a physical way. It was as if he'd pulled a black curtain between them. In a precise, intense voice, he said, "I don't like it, Haley. I told you when I came here, I wanted no part of any kind of a relationship, and what in hell's happened? I'm up to my neck with you. I want to watch you and touch you, and I want to make love to you. I don't like it, I don't want it, and damn it, I resent it."

Haley swallowed. She should move, she should back away and make some excuse to leave and let the tension disappear on its own. She had come too close after the meeting a few nights ago, close in that she'd allowed him to touch her heart. In his present mood, the only thing that could come of hanging around was pain. Not for the first time, she realized how much simpler things would be if her feelings could be reduced to only sexual ones.

The more she reminded herself that she'd already divorced a man who had tried to control her, the more she realized that with Cage, control was becoming less and less of an issue. She didn't want to think she could so easily readjust her thinking. Not for a man who'd just told her he resented her.

Perhaps it was time to take off the romantic lenses and see this for what it was. Sexual, and not permanent. As for control, Cage had been remarkably restrained at moments when he could have taken from her, when she would have been more than willing to give.

But realizing that she'd been more willing than he had was a revelation in itself. She'd had little pleasure from making love with her ex-husband, again because he liked to be in control in the bedroom just as much as out of it. Haley had found sex to be more boring than unfulfilling. Routine. The difficult thing for her had been that Philip never seemed to notice. He had acted as if she were supposed to be passive, supposed to always be under him, supposed to find satisfaction in the act even if she never was fulfilled.

Cage was nothing like Philip, she reminded herself, but she, too, had changed since getting to know Cage. And there, she realized, crouched her worst fear. She was more than just attracted to Cage; she wanted him in the most intimate way…and if she wasn't very careful, he'd know she'd fallen in love with him.

She shuddered to think how he would react to that. He would no doubt accuse her of trying to manipulate him, of trying to push her idealistic ideas of happiness and "forever after" on him when he'd clearly told her he wanted nothing to do with any kind of a relationship.

"Haley…"

She kept her lashes lowered, blinking and damning the sting of tears she didn't want. She had to get away from him. "Yes, yes, we should go."

"Look, I don't want to hurt you. I know your questions are well-intentioned, but wasting your idealistic talents on me is futile."

"You're probably right," she said crisply. "Look, we've kept things under control.…" She swallowed, recalling the times they hadn't, the time in his bedroom when *she* hadn't. "Well, under control most of the time. We've had a good working relationship. Now that the Association is regrouped and the streets are looking more civilized, I would imagine you want to concentrate on doing what you came here to do." She tossed her soda can into a nearby receptacle, and then, ignoring his deepening scowl, she stood on tiptoe and brushed her mouth across his. "Thanks for all your help."

He ignored her thanks, and her kiss. Instead, he gripped her shoulders when she started to move away. "What I came here to do? Let me get this straight. You're giving me permission to get revenge for Matt's murder?"

"Certainly not," she replied hotly. "I'm simply saying that you're welcome to go and get on with your life, whatever it entails. I won't interfere or try to run anything. That's what you said you wanted, isn't it?"

He let go of her, his eyes a little distant, as if he weren't really sure of anything. Finally, in a remote tone, he muttered, "Yeah, that's what I said I wanted."

Son of a bitch.

The wind tore across his skin as he rode. The cycle ate up the miles of asphalt, but Cage paid no attention to the changing scenery or the lessening of the traffic as he left the city. His concentration was tight enough to keep him on the bike and in the right lane, but that was it. He wasn't heading anywhere in particular, just riding to clear out his head.

His emotions—the ones he'd always believed he didn't possess—weren't so easily defined. And from the moment he'd stalked away from Haley, gotten on the cycle and ridden out of Mayflower Heights, those emotions had clamored through him, no matter how much he tried to deny them.

Nor did he have to concentrate very hard to know why.

One woman.

One bleeding-heart do-gooder whose idealistic way of viewing life should have been extinct—or, if not, then thinly shredded by the influences around her. And yet she staunchly maintained some rosy image of hope and new tomorrows. How in hell did one find new tomorrows when the yesterdays were so damn discouraging?

Grimly he realized that her optimistic outlook could have been dealt with. In fact, Cage had no doubt that if she were like the social worker he knew in Florida who refused to give up on drug addicts, or if she were like the mission workers in South America who, despite rank poverty, maintained a love and dedication that boggled Cage's mind, he could easily have handled it. Even if Haley had been like Matt—caught between a nostalgia that embraced hope and the reality that the cesspool of drugs and violence wasn't fixable by noble intentions—he wouldn't have had a single problem.

Hell, if her idealism could be fitted into any of those slots, he wouldn't be in this mess. But somehow this woman affected him personally, deeply, and that was what unsettled him the most. She had churned up and exposed a part of him he'd never allowed anyone to see. Not the old man, not Matt, and certainly not a woman.

Yet slowly she was peeling back the layers, making him look at himself, making him yearn for things to be different.

He'd known women more beautiful, more experienced, and so far from idealistic they hadn't known the word existed. Brenda what's-her-name, for starters. Now, any relationship with her, that would be uncomplicated. He wouldn't have to bare his soul, or find excuses to say no to sex, or spend any nights—as he had the past few—recalling the sweet sounds of pleasure she made on the edge of the bed when she came apart in his arms.

He should just keep riding and never go back. Cage had every confidence that Noah and the cops would eventually get Matt's killer. Even his need for revenge, so strong that it had eaten at him like a cancer, had now subsided. No doubt, thanks to Haley. Bad enough that he'd become preoccupied with her, despite his determination not to. How in hell had it all happened?

The crazy thing was, he doubted she was totally aware of how she'd influenced him. Nor did he believe she'd set out with some missionary intent to change him in the first place. From his own experience with trying to keep Matt from going back to an inner-city neighborhood that resembled the one Cage had dragged him out of, Cage knew changing

Matt's mind permanently wouldn't have been any cakewalk. And for damn sure Haley's trying to change him—or his mind—should have been impossible.

And he sure as hell didn't want to change. Not for himself, and not for Haley Stewart.

Cage slowed the cycle, taking a turn and bearing right. The truth was, he had changed. Deeply and irrevocably. Haley had found some part of him that he hadn't known existed, urged it to the surface and, in her own idealistic way, exploited it.

He couldn't stop thinking about her, stop wanting her, stop wondering about what she would do after he was gone.

He rode for miles, trying to clear his mind of her, but she clung to his thoughts with the same tenacity with which she clung to her idealism. Her words about his having another reason for avoiding marriage crowded back into his thoughts. How had she known? How had she known, when he'd so carefully kept that part of himself buried? He hated the reason because it was so entrenched, its roots so deep. It was tangled and thick and ugly, and Cage had never acknowledged it to anyone.

Even within the confines of his own thoughts, he had never wanted to deal with it, to chance looking too closely at it, so he'd pushed it back farther and farther as he'd continually tried to prove by his actions that it didn't exist.

Oh, he knew Haley didn't know anything specifically, but her quizzing about his refusal to get serious in a relationship had touched a raw nerve.

He eased up on his speed and exited the interstate. He needed to go back and see Noah. Although he wasn't sure he had any answers as to what to do about Haley, he did feel marginally better. He brought the bike to a stop at an intersection as he looked around for signs that would get him back on the highway to Mayflower Heights.

Damn.

Cage lowered his head and shook it back and forth slowly. Paradise Falls. The same intersection, the same general store. Only this time Haley wasn't behind him, with her hands clinging to his belly, her breasts pressed into his back, her legs gripping his hips.

Maybe he'd freaked out. Bad enough that she'd managed to take charge of the direction of his emotions. For him to have come here, without any conscious thought, blew his mind.

When he'd brought her here after her experience with the Venoms, Cage had chosen the town partly because of the total contrast to Mayflower Heights. But there had also been another reason.

A reason she'd love, he thought with grim sarcasm. Geoff Dane and his wife, who lived in Paradise Falls, had taken in inner-city kids in the summer to give them a chance to see a tree, eat from a vegetable garden, swim in a pool. Cage and Matt had come here for two weeks every August until they were well into their teens.

After Matt had passed his bar exam, Cage had suggested Paradise Falls as an ideal place to set up a law practice. But Matt had wanted to be closer to the city, and then he'd handled Haley's divorce, and after that he'd finally taken the offer at Donovan and Cross.

But if he'd practiced in Paradise Falls, he'd probably still be alive....

Cage stared straight ahead for long, agonizing seconds. Finally he realized the unbridgeable gulf between two realities. What Cage had wanted for Matt, and what Matt had wanted for himself. In a way, it was exactly the same gulf between himself and Haley, except with different facets. She feared him because she feared he would take over, control her. But Cage's fear was greater; he feared she'd discover the deeper and not so altruistic thoughts he had always harbored about his brother.

Stay away from her, he told himself. Don't touch her, don't kiss her, don't think about her. And, most of all, don't do what's been eating at you for days. Don't make love to her.

With that thought, he adjusted his sunglasses and headed back toward Mayflower Heights.

* * *

"I'm tellin' you, I heard it just a few minutes ago."

Haley frowned. "Kevin, I'm not doubting your word, but where did you hear it?"

"At the pool hall over on Fuller."

"So that's where you've been," Alicia scolded. "I've been looking for you all afternoon."

"Jeez, Mom, it's bad enough that you're gonna drag me away from my friends, now you don't even want me to say goodbye."

Haley touched his shoulder. "Kevin, your mother's decision to move doesn't mean you can't see your friends. I'm sure she'll be down here to visit me."

"But how come now? The place looks good, and Cage is here to keep everything in order."

"Cage told us he won't be around forever, and that how-to comic book on drug use terrifies me," Alicia said. "It's all settled, Kevin. We're moving uptown, and nothing is going to change my mind."

Kevin started to say something, but Haley stopped him. "Tell me about what you heard."

"They said a major shipment is coming in at three-thirty at the mill section. It's gonna be cut and packaged and ready for the street by Friday. Somebody joked about a candy store of coke."

From what Kevin said, and what she knew about past drug shipments, the mill section south of Mayflower Heights would attract the least attention. The buildings there edged the street, but the road also led directly to a closed access to the interstate.

Haley went into her bedroom and came out with the video camera and one of the new cassettes that Alicia had bought for her.

"My God, Haley, you're not going to go tape it?"

"I most certainly am," she said as she checked to make sure everything worked. "The arrival of the drug shipment, and anything else I can get."

"Are you crazy? After what happened in that ware-house? And they've arrested the Frazer brothers. Don't you think you've done enough? You're gonna get those dealers so angry at you..." Alicia's voice trailed off, as if she didn't even want to mention the possibilities.

Haley hugged her. "Please don't worry. I'm not suicidal, and don't forget, nothing beyond those threats has hap-pened. Unfortunately, the Frazer brothers aren't the only drug dealers. Besides, I'm not going to go alone. Norman and a few of the others will be with me."

"What about Cage?"

"No."

"No, you're not going to ask him, or no, you're not go-ing to tell him?"

"Both," she said dismissively. "Kevin, would you run over to Norman's and tell him I need to talk to him? Also John and Tony."

"All right! I'm going, too."

"No, Kevin, you can't."

Haley thought he looked as if someone had punched him. "Whattaya mean I can't? I did before."

"I know, and you shouldn't have. Cage was right. You're not old enough to be involved...."

"Not old enough?" He glared at Haley. "I've done drugs, had sex, and gotten wasted on Wild Turkey."

Alicia paled. "Oh, God."

Kevin gave her a perturbed look. "Come on, Mom, get real here. You knew about the drugs. The other stuff is no big deal. Everyone does it."

But her paleness soon turned to anger. " 'Everyone does it' is a foolish and stupid reason. If everyone jumped off the roof of this building, would you do that, too?"

He shrugged. "Depends. Could be fun."

She narrowed her eyes. "If ever there was a reason why we should move away from here, you just gave it to me."

Haley put her arm around Kevin's shoulder. "As much as I know you would be a big help, I have to agree with Cage."

He swore and jerked away from her.

"Kevin! Don't you dare treat Haley like that!" But he slammed out of the apartment. Alicia's eyes filled with frustrated tears. "Oh, Haley, I'm so sorry...."

"Don't be silly. He's disappointed, and I can understand that." After a few more reassuring words to Alicia, Haley walked over to the phone and dialed Norman's number. As angry as Kevin was, she wasn't sure he'd remember he was supposed to contact them. She quickly told Norman her plans and he promised to get the others. Whether it was Cage's influence or a sense that caution was called for, she called the police and asked for Noah Drake. She was promptly told he was in a meeting. Haley finally told the officer at the desk what was going on, and he promised to send a patrol car as soon as one was available.

Haley mentally shrugged. She'd heard *that* before, and from her own experience she knew that "when available" could mean twenty minutes or three hours.

A half hour later, armed with the video camera and an extra cassette, Haley, Norman and the others made their way to the designated area. Because of the tall, old structures, the sun had to fight its way through the shadows. The hazy light revealed a scorched despair immersed in overgrown blight.

Haley halted at one corner and glanced toward the back of one of the buildings. Two men stood there, and she watched them unlock the doors, look around and then walk away. She listened for a truck, but the only traffic noise came from the nearby interstate.

According to what Kevin had said, the shipment should be coming in within ten minutes. She wanted to get set with the camera in an inconspicuous place that would give her a view of the doors and the interior of the building.

She said, "If we can get to the second floor of that old firehouse, we could capture the arrival and unloading through that window that faces the warehouse. Maybe get some license-plate numbers, and some good face shots, too."

Norman and the others agreed. Quickly they made their way to the firehouse, where Norman pushed in a door long ago battered up by a heavy object. No doubt a drug raid in the early days, before all the junkies and dealers had learned how to avoid the cops, she decided grimly.

They crossed the trash-strewn floor, passed the pole that firemen had once slid down and finally located a set of stairs. The wood creaked as they made their way to the second floor, Norman in the lead. The heat suffocated them. By the time they got to the window that overlooked the building, Haley's clothes were sticking to her.

Nevertheless, they settled in. The windows had long since been broken, but despite a crossdraft, the breeze wasn't cooling. Haley sat on the floor with the video camera aimed and ready to tape.

"Now all we have to do is wait."

And wait they did. Three-thirty came and went.

John passed around cans of cold iced tea he'd brought.

Three-fifty.

Tony muttered, "You sure Kevin got the time right? Or even the day right?"

"He seemed positive," she said as she glanced at her watch for the tenth time. Almost forty minutes since they'd climbed the stairs and settled in to wait.

"Not a sign of anyone since those two guys unlocked the door," Norman said from his crouched position to her right.

"Maybe they got delayed. Traffic or something."

"Maybe they're not coming."

Haley again glanced at her watch. Her energy had long since been sweated out of her. Maybe this wasn't the place. Maybe she'd misunderstood what Kevin had told her. But he'd mentioned the old access road, and this street was the only one that hooked into it. And from this vantage point, even if she'd gotten the building wrong, they would have seen or heard a truck.

"Either Kevin got the tip wrong, or somebody was blowing smoke," Norman said. "I say let's forget it and get out of here."

"Yeah," Tony agreed, "Before we can't. I'm about dead from this heat."

John nodded, cursing the stifling air.

"Haley?"

She glanced at Norman and the other two men, her disappointment visible. "You're right. No one's going to come. Maybe we should just chalk this one up as a dead end."

The return to Standish Street wasn't half as energetic. In fact, Haley was worried. Now that she thought about it, a tip of that magnitude wouldn't have been bandied about in a pool hall. Certainly not when undercover cops were known to be in the most unusual places.

Kevin hadn't mentioned who had done the talking, and he hadn't gotten any other details besides the exact information he would need to galvanize the Association into action.

Had it been some sort of trap? But no one had been around, and if it *had* been intended as an attempt on Haley's life, they'd apparently changed their minds about that, too.

As they turned onto Standish Street, Norman gripped her arm. "Oh, my God!"

Haley's eyes widened with disbelief and horror. The cleaned-up Standish Street that they'd left a little less than two hours ago looked as if every vandal for miles around had descended on it. Trash littered the streets. Car tires had been slashed. And the newly hung sign that had once read The Mayflower Heights Association now sported a crudely painted and very gruesome, writhing snake.

The improvements in the vacant lot lay in ruins, the swing set a twisted mass of colored metal, the benches burning even as Al Pedenazzi beat at the smoldering flames with a broom.

But the destruction was most savage at Haley's apartment house. Coarsely written and obscene graffiti had been spray-painted in red on the building. Her window box was gone, the red geraniums trampled and crushed on the ground. In red paint that dripped ominously like blood were the words NEXT TIME YOU DIE.

Alicia was in hysterics, and Kevin was doing his best to calm her down. Apart from a few scattered neighbors, the street was coldly silent.

Haley couldn't take it all in. Not just the brutal and senseless destruction, but how easily they'd conned her. There had been no drug shipment. It had all been a ploy to get her away so that they could prove who really controlled the streets. Why had she assumed they would come at her directly? Or do something as obvious as what the Venoms had done? This had been calculated and carried out with cool precision.

Never in her life had she felt such a sense of defeat. Not just in her surroundings, but in her heart. Cage had been right. Idealism wasn't reality. Now, here, in all this destruction, she had reality. Fistfuls of it.

"Has anyone seen Cage?" she asked wearily as she handed the video camera to Norman.

"Not since he rode out of here on his motorcycle."

"When we needed him, he wasn't here."

Haley whirled to face the growing and restless crowd. "Don't any of you blame Cage for this. This was my fault."

"Haley, don't be ridiculous."

"It *was* my fault, damn it! I'm the one who thought I had it all figured out. I'm the one who should have known a few coats of paint and swept-up streets didn't mean they wouldn't come back."

"Cage will know what to do."

"Cage will have every right to say 'I told you so,'" she said in total disgust at her own stupidity. "And he'll be right."

Chapter 10

Cage was just about to leave Noah's office when Haley walked into the police station.

At first glance, he almost didn't recognize her. Her clothes were dirty, her hair was tangled, and her skin was sweaty. She looked as if she'd been cleaning out a dusty attic. The contrast to her glowing look after the cleanup on Standish Street was so striking that Cage might have assumed that either the before was a dream or this was a nightmare.

As she drew closer, Cage saw more than mere dishevelment and dirt-streaked cheeks. Something had happened to her, something had changed. Without a clue as to what it was, he reacted with a cold, hard fury that rose, unbidden, from the core of his soul.

He made his way toward her. His outrage ignited with a need to shield her, to catch her up in a protective grip, while at the same time to try to handle his own flat-out terror.

Her eyes had hardened with rage. Not anger or frustration or disappointment, but rage, an emotion he'd never seen in her.

Cage gripped her shoulders and felt the trembling. He drew her into his arms. "What in hell happened?" he asked, bracing himself for the answer.

She sagged against him as if he were her support system. Taking a shaky breath, she whispered, "They're bastards, Cage. I should have known it was a trick. I should have known...."

"Who are bastards? Should have known what?"

Noah came forward. "Haley, I'm Noah Drake. Why don't you come into my office and sit down?"

Cage followed her into the glass-paneled room. Someone brought in a glass of water, and then Noah closed the door. Cage brushed her hair back from her cheeks. "Are you hurt anywhere?"

She shook her head, taking a huge swallow of water. Cage forced himself not to bombard her with questions. She sat on the edge of the chair, holding the half-empty container and staring at her lap. "Kevin told me about a shipment of drugs that was supposed to be delivered to a warehouse near the closed access road."

Cage and Noah glanced at each other. Then Cage said, "You took the video camera and went to film it."

"Yes." Then she looked up at him and frowned in confusion. "How did you know?"

"I know you, Haley." he replied grimly. "I know you too well. Go on."

She told Cage and Noah the story, of waiting long past the hour Kevin had overheard as the time the shipment would come in, of returning to Standish Street and finding her apartment house singled out as some sort of trash target, but also of the wanton vandalism of the entire neighborhood.

Cage got to his feet.

"Take it easy," Noah said in a low murmur.

"Easy, hell. I'm up to my neck with taking it easy."

"No one was hurt."

"Of course they were hurt," Cage snapped. "Maybe not blood and bullet holes, but their homes, their sense of safety—if they even know what that's like anymore. The old line 'It's a jungle out there' is true. And Haley. For God's sake, she's their last hold on sanity and she's beginning to unravel.''

For a few seconds, all that could be heard was their uneven breathing as tempers were barely kept under control.

"They're winning,'' Haley finally said wearily. Her tone swung Cage's attention back to her. "Alicia is moving away, and the street is all but deserted, with everyone back to hiding in their houses. The park, Cage." Her eyes were so filled with sadness, Cage had to glance away. "They broke the swing set, burned the benches. Poor Al..." Her voice died, and she shuddered. Then, in a curiously unemotional tone, she added, "I know the dealers are rubbing their hands with glee, thinking they've won. And all because I stupidly followed a tip overheard in a pool hall. First the comic books, and now this. I have no one to blame but myself.''

Cage studied her, coldly furious at what they had done to her. His mind tumbled with half-formed thoughts. He wanted to take her a million miles away from here, he wanted to find the bastards who had set her up and vandalized her apartment building, but beyond all that, he felt as if the attack on her were an attack on him. As though *she* were a part of him.

The idea of calculated revenge kicked in and stunned him with its intensity. Revenge for Haley? No, that was supposed to be for Matt. His brother, the kid he couldn't save, the kid the old man loved, the kid that he'd—the word fell into place like a missing puzzle piece—the kid that he'd resented.

Mentally Cage tried to use all the old excuses, the old guilt, the old refusal to avoid confronting the deeper truth.

Beneath his concern, his love, his promise to the old man, Cage realized, he'd always resented Matt. Resented the hope the old man had in the kid while firm in the assumption that Cage would die in the streets. He had resented the obvious favoritism toward his brother. He had resented the old man's expectation that if he lived, Cage was always to care for Matt.

Who in hell had ever been there for him? Who had ever given a damn whether *he* lived or died? Who had ever felt that he mattered, that *he* was worth a damn?

Haley Stewart.

He dragged a hand down his face. The truth that he'd denied lay blatantly clear before him. The emotion felt so new, Cage wasn't sure what to do with it. Haley believed in him, not just in his ability to help her or to protect her, but in him as a human being. Commitment to someone else suddenly slipped into his thoughts, along with the belief that there would be a tomorrow, the knowledge that if he died, someone would care.

He had no idea what kind of expressions had passed over his face, but undoubtedly they'd been a little strange.

Haley peered at him worriedly. "Cage, please say something. You're scaring me."

He drew in a breath, seeing her differently now. He should be pleased, should be thanking her, but instead he felt unsteady, unsure. He'd never had anyone simply care about him, and he didn't know what to do with the feeling. Should he be grateful? Suspicious? Worried? Maybe he shouldn't do anything. After all, she cared about a lot of people. Caring about one more hardly made for a brass-band announcement. He managed a slight smile. *"I'm* scaring *you?* You're supposed to be worried about yourself, not me."

Noah got to his feet. "Look, let me get someone over to Standish Street to take a look. Maybe he'll find some clue as to who might have done this. In the meantime, I have a suggestion for you two." When both remained silent, Noah added, "Some time away from Mayflower Heights. Even if it's just a day or two. You both need some distance and some perspective."

Neither of them said anything.

An officer knocked on the door and then came in. He set up a tape recorder, and Haley repeated in detail what had happened. She also told of calling the police before she and the others went to the designated warehouse. Cage felt a moment of vindication for Haley when Noah called in the officer who had taken the call. Noah chewed him out, reminding him that Standish Street should have had highest priority, since Matt had been shot there. He also, to Cage's satisfaction, informed the officer that if it weren't for Haley and the Association, they wouldn't have the Frazer brothers cooling their heels without bail.

Haley finished up her statement, and she and Cage left the police station.

Outside, Cage took her arm. "You up to a ride on the cycle?"

She nodded, but she was clearly distracted. "Sometimes I want to just run away. Run away to somewhere safe and clean and empty."

Cage needed to hold her, needed to know she was okay. Tugging her into his arms, he muttered, "So much for my great idea of a working relationship, huh? I shouldn't have just ridden off. Or at the very least, I should have stopped to see you before I went in to see Noah."

"But you couldn't have known this was going to happen."

He brushed his mouth across her forehead. "Nice try, Haley, but I should have seen this, or something like it, coming. After what we heard at the warehouse, I knew the lull wouldn't last forever. I just underestimated their timing." He shook his head, cursing under his breath.

But Cage's anger at himself didn't reach its full potential until he saw her apartment building. He'd seen death threats, he'd seen brutality, he'd seen vicious hate before, but the graffiti-scrawled warnings in dripping red paint sent an ominous chill through Cage that he'd never experienced.

Haley seemed to sag under the weight of what surely was every ideal she'd ever held having been shredded and violated. "You know what I feel, Cage? Hollow. Like someone pulled some plug and everything that was inside me poured out."

He knew how that felt, he thought furiously. He'd just experienced it, listening to her at the police station.

Cage went with her into her apartment, which, amazingly, hadn't been touched. He scowled as he glanced around. As much as he wanted to believe they hadn't had the time or the nerve to get inside and tear the interior apart, he knew better. If they'd planned this out to the extent of fabricating a drug shipment to get her out of the neighborhood, they wouldn't have missed the sick pleasure of slashing up her personal things. No, they had left this intact deliberately, he concluded as he glanced around the apartment's contents.

He had no doubt that they would be back.

Cage glanced at her. Her relief that the interior had been spared was obvious. False hope, he decided grimly, the mainstay of a do-gooder.

He sighed, both pleased she had some hope—even if it was false—and worried about what was coming next. "I want you to pack some things, Haley."

"Pack? You mean to move?"

"We're leaving here." He knew she had taken too much comfort that her personal things hadn't been disturbed.

She shook her head. "No, I can't."

"*You can't?* I don't want to hear *can't.* I should have taken you out of here days ago. Didn't you just tell me you wanted to go away to somewhere safe, that you felt empty, violated?"

"Yes, but I can't leave here permanently. Maybe, as Noah suggested, for a day, or even just a few hours." She scowled. "You know, like we did after the Venoms?"

"A few hours in heaven before we return to hell. Is that it?"

"I just need some time to get my bearings and decide what to do. But I can't just pack up and leave. This is my home, and besides, what about the others?"

"You're not responsible for the others. They're all adults, and no one is forcing them to stay here."

"But they have no place to go. If I just up and leave, the dealers will surely move in like locusts. Like they were before. I know what they did here was aimed at me, and I shouldn't have been so shocked. Now that I've had a little time to think this through, I know I can't let them think they've beat me."

Cage's fury erupted. "Beat you! Of all the damned asinine reasoning! Who in hell do you think you're dealing with? A bunch of reasonable-thinking intellectuals who are playing devil's advocate about inner-city blight? These guys play for keeps, Haley. I told you days ago that this is about money and power and greed and turf. They don't give a crap about you and your lofty hopes for greenhouse conditions and neighborhood unity."

She lifted her chin. "And what is your solution? To cut them up with your switchblade?"

"Don't tempt me," he said darkly.

Her cheeks paled. "You're serious."

"As serious as I've ever been about anything."

Cage crossed to the window. It was an astounding sight, like one of those split screens that showed a before-and-after shot of changes. The face of his apartment building was almost pristinely clean, yet Haley's looked as if it had been through a war. They had methodically drawn a circle around her, in much the same way that the Venoms had formed a circle when they'd cornered her on the streets. In the latter situation, Cage had used some heavy-handed persuasion and had gotten her out. Next time, he knew, he'd need more than a switchblade. With a start he realized that his own thoughts scared him now because of the potential rage he knew lay so close to the surface. He'd thought he'd felt responsible for and protective of his brother, but that paled compared to the tangle of reactions he felt at even the possibility of Haley's being hurt.

Despite his jabs at her idealism, he knew it was a quality that attracted him to her, but when her ideals came up against her own safety, he drew the line.

Cage sighed again and dragged a hand through his hair. So, what to do? Forcibly hauling her out of here didn't appeal to him, and he knew it would accomplish nothing. She'd simply come back. But maybe if he could get her away for a few hours so that she had a chance to put some distance between what had happened today and what could

happen in the next few days . . . He knew one thing. He had
no intention of letting her out of his sight.

He turned from the window and said, "Okay, Noah did
suggest we get away. Let's do that."

"Is this a trick?"

He raised an eyebrow. "You mean am I planning on kid-
napping you and locking you away in an old tower?"

"Please don't be sarcastic."

"All right, how 'bout if we call it a night out in a small
town with graffiti-free buildings and quiet streets?"

"Paradise Falls?"

"Yeah." Cage surprised himself with the suggestion.
Hadn't he been warning himself about staying uninvolved,
of keeping his focus off Haley? Yet, he realized that he, too,
needed reassurance. He needed to see her happy, her eyes
sparkling with wonder and excitement, not ringed with
horror and disillusion.

She smiled then, the pleasure that replaced the pain in her
eyes making him realize that this was one decision he'd
made that was exactly right. Softly she said, "I'd like that.
Yes, I'd like that very much."

Two hours later Cage brought the motorcycle to a stop in
front of the Paradise Falls Inn. The Victorian inn had rolling lawns sprinkled with white wrought-iron umbrella tables. Geometrically shaped beds of rosebushes were
scattered about as though sprinkled by a master gardener.
Yellow-and-white awnings shaded the windows that faced
the strongest glare of the sun. A veranda-size front porch
with plump-cushioned wicker chairs, a swing attached with
brass chains to ceiling hooks and hanging baskets of geraniums and petunias mixed with green-and-white caladium
completed the picture of warmth and charm.

Haley stared, her eyes alight with anticipation, as she got
off the motorcycle. Definitely calmer now, she realized that
just knowing they were coming here, along with the little
time she'd taken to pack an overnight bag, had all helped to
lessen the stress of seeing the senseless vandalism in Mayflower Heights. Thinking back, she realized she'd been

shocked and horrified by the physical rampage but was more affected by the numbing sense of her own failure that the incident served to underscore.

Here she felt as if she'd been transported from horror to happiness. A state of mind, she knew, and yet she felt renewed, no longer numb, no longer drained of energy.

She glanced at the inn and at Cage and a new realization shimmered over her. One she should have been thinking about on the ride here, but she'd simply been so glad to leave behind the destruction that her mind hadn't considered this new possibility. Would they sleep together, or would they get separate rooms? Cage hadn't said a word one way or the other, but Haley had no problem with the former. She loved him; she'd known that despite the ongoing disputes and disagreements. However, she certainly didn't want to seem forward or, worse, act as if she was planning something he had no intention of doing. Maybe it would be best to assume they *weren't* going to sleep together and then see what he wanted. This way, she wouldn't be disappointed.

Affixing a bright smile to her face, she glanced once again at the grounds and at the inn.

Cage grinned. "I take it you approve."

"It's wonderful. But why didn't we see it the first time we were here?"

"It's quite a ways from the road and the Danes don't advertise."

"The Danes? Do you know them?"

"He's a retired attorney. He and his wife used to take in some of the inner-city kids in the summer for a few weeks. To give them some weeks with clean air, cookouts, and swimming in a real pool rather than standing in front of an open fire hydrant."

"And you were one of those kids."

Cage unloaded the few things they'd packed for the overnight stay. "Yeah. Matt, too. I've kept in contact with them over the years. Geoff and Lily came to the funeral, and I stayed here for a few days afterward."

"Then, when we rode here that day, it wasn't just by chance?"

"Actually, I hadn't decided to come here until we were on the road. I wanted to take you somewhere totally opposite to what you'd just been through, and Paradise Falls seemed the perfect place."

"Well, it *was* perfect," she said, taking a deep breath and squeezing his arm. "And it's just as perfect today."

They walked up onto the porch and smiled at a young couple who were sitting on a wicker love seat sipping something that looked lemony and cold. Haley whispered to Cage as they stepped into the cool interior, "Are we going to get separate rooms?"

"That's up to you."

"Then you weren't?"

"I didn't bring you here to sleep with you, Haley."

"Oh."

"You're disappointed?"

"I don't know, but yes, I think I am."

"Because of what happened the other afternoon."

"Yes. I thought you wanted . . . me."

"I do, but I've no intention of putting you into some seductive situation so that your defenses are down or, worse, you accuse me of trying to control you with sex."

Geoff Dane, a lean man with a shock of steel-gray hair, rimless glasses and a welcoming smile, crossed the shadowed interior and extended his hand, effectively forestalling any further conversation.

"Cage, good to see you again. Had no idea you were still in Rhode Island."

"For a few more days. Geoff, this is Haley Stewart."

He greeted her warmly. "Welcome. Let me get you registered. We're not too full right now." He went on to describe the available rooms, as if the choice of the right one would add to the enjoyment of their stay. Included was a room on the third floor that overlooked the gardens.

Cage glanced at Haley, and she knew he was letting her make the decision they'd been discussing earlier. Or perhaps he was giving her control of the room choice. For she had a very real sense that whatever decision she made would be fine with Cage. It was a bit unsettling, she realized. If he'd simply taken a room and she'd had to agree or embarrass everyone by making an issue of not wanting to stay with him, then she could indeed have safely blamed him for trying to set up some seduction scenario.

Oh, she knew he was surrendering control to her, and she should be pleased. Instead, she faced a whole different issue. How she really felt about making love, about falling in love with Cage. For she'd realized after the comic-book incident that he was already deeply entrenched in her heart. But, unfortunately, she wasn't as sure if she should abandon her more logical reasoning that she would get hurt if she stayed on this path with him.

Unquestionably she'd fooled herself into thinking she could keep from wanting him, all the while hoping that he might just sweep her away so that she wouldn't have to decide. Wasn't that what had happened in his bedroom? She should have been relieved when he'd stopped, when he'd said he had nothing to protect her. Yet she'd clearly felt rejected, hurt, embarrassed and, most of all, frustratingly disappointed. In the end, Cage's only consideration had been to give her those moments of exquisite pleasure.

On some subconscious level, then, she'd obviously wanted to be seduced. That way she could use the excuse that she had simply reacted to the moment, to the passion, to Cage.

He'd told Geoff that he would be in Rhode Island a few more days, and that meant their time together was short. Tonight would be a one-time joining with him before a whole lifetime of nights without him. Perhaps the safe way was to take separate rooms, but tonight she could choose to be with him. In a few days, even that choice would be gone.

"The room overlooking the garden sounds wonderful."

Geoff Dane smiled. "I thought that might be your choice."

Cage's expression was totally neutral. He pulled out his wallet, but Geoff shook his head.

"This is on Lily and me."

"Geoff, that's not necessary. You're not going to make any money giving away the best room in the house."

"But seeing you with someone is better than money. Now, why don't you go on up and get settled? We serve dinner here at seven, but there are also a number of fine restaurants in town, if you don't feel like being on a schedule." He handed Cage a key and added, "It's the first door on your left at the top of the third-floor landing."

Cage pocketed the key, picked up their small bags and gestured to Haley to go ahead of him. The stairway was carpeted in a flecked burgundy that continued past the second floor to the third.

Nothing was said until Cage had the room unlocked and they were inside. The first thing Haley noticed was a four-poster double bed with a white-and-rose lace quilt. The walls were painted a creamy white, with a ceiling border of pink rose wallpaper that matched the quilt. Garden prints in long, rectangular gold frames gave a sense of undisturbed beauty. Cage flipped a switch, and a brass ceiling fan began to whirl slowly.

Haley crossed to the window that overlooked the garden. White lace sheers shimmered in the light breeze, bringing the fragrance of roses indoors.

She turned and glanced back at Cage, who had settled in a high-backed upholstered chair. He watched her, his eyes steady, his forearms resting on the arms of the chair. If someone had stepped into the room, they would have assumed he was relaxed and languid. Haley knew better. She realized, in that moment, that she could sense the change in him because she'd come to know him so well.

Their bags lay on the floor, and his posture related a sense that there was no rush, yet she knew that her decision about the room had changed the dynamics. Whether they were together a few days, a few hours, a few minutes, she knew that coming into this room with him meant they would make love. But it also meant that when she left here, she would be different. That both scared and intrigued her.

Haley was glad for the distance between them, wary of the sudden clamoring need for him. Surely he couldn't see the hunger in her eyes, the slight tremble in her hands, the tightness in her body? Her arousal had come too quickly, she thought, but then, perhaps she had been waiting too long, in some secret part of her, for this moment. Coming with him, taking this room with him, seemed like two small steps compared to the giant leap ahead of her.

She could put a stop to the direction things were taking, turn away, say she'd come to her senses. She knew Cage wouldn't take what she couldn't give. But then, who would be the real loser? She would. For she desperately wanted him, and she was just as desperately afraid that this might be her only opportunity.

"You're not sure, are you, Haley?" he asked, in a low voice edged with what sounded like disappointment.

She pressed her lips together and closed her eyes. His chagrin cut into her, too deep for her to answer his question with an honest *yes*. Yes, she was sure she wanted to make love. She just wasn't sure how he would react if he guessed she was fearfully close to falling in love in him.

In a husky voice, she turned his question around. "You're sure, aren't you?"

To her surprise, he didn't answer right away. "Being sure implies knowledge that nothing can go wrong. I've already discovered that with you my knowledge has been both limited and wrong."

"I don't understand."

"Me neither," he said grimly. I'm still trying to figure you out. Let's just say that I've learned a few things about myself I don't like."

Haley wanted to ask, but she feared the answers. No doubt at some level he was still fighting the attraction between them.

Still, they were here, and he was as much as saying it was her move, her call, her decision.

She turned back to the window. The sheers billowed around her, fanning her cheeks, her arms, cooling the restless, swirling heat within her. She wanted to throw off her clothes and stand in hedonistic freedom. She wanted to find pleasure with him, in him, but most of all she wanted to give to him. Her thighs ached, the heated core of her burned, and the memory of his fingers sliding deep inside her sent a shiver rippling down her spine.

She tried to clear her throat of its rasp. "This is a wonderful place," she murmured, "Like something out of a dream or a fantasy."

"I'm glad you're pleased. I considered a hotel in Providence, but I know you were really taken with Paradise Falls."

She turned just enough to see him in the waning afternoon light. "Thanks to you."

He shrugged.

They stared at each other a moment, then both fell into a strained silence. Haley turned back to the garden, suddenly feeling awkward with her need for him, with the arousal that was now churning to new levels. She heard him come to his feet, and her mouth went dry.

She didn't move. She didn't dare.

Her body tensed in anticipation. His fingers brushed her skin, and she jumped.

"Easy, baby, easy..." He touched the back of her neck, then swept her hair aside as he bent to kiss her. She caught her breath at the hot hunger of his mouth. Her eyes drifted closed.

His hands splayed at her waist, urging her back against him. Then, with a lazy skill, he fitted himself against her with a naturalness that made her shudder.

Cage went still, amazed that so common a gesture could cause such intense reactions. Cause them in her, cause them in him.

Her arousal startled him.

His arousal startled her.

He had barely touched her, and yet it was clear she'd plunged into a state of languid desire. Her body swelled and smoldered. His hand feathered across her hips, dipped between her legs, lingered, enticing her to arch into his palm. Following his silent instructions was as natural as taking a breath.

"I want to feel you wrap around me," he whispered. She could only nod before his hand was gone.

She sucked in her stomach, her hips and lo̶̶
less with anticipation. His mouth drifted to her
shouldn't be able to do this to me," he murmured
woman should have this kind of power."

For a few seconds, her mind flailed around in an erotic haze, trying to put his words together. The curtains blew around them, their long shadows drawing provocative patterns. Her body swelled with each touch, each kiss. His fingers skimmed open her blouse buttons, then deftly unhooked her front-closure bra. The cool air swept her skin before his hands cupped her breasts, finessing the nipples.

"Cage, please..."

Once again he slipped one hand between her thighs, nudging her legs even farther apart. She knew she was teetering very close to release, and she knew he knew it, too.

"No... Someone will see...." She wasn't sure she cared, and she knew she wouldn't stop him.

"Only the roses," he murmured as his fingers opened the closure on her slacks. He drew a finger along the lace panel of her panties.

Breathlessly she whispered, "You're very persuasive, you know."

"You're very seductive." With his other hand, he palmed her breast, and she felt her nipple burrow eagerly into his cupped hand.

Then he eased her around so that she faced him. Haley slipped her hands around his waist and tipped her head back. His eyes penetrated hers as he pushed her blouse off her shoulders and brought his mouth down on hers in a crushing kiss.

Haley couldn't get enough. Her fingers dug into his waist, skimming along his belt to the front of his jeans. She brushed her fingers down the straining zipper, her mind exploding with sensations and images. She wanted to see him, touch him, feel him against her, bask in the heated intimacy of having him inside her. She wanted him to take her quickly, take her gently, take her on the floor, across the bed, in his arms, between his legs—

"I can't stand this...." she whimpered with a shuddering softness. She burned and ached, her body yearning to yield. Standing before him, naked to the waist, she began to shake with the driving need for fulfillment with him.

Cage stepped back, and she swayed, her hands clawing for him. His gaze wound deep inside her, probing and stirring her, far beyond any point of mere sexual arousal. His consuming power over her body paled by comparison to the surreal hold he had on her soul. Haley realized it as though from some far-off distance, as if the sumptuous banquet they'd delved into was only the beginning.

Cage opened his belt. The ends dangled as he reached for the button to his jeans. She stood wantonly exposed, her mouth slightly open, her hair moving from the breeze blowing behind her. Her eyes followed his fingers. He eased the button open.

"Come here."

"God, Cage..."

"Come here, Haley."

She kept licking her swollen lips. She felt swollen in every part of her being. How she moved, she couldn't have said. Her breasts felt heavy and separate from the other parts of her body. Her slacks itched, and she wanted them off. Never had she been so quickly and deeply aroused, and she knew it had little to do with the surroundings, and everything to do with Cage.

The open jeans drew her eager hands, and she slipped her fingers inside. He, in turn deftly, peeled her slacks down, along with her panties. He urged her against him, and they tumbled back onto the bed. For a moment, Haley wondered if the sudden weight would crack the wood. Cage fumbled with a foil packet and managed to get its contents on in such a smooth motion that if she hadn't felt it, she wouldn't have known he'd done anything.

He speared his fingers into her hair, rolled her beneath him and entered her.

She opened her legs, the feel of him inside her so exquisite that she wanted to capture the sensation and store it away in a safe place.

He lay perfectly still, and when she opened her eyes he was staring down at her. His level of arousal had just about neared its peak. "I'm not hurting you, am I?"

She shook her head, drowning in the pleasure she saw in his eyes. "Come deeper," she urged.

He stared at her for a long second, his tone oddly intense. "I'm already in too deep now."

She brushed her fingers along the back of his neck, rubbing the thick texture of his hair between her fingers. "I'll let you go," she whispered, wondering if she would be capable of ever doing anything that heartbreaking.

He lowered his mouth without answering, and his kiss carried a possessiveness that Cage didn't want to think about. He reveled in the magnificent taste of her, in the thirst she'd created in him, a thirst that would never again be quenched except by her. Dangerous thoughts, he knew, but even more dangerous because he knew how thoughts too often became hopes. And he was a man who couldn't believe in hopes.

His mind couldn't concentrate; his thoughts were too fuzzy, too elusive, too centered on trying to hold back his own raging body.

She slid her hands over his hips, tugging him deeper.

Heat burned away at his control, and he was recklessly close to losing it. "Slow and easy... Once I begin to move, Haley, it'll be over."

In answer to that, she wrapped her legs around his hips, and her hands urged his mouth to hers. "Once you kiss me, it'll be over for me, too."

His mouth took hers in a hot, raw kiss that had her raising her hips to meet his thrusts. Cushioned by the plump quilt, they rose and fell, moved and swayed, his body finding an immeasurable array of sensations that carried him beyond anything as tactile and ordinary as mere pleasure. He felt ravished and savaged and extraordinarily alive.

Haley gathered him in.

Cage feasted.

Outside the window, guests at the inn strolled in the garden, slowly making their way to the veranda for cocktails before dinner was served. Music drifted in, a soft ballad crooning of love lost, love found. One guest remarked on the black motorcycle and wondered who owned it. According to what she'd heard, a matronly guest commented, the cycle belonged to a handsome young couple. On their honeymoon, perhaps.

"On their honeymoon? Ah, yes..." a guest remarked.

"They went to their room, and no one has seem them since."

Ahh, yes... as it should be...

The soft laughter then stole into the room, along with the strains of music and the scent of roses, to curl in secret seclusion through the sounds of steamy whispers and satisfaction.

Cage dragged his lungs for oxygen. His climax roared up, armed with enough power to blow away any chance that he could wait for her. His body shuddered, bearing down, as pins of light exploded behind his eyes like a thousand tiny prisms.

He whipped his head back, his body convulsing and rocking as he poured all of himself into her.

Haley cried out, her body folding and pulling from him, while at the same time her own ultimate fulfillment was reached and raged through her. She wanted to hang forever suspended in this moment. To be so in sync with him, so lost with him, so fused to him, that nothing could ever break them apart.

He lay spent, his hair damp with sweat, his mind as heavy as his body.

Haley wanted only to sleep, to stay wrapped beneath Cage in a cocoon of pleasure. No, she thought dreamily, better than pleasure, better than satisfaction. She knew their joining had forever sealed her love for him.

Moments passed with each of them silent, their breathing ebbing to a normal speed.

Haley kissed his ear. She wanted to tell him she loved him, adored him, wanted to stay forever in this room with him. But she knew she couldn't. Instead, she said, "I think we're going to miss dinner."

He mumbled something.

"What did you say?"

"I already ate."

She grinned into the ever-deepening shadows. "Me, too. How about dessert?"

He lifted his head then, and for the first time she saw no sign of the usual wintry blue, only a warm blue, a contented blue. She tucked the image away in her heart.

He peered at her as if she'd suggested some foreign concept. "Dessert. The downstairs-in-the-kitchen kind?" At her grin, he grumbled. "Why did I ask?"

"Hmm," she said, delighted with the intimacy that allowed her to be just a little naughty. "I was thinking of something thick and warm that would taste good on my tongue."

For a full three seconds, he stared at her. Then his mouth broke into a grin. Kissing her luxuriously, he murmured against her mouth, "I think I've discovered gold."

"Me, too," she whispered as she nipped at his lower lip, then sank once again into a long kiss. She hugged him, her hands working down his body, wanting their time together to last forever. If only it would, if only in some magical way she could transfer the wonder and the treasure of Paradise Falls to Mayflower Heights.

If only she could capture the mystical wonder of being in love with Cage and make it a reality.

If only.

Around midnight, they sneaked down the stairs and outside to the porch. The night was warm, the stars' silver sparkles in the velvety black sky.

Barefoot and wearing only Cage's shirt, which she'd haphazardly buttoned, Haley settled in the corner of the same swing where they'd seen the couple sipping drinks. The cushions were cool against her thighs, the late evening breeze only a whisper. Her hair was tangled, her neck damp from a long trail of kisses Cage had brushed across her skin. She'd kissed him, too, in places she'd never kissed any man, and she reveled in the knowledge that she'd gotten as much pleasure as she'd given.

Cage leaned down, feathering fingers down the barely buttoned shirt, and whispered, "Why are we down here where I can't do what I want to do?"

She grinned, tucking her palm into his unbuttoned jeans. "What do you want to do?"

He cupped her breast, his hand feeling familiar and wonderful, as if he'd been touching her for years. "Things that would definitely be difficult on a swing." He dropped a kiss on her mouth, then another, lingering and savoring.

"We decided we were hungry, remember?" she asked, her breath reedy, her voice husky with new arousal. She threaded her fingers through his hair.

"Yeah, well, on second thought, I could get along for a while longer on an empty stomach." But he straightened after kissing her once more. "Let me see what I can find. I'll be right back."

He moved away into the shadows, and Haley heard the soft closing of the screen door. She watched a rabbit scurry across the dewy lawn. Sitting back, she drew in a breath, gathering in the scent of the roses, made more fragrant somehow in the darkness. She felt replete and ravished, and wondered what it would be like to stay here forever instead of just this one night. No worry, no hassles, no disappointments. Just Cage and Paradise Falls.

He returned, carrying a bottle of champagne, two flute glasses and a plate of cold lobster tails. Haley uncurled her legs and sat forward, her stomach growling with the realization she hadn't had any real food for hours. Cage handed her the lobster.

She licked her lips in anticipation. "I adore cold lobster."

He chuckled and set the flutes down on a small wicker table. "I hope Geoff and Lily don't mind."

"Oh Cage, maybe you shouldn't have. We didn't show up for dinner and to just raid the refrigerator *is* a little presumptuous."

He raised an eyebrow, then reached for the dish. "Yeah, you're right. I'll put them back."

Haley wouldn't relinquish the plate. There had to be a dozen of the pink and white pieces, garnished with lemon wedges and a small cup of cocktail sauce. "Maybe I could just take one."

"Or two or three," he said with a teasing grin. "Tell you what, I'll make sure they're replaced in the morning. Since Geoff insisted on giving us the room for free, the least I can do is buy a few lobsters."

With that settled, Haley picked up one of the tails and dipped it into the cocktail sauce. She ate slowly, relishing the rich taste. Cage popped the cork on the champagne. At the *whoosh* of air, she lifted her lashes. "You're spoiling me, you know."

"Good. After what you've been through a little spoiling sounds like a great idea."

His comment made Haley realize that this was the first time even a mention of Mayflower Heights had come up. The last time they'd been here, they'd both been careful not to talk of the Venoms or the trouble in Mayflower Heights. But now she didn't object, deciding that whatever relationship they had, the topic of Mayflower Heights wouldn't be intrusive. She had to credit her conclusion, though, to seeing this side of Cage. Relaxed, not so strained, actually teasing her. The past few hours, in fact, had proven to her that despite his cynicism, his coldness and the refusal to let himself believe in anything, he hadn't totally obliterated his capacity for warmth and happiness.

He finished pouring the champagne in the delicate glasses and set the bottle down. Handing her a glass, he settled down beside her, and tucked her close to him.

Haley took a bite of a second lobster tail and then fed the rest to him. They sipped from their glasses, the silence settling around them. Haley liked this sense of just being quietly together, of not feeling the necessity to talk, experiencing the ease of sitting close, of touching sweetly and softly, of giving in with a joyous abandonment.

Cage set his glass down and leaned back, setting the swing in motion. Crickets buzzed in nearby bushes, the only sound in the serenity of the night.

Haley wiggled closer, then moved enough to press her wet mouth to his bare chest, moving her lips lower. "You taste better than lobster and champagne," she murmured as once again she felt her body begin to hum with new desires.

Cage drew in a long breath, sliding his fingers into her hair. "Now who's spoiling who..." He let her kiss and nuzzle and tease, basking not only in the feel of her but in all that could have been. An ideal life with the ideal woman living in an ideal place. Dreams and fantasies, he realized, not reality. And yet he kept coming back here. He kept wanting to prove to himself that an idealistic world could exist with the same possibility as these ideal moments. He slid his hand down her back, cupping the soft warmth of her bottom beneath his shirt.

Her hands were busy, enough so that she had his jeans open. He took her by the shoulders and lifted her. "We can't do this in the swing, baby."

Her disappointment was so immediate, Cage chuckled. Nevertheless, he moved her so that she straddled him, her thighs tucked along the side of his. The swing rocked precariously.

Her eyes were hazy, her mouth slightly swollen and Cage simply couldn't resist. Tugging her closer, he urged her against him, then kissed her. The motion of the swing slowed as they once again sipped from one another. Tongues greedy for more, hands exploring and touching, mouths arousing and tantalizing.

Haley wiggled closer.

Cage felt the urgent heat of her beckon to him.

She wiggled again, then lifted her mouth, her voice husky and rich. "I bet we can."

Cage drew in a long breath, no longer caring about whether they could make love in the swing, only caring about how soon he could bury himself inside her. "I think you're right."

She stretched and lifted, and with an ease that amazed him, she positioned herself so that sliding into her was not only possible, but erotically pleasurable.

Cage groaned, his thoughts so tangled with the taste and scent and wonder of her, that he pushed away any thought of what he would do without her. Dreams and fantasies, he tried to tell himself. They weren't reality, but she was.

Haley gave all of herself.

Cage couldn't get enough.

Their bodies moved languidly together, wanton and yielding and masterfully playing out the ancient mating ritual until they reached the miracle of completion. And in that final moment of exquisite pleasure, Cage realized that every dream and fantasy he had in the future would not be complete without Haley Stewart.

Chapter 11

"Is this the reason you were so quiet on the way home?"

Cage went into her bedroom, put her bag down and returned. "I don't want to argue with you, Haley."

She hadn't moved. She was still standing just inside the door, her handbag slung over her shoulder. Her eyes were accusing, no longer soft with the sensual teasing he'd seen in Paradise Falls.

That was then, he reminded himself, this is now.

In an exasperated voice, she said, "In other words, I should just be a pushover and say, 'why, of course, Cage, move right in. Never mind that I don't want you to. Heaven forbid that I might have a different opinion.'"

Cage dragged a hand through his hair. He mentally tallied up the disagreements he'd had with Haley since his arrival that first night and realized they all came back to the one source. She didn't want to be told what to do—controlled, she would call it. Fine with him. He had no desire to control her, but he definitely wanted her to stay alive.

Since Paradise Falls had been a respite, a distancing from the problems, by a silent mutual agreement they'd discussed nothing related to gangs or drugs or the recent trashing of Mayflower Heights.

Cage had been planning to tell her that he intended to move in with her since before the vandalism. Not that he'd thought she'd be any more receptive to it then than she was now. And from the glaring coolness in her eyes, he decided ruefully, she wouldn't be receptive anytime soon.

He understood her need for independence and realized that she probably viewed this as his taking charge, but Cage saw it as just plain good sense. He'd lost Matt; he had no intention of losing Haley.

Crossing the room to the windows, he opened the one that had once displayed Haley's flowers. Leaning out a little, he glanced up and down the quiet street. Not peaceful, but frighteningly calm.

While they'd been gone, someone had tried to whitewash the graffiti on the side of Haley's apartment, but Cage had already seen the similarities between the ones after Matt's death and these coarse drawings. He'd called Noah just before they'd left for Paradise Falls, and the detective had promised to send someone to get pictures of the graffiti. From the evidence already gathered, in addition to Haley's confrontation with the gang and the overheard warehouse conversation—and now this most recent threat—both Cage and Noah were positive that Matt's death had been a deliberate attempt to scare Haley off. The recent vandalism had been just another step to make their point. Cage had no doubts that, given an opportunity, they might just try to kill her.

He turned from the window to find her regarding him with none of the passion he'd seen just hours ago. Maybe that was best. What had happened in Paradise Falls just didn't belong here, amid the rubble and ruins. Those hours were a step outside reality, and the flood of feelings that he'd felt for her must have been part of the fantasy.

But nothing here on Standish Street resembled fantasy; this was just a stark defeat that was all too sadly real.

With a jolt, Cage realized the lasting impact her idealism had made on Mayflower Heights and on those she loved.

Yes, Haley had a fierceness that sometimes exhausted the limits of good sense, but her do-gooder attitude—the one he'd cynically dismissed—had slowly crept into him. Not radically, not in a screeching attempt to convert him, but with a dogged pervasiveness that somehow had settled into his heart. He knew he could no longer totally separate himself from her. Cage wasn't sure what terrified him more, needing her or losing her.

In a matter-of-fact voice, he said, "I'll get Norman to give me a hand switching the beds."

"You're not listening to me, Cage."

"No, *you're* refusing to listen to *me*. This has nothing to do with controlling you, this has to do with you staying alive."

If he'd thought that might make her reconsider, he was wrong.

"Is that why you hustled me out of here? Is that why we made love? Pretended that life was grand and we were in our own little world? It was all some design to make me pliable so that I would agree to this?"

Cage sighed. "No. I'd made up my mind on this before we left."

"Well, you can unmake it."

He wanted to take her by the shoulders and shake some sense into her, while at the same time he would have preferred to carry her off to somewhere safe permanently, not just for a few days. He'd decided on moving in here because it was the best he could come up with and still allow her to stay. Ordering her to leave, or physically taking her out of Mayflower Heights, was not a job he relished. Not yet, at least.

Frowning at her, he decided to try another angle. "You know Haley, in the past, I've accused you of being a bleeding heart, a do-gooder, sometimes too generous and too concerned for other people. But I would have never accused you of plain stupidity."

"Thank you very much, Mr. Murdock," she snapped coldly. "Your analysis of my character is enlightening."

"Cut out the haughty, offended attitude. Me staying here is not going to complicate your life. I have no intention of trying to run roughshod over you, but until I know exactly who killed Matt and—"

"You bastard!" She flung her handbag onto the couch, began to pace the room, then stopped and whirled on him. "That's all this is about, isn't it? That's all any of what has been between us is about. You wanting to avenge your brother's death. So now you see me as more useful than you did before. Would this be because you've slept with me? Sex becomes a handy new tool of control? Give the lady great orgasms, then she'll be putty in your hands? You think that gives you some right to move in here and act as my supposed protector, when all you really want is to make your revenge a little easier?"

Cage stared at her, nonplussed by her vehemence, not sure which accusation he should answer first. Haley's shoulders trembled, but she stood staunchly still, as if to say she could handle whatever answer he gave her.

"You don't really believe I would use you like that, do you?" he asked softly.

Suddenly her anger was gone, as quickly as it had come. "I don't know, Cage. I don't even think I know you." She turned away, her voice catching.

He considered taking her into his arms and reassuring her, but he'd resolved on the way back here to keep things professional. Besides, he wasn't sure he trusted himself to touch her. She'd already gotten too deeply inside him, raising havoc not just with his body, but with his heart.

In a nonconfrontational tone of voice, he said, "Just to set things straight, I repeat, I made up my mind to move in here before you came to the police station. And you're dead wrong about why I slept with you. I don't sleep with a woman for any other reason than what's going on between our bodies. And you and I had a hell of a lot going on."

She took a deep breath, and he knew she wasn't going to deny what he'd said. Yet he noted the shadow of disappointment that crossed her face. He wasn't stupid, nor was he blind to or ignorant to what she probably wanted to hear.

But he couldn't say what he couldn't believe in. He couldn't make promises he couldn't keep. And it was a lot less complicated if he deliberately made himself deny that anything more than sensational sex had gone on between them. But he cursed inwardly at the unbidden ache to tell her how he really felt.

Finally she asked, "Then why didn't you tell me about your plan before we left?"

"Would you have been more agreeable?"

"No."

"Then it's a moot point. All we did was postpone this argument."

"All we had *was* a fantasy," she said softly.

Cage grimaced. He didn't want to talk about this. Maybe he wanted to maintain the purity of Paradise Falls and the solace he'd found there with her. Maybe some of those deeper feelings that he wanted to deny weren't going to go away. Yet, even if he admitted them to himself, they were still too fragile to put under any glaring lights of truth. Maybe he still didn't believe in anything, any tomorrows, anything permanent for him, despite the moments of wonder and hope he'd shared with Haley.

In a cool, distant voice, he said, "And if I remember correctly, you were the one who okayed the room Geoff offered."

"And you brought condoms."

She didn't miss a beat, he decided grimly. "That's called being prepared. I still recall that time in my bedroom when we weren't."

To his astonishment, her cheeks flared with color. Then, as if not wanting to chance a conversation about that first time, she added, "If we'd had separate rooms at the inn, it would have been because I didn't want us to be intimate."

He gave her a long, direct look. "You're wrong, baby, and you damn well know it."

"Are you saying that I don't know what I want?"

"Oh, for God's sake," he muttered under his breath. Then he said, "I'm saying that what happened between us had been coming for a long time. To deny that is silly. Now, we could have played games with separate rooms at the inn, but all that would have done was make being together a trip across the hall or up the stairs."

"I might have said no. I might have refused to let you in the room," she said staunchly.

He raised an eyebrow.

"Damn it, Cage Murdock, I might have!"

He shook his head in disbelief. "Why is it so difficult to admit you wanted me as much as I wanted you? You had no trouble while we were making love."

"Because you're too good, and—" She took a deep breath, and he had to check himself against urging her to finish the sentence. She moved her hand in a gesture of dismissal. "None of that has anything to do with now. If you're living here with me, then you're going to expect to sleep with me."

"Haley, I didn't say anything about sleeping with you."

"But you said you wanted to switch the beds."

"Because it's your bed, and I probably won't be moving back into that apartment. I can sleep on the couch. In fact, I think for both our sakes that would be a better idea."

She stared at him for a long time. "Paradise Falls wasn't real, was it? I mean for us. It was just a step out of the dismal truth of Mayflower Heights into some unspoiled world that is more fantasy than reality."

"It accomplished what it was supposed to do. It gave some relief from what you experienced here. It gave you hope."

She gave him a puzzled look. "You don't believe in that sort of thing."

"But you do." He paused, debating with himself about revealing any of his shut-off feelings. Unused, dormant, dead, he wasn't sure, but they were long-abandoned emotions that had all surfaced with a fury at Matt's death.

Revenge. Cage had tasted its acid, and its sweetness. It had been born of love and hate and sorrow and regret; yet Cage had hoped for Matt and for his future. And from that hope he'd reaped pain and despair. Not counting on tomorrow, not believing in any kind of permanency in his own life, lessened the possibility of disappointment. For Cage, Paradise Falls represented emotions and desires he couldn't count on, not in the real world, where he lived.

For he still felt gripped by the deep sense that he didn't matter, that his life was destined for some messy and bloody end, like the old man had always said. And yet, here *he* was alive and Matt had had the messy and bloody end. Matt had yearned to return to the inner city, and Cage had been furious. Perhaps that anger had only been more of his newly admitted resentment. Exasperation and, yes, outrage, at the utter stupidity of not taking what Cage had worked so hard to hand him.

My God, he thought wearily. Why in hell would Matt have wanted Mayflower Heights when he could have had Paradise Falls?

And Haley. She, too, insisted on living in dangerous conditions because of some idealized notion that she could change things. Paradise Falls was the change she wanted. But why not just take that, instead of trying to reconstruct a ghetto?

In a distant voice, he said, "When I was kid going there in the summer, I saw it as if it were a picture of hope, of happiness. Perfect conditions, the ideal life. The one the old man wanted for Matt."

"And for you."

He scowled at her. "Why do you keep insisting on that? I told you that first day that I didn't matter to him. I had a switchblade to keep me safe, a cocky attitude, and a street wisdom that would never have fit into a place like Paradise Falls. When I went there in the summer, I was on my best behavior."

"So you wouldn't get kicked out."

"Probably. At the time I was too damn arrogant to think that would happen, but some part of me knew that more was expected of me there than at home."

Her voice hesitated and then softened. "I noticed a difference in you while you were there. That first time, you were relaxed, and you never mentioned the Venoms, or what had happened. It was like some surrealistic atmosphere.

And then this time. The inn, making love, not arguing or disagreeing or worrying. Using any inclination we had to touch and kiss and discover each other."

"The place was aptly named," Cage said, already regretting that he'd said he wouldn't sleep with her here.

"But now we're back to reality."

"And me moving in with you."

She sighed. "I don't like it."

"Yeah, I could tell," he said succinctly, while at the same time telling himself that her liking it or not liking it had not one damn thing to do with anything. Not with the knot in his gut or the odd pain somewhere in the region of his heart.

Not one damn thing.

Moving in, Cage soon realized, was not as simple as he'd made it sound. Their relationship became more strained, despite Cage sleeping on the couch, despite Haley maintaining a cordial, but definite distance. The hours in Paradise Falls were no more than a memory. Their lovemaking, their ease with each other, even the jumble of emotions he'd felt and couldn't deny, were now a part of the past. Or so he told himself.

Here in Mayflower Heights, they'd achieved the essence of a working relationship. No personal involvement. They moved away from each other instead of toward each other. They talked in generalities that belied the intimacies they'd shared for that one night. Worst of all their caution, whether they were alone or with others, increased rather than defused the tension between them.

Cage found his sleep interrupted by memories of her sprawled on top of him, by fantasies that had him searching for her, by exquisite moments when he was sure that the essence of life was being with Haley Stewart.

Haley found her dreams filled with his body tugging hers into a feast of the senses. Then awakened to the realization of Mayflower Heights and an even more vivid reality—loving Cage and wanting him were now so blurred that acknowledging one without the other was an impossibility.

Added to the personal strain was a more insidious problem. If Cage had entertained any hope that his moving in would have had a marked effect on the swirl of indirect threats against Haley, he was wrong.

Pockets of violence erupted in the streets. Store windows were smashed, and flagrant looting escalated. Drug deals became more prominent, with an in-your-face haughtiness that made Haley furious and Cage all the more careful. The police sent patrol cars to cruise the streets, but often they arrived too late to do anything more than arrest a few punks.

The cleanup and the general feeling of progress and goodwill in the neighborhood that had been so prevalent before had deteriorated. Word spread that Boa had regained his power, and that he and the Venoms were on a rampage.

Four days after Cage moved in with Haley, he sensed a marked change in the streets. Tension that before had been scattered or only evident after some act of vandalism now began to come together and build as if the neighborhood were a pressure cooker.

The unrelenting stress peaked when a fire was started in the park next door to the Pedenazzis'. When Al tried to put it out while waiting for the fire department, someone torched his house. Fortunately, both fires were extinguished with minor damage, but the incident set a tone that unnerved the neighborhood. This violence, unlike the vandalism aimed at Haley, stalked and swaggered through the streets, more encompassing, more boldly executed. Mayflower Heights got restless and angry.

Against Cage's wishes, Haley called a meeting of the Association. Fury and a disturbing "we've had enough and we're gonna act" glower marred the faces of many of the members as they found their way to seats.

Cage stood to one side, watching with a worry that concerned him for two reasons. One, he knew that whatever decision was made would matter little to the gangs and drug dealers. Two, his concern bit deep inside him, and he clearly recognized that if anyone hurt Haley, there wasn't a revenge he could carry out that would be good enough. He recalled his deep rage after Matt's death, but he knew that now much of that had been tangled with his long-buried resentment at the old man for always having favored Matt. That resentment had quite probably spilled over into his annoyances at his brother. Then, with the pain of his loss and the guilt of not having been able, in the end, to protect his little brother, Cage had leapt to the most obvious reaction: avenge his brother's death and make up for his own unacceptable feelings.

Yet with Haley there wasn't any guilt or resentment to blame, there was just this endless hollowness at the thought of losing her.

A vacuum in his heart, he decided truthfully. The question was, did he fear that she'd filled the vacuum forever? Or did he fear he couldn't abide its being empty again? Or had the vacuum begun to simply dissipate since he'd walked into the Association that first night?

Whatever was going on inside him, one thing was clear. She meant too damn much to him in a too damn personal way.

Watching her now, as she valiantly tried to bring some sort of calm to the chaos of grumblings, murmurings and general discontent about her continued call for nonviolence, brought to Cage's mind an out-of-nowhere possibility.

Maybe he'd fallen in love with her.

Just the few words, floating into his thoughts without any kind of fanfare or startling revelation, so startled him that Cage was glad no one had been paying attention to him at that particular moment. He was sure the color must have drained from his face.

Leaning against the wall, he closed his eyes. A combination of exhaustion and worry about her, he concluded firmly, that was all. God, that had to be all.

Finally the room grew quiet enough for her to speak. "This is not the time to desert our principles of nonviolence. Nothing will be accomplished if all of you are out there waving guns around," Haley said, her voice amazingly steady.

"Hell, a few guns will show them we're not a bunch of old men!"

"Or scared of them!"

"Yeah, we tried your way. It ain't workin'. We gonna wait around until someone else gets killed? Cage, here, has already lost his kid brother, for God's sake. Anyone found out who blew him away? Does anybody care but us?"

"But it's because you *do* care that we can't resort to blood on the streets," Haley replied loudly as everyone began shouting at once.

"So what are we gonna do? Ask them all to please go away and don't hurt us? That oughta make a real impact. They'll be sprayin' us with bullets while they're laughing."

Cage stepped forward and stood beside Haley.

The crowd quieted some, but not much. Quite a contrast, he decided, from the meeting less than a week ago when they had praised Haley and agreed with Cage's cleanup suggestions. More than ever, he was convinced of the danger of mass alliances, whether they be gangs like the Venoms or groups, such as the Association, intent on good works. Unfortunately, they were often governed by the strongest voice, and if that voice wanted trouble, the others usually followed like sheep behind their master.

Cage understood their anger and their need to express it in tangible outrage. Perhaps understanding, but not approving, was why he stood beside Haley instead of with the crowd. God, her idealism had rubbed off on him, whether he'd wanted it or not.

"Cage, they're not even listening," she said, so close to him he could smell her skin.

"Then we need to get their attention." He reached down, pulled the switchblade from his boot and snapped it open. Turning, he threw it at the The Mayflower Heights Association sign that had hung outside until someone had shot at the hinges and it had crashed to the ground. The knife gouged into the wood with a dull *thunk* and stuck there.

Haley shuddered. "Oh God."

Suddenly the audience was fixated on the blade. Silence rolled through the room like a thick fog.

Cage spoke. "Are you going to give me a minute of your time, or are you going to go off half-cocked and get your-selves killed?"

Haley touched his arm. "Cage, please..."

When he glanced at her, he felt a rising fury at her persistence in clinging to a method that clearly wasn't working.

In a low voice, he said, "I want you to stand here beside me and shut up. They're not going to listen to your pleadings, no matter how sincere they are."

"Of course they're not, because you represent violence and revenge and, most of all, because you have a reason. Matthew."

"Never mind my reasons. Right now, you not getting killed the way Matt did is a hell of a lot more important to me than the egos and pride of the Mayflower Heights Association."

Her cheeks were pale, and her eyes were wide with concern. Cage saw a huge difference from the woman he'd encountered once in this very room, who had been so determined to get rid of him. He hated the word *defeat,* but there was no question now that defeat ringed her eyes and her mouth.

He turned back to the crowd. "No guns."

"Hell, Cage, that's the only thing they understand."

"Yeah, and their life expectancy is hellishly short," he replied bluntly. "Average age about twenty-five. If you people want to come out of this in one piece and not spend a few weeks attending the funerals of your neighbors, then forget the guns. Norman, get on the phone and call the cops. Ask them if they'll get some patrol cars to move through here every couple of hours."

Norman nodded and moved toward a nearby pay phone.

"My God, this sounds like war," someone said. Nods of agreement, and just a tinge of new fear, passed through the room.

Cage took the knife from the sign, closed it and put it back in his boot. To the murmuring crowd, he said, "Those of you who have agreed with Haley that nonviolence is the best way would be wise to consider that, as an option, peace may no longer be possible. If you want no part of what could happen down here, I would suggest that you take your summer vacation now." Cage narrowed his eyes and raised his voice. "And those of you in the back who are planning a sneak attack on the dealers or the Venoms, forget it. You don't stand a chance."

The four in the back who'd had their heads together, whispering, all turned suddenly and scowled at Cage.

"We heard they're after Haley for what she did to the Frazer brothers," one of them yelled at Cage.

"Yeah, and for what you did to Boa, Cage. They got lots of reasons to come here and do serious damage."

"Let's call a spade a spade. They want revenge. Or rather they want to use revenge as an excuse to take over Standish Street."

"So you're saying we can't stop them? That no matter what we do they'll win?"

The back-to-back questions instantly resonated deep in his gut. His old man had said something similar the night he was knifed. "You can't stop this from happenin' to Matt. They'll win unless you get him out of here." But his father hadn't been right. They'd won despite Matt's leaving. And they'd won again when they'd killed him.

Something hot and dangerous fueled inside Cage. Damn it, they would not win by taking Haley. Not if he had to breathe his last breath to stop them.

"So what do we do, Cage?"

"Yeah, man, just what in hell are we supposed to do?"

Cage waited until the room was silent. In a low voice, he said, "We take away the prize that they're after. Haley Stewart."

Hours later the heat of the August night lay on the neighborhood like a suffocating blanket. Sirens whined and snatches of worried conversations spilled from one house to the next. At Haley's, Cage stood in the bedroom doorway, watching her undress.

He'd been there just a few minutes. Getting her out of Mayflower Heights was no longer a choice or an option, yet despite the danger, he desperately wanted her. Fool, he cursed himself furiously, you're a damn fool. Take her out of here and then make love to her. That was the smart thing to do. But he didn't want that; he wanted her here.

God, maybe it all had to do with the wide gap between Paradise Falls and Mayflower Heights. Maybe, for some incredibly odd reason, he needed to know her intimately here. Here in the rubble and the ruin. Here where anything that resembled love and hope could only come from people like Haley.

Despite the window fan, the air was sultry, thick, and hotly intense with the smell of violence and fear and roses. Cage concentrated on the rose scent of her, which had penetrated so deeply into his senses he could smell it even when he was nowhere near her.

He was barefoot, wearing only jeans and his silver chain. She hadn't seen him yet, or she'd chosen not to notice, but just the same he prepared himself for any number of reactions. He intended to make love to her, and then he intended to take her out of the neighborhood. In that order.

Desire beat deep inside him with a primitive need, but it was still her choice.

But getting her out of Mayflower Heights was his call. She would go if he had to physically remove her. He suffered under no delusions that Haley would simply cooperate without giving him a hassle. But it didn't matter. He'd take the heat and the hassle; he'd handle and ignore her fury and pleas. For, in the end, she'd be alive.

She turned then, having dispensed with her shorts and blouse. Wearing just white satin panties and a matching bra with tiny rosebuds edging the lace border, she looked directly at him. Cage didn't move, feeling the heavy shudder of arousal roar through him, so darkly intense that he had to lean a little harder against the door.

What astounded him was the sizzling level of intimacy that wired them to one another.

She made no attempt to cover herself, no attempt to turn away from what he knew she must have seen—his arousal, and the naked desire in his eyes.

Haley's own feelings of desire were a reflection of Cage's urgency. Feelings of wanting him, of taking all that she could before their time ran out. Days of awkwardness between them had worn her down. Nights of intimate images shimmered too brightly when she was supposed to be putting their relationship behind her.

For Haley, love had defined itself in Cage. How much simpler and straightforward these moments could be if only her body and not her heart wanted him. Inwardly she shivered, unable to deny the physical need but knowing that as satisfying as it was, sex was fleeting.

Haley wondered what he'd do if she simply said, "Come love me, for I love you so much that I need to show you." Who was she kidding? Cage wanted nothing so permanent. He didn't even *believe* in permanency, not when it came to expecting any tomorrows to come. To think he would attach himself to something as ill-defined as love was absurd.

Yet tomorrow would come. And following the days were the nights that promised a dark loneliness with only the scraps of memories. A hundred, a thousand, days and nights; all without Cage.

She had tonight. She had his desire for her. And maybe, if she met him on the same level of need and passion he felt for her, it would be enough.

She watched him, observing the tension, the raw sexuality that somehow seemed restrained and yet so blatant. She couldn't turn away, she realized, she couldn't let him leave her to sleep alone tonight.

She could do this. She could just enjoy and then let go.

Seduction; a little wild, tantalizingly wanton.

Ravishment; provocative and spicy.

Abandonment; flowing in sultry streams and ignoring that beneath every touch, every kiss, every cry of satisfaction that she gave, she was really giving love.

Taking a shallow breath, she whispered, soft and low, "You want me, don't you?"

"Yes."

"One final time, is that it?" Her heart clenched as the question swirled between them.

"Are you going to say no?"

"You'd accuse me of self-denial."

"I'm giving you a choice. But please make it now." He tossed three unopened foil packets onto her bed.

She looked at them for a few moments, then slowly reached across the bed and picked them up. First one, then the second, and then the third.

Staring at them, she realized that they represented more than just protection from pregnancy. They meant no left-behind reminders, no ties to her, no legacy for his future.

Tears threatened to blur her eyes, and she blinked furiously. No, she would not think ahead. Just tonight. Just these next moments.

Cage watched her lower her head and methodically fit the packets together in her hand, as if debating tossing them back to him. Her hair swept across her cheek, leaving her face shadowed.

He hadn't moved; he hadn't dared for surely once he touched her there would be no turning back. In the stillness, he tried not to allow any feast of the senses to show in his expression. Her breasts spilled over the top of her bra, and the low band of the panties reminded him too vividly of the treasure that lay beneath.

"Is three all you have?" she asked with an inquisitiveness that could have indicated she held a handful of collector's items.

The impact of her question made his mouth go dry, and for a few seconds he was speechless. "God, I expected an argument, and I get this," he murmured, wondering why in hell he'd thought he had her figured out. "They're what's left from Paradise Falls."

In a too-soft voice she murmured, "I didn't think there was anything left from Paradise Falls." The words stretched between them, their real meaning clear. All that had happened between them in Paradise Falls had been left there. Then, a little louder, she added, "I thought we ran out."

Cage watched her with an intensity that wired him to her. "No. You wore me out."

"And three won't wear you out tonight?"

"No."

"But three is enough." Then he heard the resignation in her voice. "Afterward you're going to send me away and make sure Matt's killer is arrested, and then you'll be gone."

Cage scowled. How in hell did she read him so clearly? Yeah, that was what he wanted, what he'd intended, yet when it was put so bluntly, and when it came from Haley, he didn't like the sound of the words, or all the hidden meanings behind "afterward."

Not even attempting to shade the truth, he said, "Yeah, that's the plan."

She carefully placed two of the packets on the small table beside her bed. Then, with the third one in her hand, she crossed the room and stood in front of him. Watching his face—her own resigned in a pain he saw and wanted to ignore—she pressed the packet into his palm with great care. Then, as if she'd done this every night for years, she trailed her fingers along his stomach, coming to a stop at the button of his jeans.

Slowly she eased it through the ragged hole. Cage cupped her hips and dipped his thumbs inside the lace of her panties.

His zipper hissed down.

Her panties shimmered down.

When he brushed his knuckles across her, he sucked in his breath at the rich dampness he encountered.

Then her mouth brushed his chest, his stomach, lower, then back up and down, and lower still.

Cage gripped her shoulders, trying to pull her up.

"No," he muttered through clenched teeth.

Her lips dusted his belly before she lifted her head, tipped it back and asked, "Why not?"

For the life of him, he couldn't think of one reason except the obvious one. "Because I'll explode."

"I know."

He stared at her for a long moment. "Is this a power trip for you, a control trip, a way to prove that you can turn me into putty in your hands?"

She glanced at her hands where they toyed with him, brushed him, played on his body as if he were an instrument made especially for her. "You'd like to believe that, wouldn't you? That would be easier than the real reason."

"Which is?"

Something slipped over her face, some sadness, some emotion he had a sense he was supposed to understand but didn't.

She drew in a shallow breath. "It's very simple, Cage. I like having sex with you."

The words rang hollow, and he knew she lied. While the statement might be true, it wasn't complete. Even the careful way she said it indicated she'd chosen her words so as not to say any more. Since mind reading was a guess at best, Cage wasn't sure how he knew that. Instinct, perhaps, but whatever the answer, the heat and erotic pounding of the moment diffused his thought processes.

Silently she began her pleasuring again. His senses came just near to short-circuiting as her mouth moved over him. He lost the will, the need, the desire, to think or rationalize, let alone say no.

Pleasure gripped him in a fist of heat that punched every other sensation into oblivion. When finally he lifted her into his arms and they spilled onto the bed, Cage realized that leaving her was going to tear him apart.

Much later, he lay with her curled up against him, her nakedness cool against his sweaty body. She slept fitfully, coming awake to kiss him and move closer, but then drifting off to sleep. He reached over and picked up his watch from the night table. Nearly 4:00 a.m., and in a few hours he'd be taking her away from here.

He tightened his grip on her as he punched the pillow beneath his head. The fan whirled softly; the breeze was no cooler, despite the deepening night. From outside came the wail of a siren, the stench of someone's garbage, the ominous lassitude of a dangerous lull in time.

Cage watched the shadows play across the ceiling, listened to their hearts beating in tandem. The smart thing, the most logical, surely the most sensible, would be for him to leave, too. Leave Mayflower Heights to the cops or to the gangs and the dealers. Why in hell did he care who won? And in the great expanse of drug-infested neighborhoods across the country, why did this one make one damn difference?

He knew the answer. Haley Stewart. She didn't make the difference, she *was* the difference.

"Damn," he muttered in disgust. How in hell had he allowed himself to become so enmeshed with her? He slowly untangled their bodies, expecting her to cling, but she let him go. He rolled out of bed and made his way out of the darkened room.

Haley lay still until he was gone, then turned her face into the pillow that held his scent. Pushing her face deep, she prayed she could muffle her sobs. But tears wouldn't come, and she knew the pain of loving Cage and letting him go was too deep, the wrenching too raw, the break too sad, for mere tears.

In the days since they'd returned to Mayflower Heights, Haley had endured and existed, rather than lived. She'd thought that knowing she loved him would be painful enough, but knowing and not saying the words made the hurt worse. She'd tried anger and outrage. She'd tried silence and disinterest. And finally she'd tried to convince herself it wasn't love, it was just sex.

She'd known he wanted her, just as she'd known that he would send her away from here despite her most vehement objections.

When she'd sensed him in the doorway, she'd known exactly what she was going to do. Ignoring him, undressing for him, enticing him had been both calculated and necessary.

Calculated because she wanted to prove to herself that she could just have sex. She could turn off her love because he didn't return it. She could be sexual without being bonded to him emotionally.

But, of course, that left her other reason. Necessity. She'd needed him around her, filling her, coveting her and unable to walk away. At least for tonight. Maybe it had, just a little, been a power trip, a need to control him, but she knew her real motive had been deeper, more intricately tied to her heart. She had needed to love him with her body, since she couldn't love him with words or promises or tomorrows.

She heard him return, hesitate in the doorway, as if entering a second time were difficult.

Slowly she sat up, pushed her hair back and got off the bed. As she had the previous time, she went to him. He'd pulled on his jeans, leaving the waistband open. She pressed her mouth to his chest. "Cage..."

He tangled his hand in her hair. "Shh..."

His skin burned hot against her cheek as she slid her arms around him, unable to get close enough.

Then she felt a change, a rigid alertness.

"What is it?" she whispered

"Stay still, Haley. Don't move."

Her heart began to thump, and she heard a car engine. Headlights flashed across the wall and then were gone.

Suddenly Cage had her in a locked hold, flinging them both to the floor even as a crashing sound startled her. She only struggled with him for a second. She heard him swear as he rolled her against the wall and crushed himself against her.

Against her, a miniscule moment before the explosion blasted through the bedroom.

Chapter 12

Amid the debris of broken plaster, shattered glass and thick, air-soaking dust, Haley lay wedged beneath Cage and the farthest wall from the bomb. All she remembered was Cage grabbing her, her window fan crashing to the floor, and a deafening noise. Her arms were twisted between them.

He'd coiled around her so thoroughly, anyone would have thought they'd practiced this for weeks. Her body hummed as if echoing the explosion, while her ears rang and her lungs struggled for oxygen.

Cage didn't move, and she couldn't.

A tiny, terrified voice whispered, "Cage is dead."

Instantly she recoiled. *No!*

But her denial stayed locked in her throat. He didn't move, and her own heart hammered so hard she couldn't have said if his heart beat or even if he breathed. Somehow her face had sought refuge against his neck while his arms cradled her head.

No! He's not dead! I won't let him be dead! I love him! Muffled against him, she tried a croaking whisper of his name, but her mouth was so cottony, nothing came out.

She tried to move, her hands flexing, struggling to find their way around him, desperate to find some hope that this was a nightmare, a horrifying dream. Cage couldn't be dead. Not Cage. *Oh, God, please, not Cage.*

Pleas and whimperings bubbled in her throat as she desperately moved her hands, looking for life. She encountered fragments of plaster and the litter of what had been her bedroom. But, against his back, she also encountered a wet smear.

Blood!

Her heart screamed with a denial so wrenchingly painful that she felt the rise of nausea. No. Not true. Can't be true. Won't let it be true.

Now her lungs were burning, and her throat was gasping as she struggled to make herself heard.

"Cage! Oh, God, Cage!"

He moved then, just a fraction, wincing.

Haley went totally still, then gripped him euphorically. "Cage?"

"I think so," he mumbled.

"Thank God," she cried around sobs and hugs that were fierce. She knew he'd somehow come back from the doors of death.

"I'm okay," he reassured her.

But she wouldn't let go. She buried her face even deeper into his neck and locked her arms around him. "I thought you were dead. Oh, Cage, I thought I'd lost you...."

He tried to pry her hands loose, without success. Then he winced again, groaning this time. "Easy, Haley. Could you let up a little?"

She did, but when he lifted himself off her and her hands left a trail of blood across his ribs, she scrambled up to examine him. Her back ached from the impact of hitting the floor, but she paid no attention to the pain.

"It's just some cuts," he said dismissively.

"Just cuts? No, you're hurt and bleeding." Her hands crept over him, searching for wounds and bruises. The darkness of the room prevented her from seeing much, but every time she touched blood, she felt her own nausea return.

Finally Cage levered himself up and grabbed her wrists, holding them away from him. "Haley, it's okay. I'm not going to die or bleed to death."

She huddled before him, shivering.

He knelt down, his voice low, soothing. "How about you? No cuts? Nothing broken? I wanted to warn you to just fall to the floor and not try to fight me, but there just wasn't time."

She shook her head, astounded that he could be evaluating her, concerned that he hadn't had time to tell her what was going on. He'd simply acted, unconcerned about blood, pain or dying, concerned only about her.

She felt chilled, and her shivers escalated into an all-over shaking.

"Haley?" His voice swam around her, rather than penetrating her, and she tried to grasp the sound to clutch it to her. With great effort she attempted to curl into a ball, aware now that she wore nothing, aware that if the bomb had come moments earlier they would have been making love—and they would, no doubt, both be dead now.

"Haley, baby, come on. Don't go into shock on me," he said as he turned her head, looking for the smallest amount of response in her eyes.

She stared up at him, her heart tumbling with a thousand emotions. Cage had grabbed her and flung himself so that his body had protected her. All her concerns about him trying to control her seemed so frivolous, so *nothing* compared to living and dying, to loving him and then losing him.

I love you.

She wanted to say the words, desperate to make him understand how full of gratitude she was that he was all right. Haley swallowed hard, caught now with the need to confess all her feelings, unconcerned about whether he would reject her, ignore her, or even leave her.

"Cage, I need to tell you how I feel...."

He looked at her sharply. "Are you hurt somewhere?"

"No, not in that way. I meant—" She lowered her head and pressed her lips together. No, she couldn't say the words, not here, not when he would think they came only from gratitude.

From somewhere came familiar noises. Neighbors, doors slamming, footsteps running.

Then hammering on her own front door.

"Haley! Cage!" shouted Norman Polk.

Cage got to his feet, reached down and gently pulled her to her feet.

Still she trembled. "I'm okay. Just the aftereffects, I guess."

"I want the EMTs to take a look."

"I'm fine—"

"No arguments," he said firmly. Steadying her, he added, "Stay here. There's glass and broken plaster everywhere, and nothing should be moved around until the police take a look."

Numb and cold, she simply nodded, leaning against the one wall that was still intact.

He made his way through the rubble to the bathroom and returned with her robe. After he helped her on with it, he scooped her up into his arms and carried her into the living room. By that time, Norman had used a club to break down the door.

"My God, is she all right?" Norman asked as he hurried into the room. Sweat streaked his face, and his eyes were wide with fear.

"Just shaken up." Cage settled her on the couch and brushed his hands quickly over her, as if to assure himself that she was indeed unharmed.

"Your back, Cage. You're bleeding."

"I'm okay."

Norman looked dubious, but didn't fuss at him. "What in hell was that, anyway?"

"My guess is a pipe bomb. Fragments of metal are wedged into the wall."

"It's a wonder you two are alive."

"We got lucky. Whoever threw it had a lousy aim," Cage muttered as he tipped Haley's face up to examine her eyes. She knew she wasn't in shock, but she felt a little woozy.

To Cage she muttered, "I thought it was fairly accurate. My bedroom probably resembles a war zone."

He grinned. "Now I know you're okay." But, though his words were teasing, she didn't miss the relief in his expression. He added, "Tell you what, though, if ever I need a lifeline, I'll be sure and call you. I probably have a few broken ribs from that stranglehold you had on me." When he saw her face go suddenly pale, he said quickly, "I'm kidding, okay?"

She relaxed somewhat, then nodded.

Norman started into the bedroom.

"Better stay out of there until the cops get here, Norman," Cage said. "They'll want to take some pictures and gather up anything that remains of the pipe bomb. They tend to get testy if anything's been disturbed."

"Oh, sure, right." He peered into the room. "From what I can see, it looks as if you were right about their aim, Cage. Looks as if it landed between the bed and the outside wall."

Blue lights flashed outside.

Haley reached for Cage's hand when he started to back away. In a muted whisper, she said, "You saved my life."

"You saved your own life, because you got out of bed when you did."

She shook her head vigorously. "No. You risked your life for me."

He scowled as if he'd never heard anyone say anything like that to him. "Instinct, Haley. That's what I'm trained to do."

She sighed with relief, glad now that she hadn't said she loved him. No doubt he *would* have said that her feelings were just gratitude. Feeling a little empty, she asked, "How did you know about the—" she could barely say the word "—the bomb?"

"I didn't. Just as you put your arms around me, I saw the car stop and back up. I didn't wait to see if he was going to ask directions or fire a gun. The pipe bomb was unexpected.'' Left unsaid, but certainly true, was that if the bomb thrower's aim had been better, or Cage's reaction time slower, they would both be dead.

Within ten minutes Haley's apartment was filled with police and neighbors. Even Al Pedenazzi, wearing his slippers and a plaid robe, peered in. Then, having satisfied himself that she was all right, he went back home.

An emergency rescue vehicle arrived, but when they took a look at Haley they found no signs of shock. She was just badly shaken. Cage refused to go to the hospital, but allowed them to clean and bandage the cuts on his back. The police asked Haley questions about who she thought wanted to kill her, and whether she thought this might be connected with her run-in with the Venoms.

"It's connected to my brother's death," Cage said as he sat down beside Haley. "His name was Matthew Murdock. He was killed a few weeks ago in a drive-by."

The bushy-eyebrowed cop asking the questions paused, studied Cage and then nodded. "So you think whoever killed your brother also tried to kill your girlfriend here."

Haley grimaced at the term, but said nothing.

Cage added, "Yeah, that's what we think."

The cop studied her. "Any threats made on your life that would have indicated this might happen?"

"Come on," Cage interjected impatiently. "You know who she is and what she's been doing. Hell, to the dealers she's a threat just because she walks and breathes."

"Look, buddy, just because you're friends with Drake..."

"Hasn't got a damn thing to do with anything!"

"Hey, I'm just doing my job."

"Then do it, but you're asking the wrong person the questions. Try the Frazer brothers. They made an obvious threat. Or how about that slime Boa and his pals, who like to terrify people because it's fun."

The cop scribbled down some information. Haley whispered to Cage, "You didn't tell me about a threat from the Frazer brothers. How long have you known?"

"Since the phone call from Noah, right after their arrest."

"He never mentioned the threat to me when I talked to him."

"We didn't think it was a good idea." At her deepening scowl, he added, "It wasn't an attempt to keep you in the dark, Haley. But you had your hands full with the Association and with worry about what we'd heard at the warehouse and where that threat might lead. I told Noah that I'd do the worrying about the Frazer brothers' threat."

She lowered her head and shook it slowly. "Please don't lie to me."

The cop asked a few more questions and then moved into the bedroom. After the police took their pictures and marked and bagged all the evidence they could gather, they left the apartment. Norman and the rest of the neighbors trailed out, leaving them alone.

They sat for a few seconds in the empty and suddenly silent room. Finally Cage picked up on their conversation and addressed her last comment. "I didn't lie to you, Haley. Why would I?"

She'd picked up a light green throw pillow, and now she hugged it to her. "Because you don't want to tell me that I was too preoccupied with you when I should have been paying attention to what was really going on."

"You're not talking about what happened after the phone call?" At her barely discernible nod, Cage pulled the pillow away and tugged her fully into his arms. "I'm not sure if I should be flattered or furious."

She lay against him with a kind of resigned willingness.

"No one has ever admitted to being preoccupied with me," he muttered. "But you're wrong about me thinking that your reactions to me would have interfered with your plans for Mayflower Heights. You've made it clear from the beginning what your priorities are. Just as I made it clear why I was here. As to what's happened between us, that was a separate issue."

Haley felt as if she were part of some kind of official report that he would have to make to his superiors. More than a little piqued, she decided to be very clear about what she was saying. "Under the heading of sex . . ." She took a long time before she continued. "Obviously, our involvement was beneficial. If we hadn't been sexually attracted, then you wouldn't have been with me tonight. More than likely I would be dead. Instead, it was you who almost got killed for me." She pushed away from him and got to her feet. Cage sank back on the couch. Haley walked into the kitchen and returned seconds later with a plastic trash can and a broom.

Cage frowned. "What are you doing?"

"My bedroom is a mess, and I'm going to clean it up."

"No." Wearily he rose to his feet. He took the two items from her hands. "You're going to go and stay with Alicia and Kevin."

"So you can stay here, take control of everything and get yourself killed."

"Your confidence in me is overwhelming. I already had one brush with death a few minutes ago, so staying alive is a habit I don't want to break."

Haley blinked. Had she heard him right? Staying alive was a habit he didn't want to break? This from the man who had told her he didn't believe in tomorrow? That permanency didn't exist for him? That he didn't matter?

Giving her a long, steady look, he asked wryly, "Since you're not arguing with me, can I hope that you won't refuse to leave?"

She lifted her chin. "Of course I'm refusing to go. Running away is exactly what they want me to do."

"Correction. Running away is exactly what *I* want you to do, *and* what you're going to do."

"Cage, don't dictate to me."

He gripped her shoulders and shook her slightly. "Listen to me. No arrests have been made, and by now whoever was behind the pipe bomb knows that you're still alive. The next time, either they won't miss or they'll double back for an insurance hit. I don't want there to be a next time. When I leave here, I want to remember you watering flowers and visiting charming old geezers like Pedenazzi. I want your idealism strong and working, not blown apart like your bedroom is.'' Cage paused, as though gearing up to make his point. ''If you give me a hassle over leaving, then I will bodily take you out of here. No joke, Haley. Now, if you want to call that controlling you, so be it. I'll live with the stigma. What I couldn't live with is being responsible for your death.''

Like you think you were for Matthew's, she thought silently. She didn't say the words, for she knew that Cage would disagree with her comparison. Cage viewed her in a totally professional manner. She meant no more to him than anyone he could keep from getting hurt while at the same time accomplishing what he'd come here to do.

Strangely enough, she didn't consider his logic a minus so much as a disappointment. She wanted to be a part of him because she loved him, not because they were linked by some outside problem.

During those moments when he'd been so still on top of her, she'd felt the hollow, endless emptiness of loss. She'd thought he was dead, and suddenly nothing else in her future had had any significant meaning. She couldn't call her terrified reaction a revelation so much as a firm conclusion. She didn't want Cage out of her life. And yet he wanted out. Of that she had no doubt.

Sending her off to Alicia's would get her away from the threats on her life, but it would also accomplish a larger purpose. He could easily and smoothly slip from any entanglements with her.

Haley thought suddenly of the woman he'd lived with. From what Matthew had said, and the little that Cage had told her, he'd eased out of the relationship when she'd wanted more than he could give. Marriage and commitment had been the issue then. Haley hadn't even come close to broaching either of those topics, and yet Cage was easing away from her, too.

Nothing painful. No breaking-up arguments. No harsh words flung at her. Not even a lie such as ''when this is over we'll see if there is really anything between us.'' She could have wrapped those words around her pride, clung to them until she had the internal fortitude to face the truth, that in a very important way she had already lost him.

He wasn't dead, but the close brush with that possibility had diametrically altered the order of important things in her life. Perhaps past experience could be the reason. The death of her parents had altered her marriage from discontent to divorce. Philip's desire to control her had been problematic, but she'd never just wimped out. She'd kept her opinions, she'd often stood her ground, and in many ways she'd tried to concentrate on the traits that had drawn her to Philip in the first place.

Yet her marriage to Philip seemed so inconsequential compared to what she'd experienced with Cage. Rollercoaster emotions of gratitude, of security, of passion, of dependence, of admiration, and of a wrenching need to understand him.

She sighed. She'd tried to tell herself she didn't love him, that when he walked away her life would simply continue as if he'd been only a temporary guest. Cage Murdock, she concluded wistfully, should have been no more than an aberration of consuming interest that, like hot passion, eventually cooled and finally faded away.

Definitely a practical way to feel. Definitely a way to not allow what small control she still held over her heart to slip away.

Yes, she would go to Alicia's, but not to flee any danger, or even to placate Cage. She would go because going to Alicia's would give her some distance, some perspective, some excuse to allow him to slip away without her doing anything incredibly stupid—like begging him to love her the way she loved him.

At dawn, about a mile from Mayflower Heights, Cage walked with her across a postage-stamp-size lawn to Alicia's cedar-colored house.

Little had been said in the past few hours while she'd packed up her things. Haley wondered if he had simply run out of words, as she had.

Before he knocked on the door, he turned to her. His face was drawn and weary, much as it had looked at Matthew's funeral.

"While you were getting your clothes together, I talked to Noah. They were able to get some fingerprints off some of the metal fragments of the pipe. So if the prints are good he'll make an arrest."

If she'd thought it would do any good, she would have asked why, if they were about to make an arrest, she was at Alicia's instead of at home? But arguing and questioning wouldn't change anything.

In as upbeat a voice as she could muster, she said, "I'm sure an arrest will be made soon. Then you'll be able to leave and get your life started again."

"Yeah, such as it is," he said grimly, then stared down at her. He searched her face, and for a moment she thought he was going to say something, but he didn't. Instead he slid his hands into her hair and eased her face upward, his own eyes dark and disturbed.

Haley slid her arms around him, knowing this might be the last time she could touch him. Terrified that he might just let her go, she murmured, "Kiss me goodbye, Cage."

He brushed his mouth across hers. "You're an incredible lady, Haley Stewart. Matt was always so impressed by you, and I have to admit that all that he told me wasn't even close to what you really are."

She blinked, taken aback by the compliment. "I want to see you again before you leave." Then, before he had a chance to protest or find an excuse to say no, she added, "Just to say a final goodbye. I mean, friends should say goodbye, shouldn't they?"

He searched her eyes, then murmured, "And onetime lovers should at least share a kiss."

Her heart sped up. She wanted to spill into the kiss every feeling, every restrained emotion, all her love and desire for him.

His mouth touched hers, softly at first, but then, as if the merest of contacts between them had the potential to burst into deep passion, Cage gathered her against him. His hands slid to her hips, holding her solidly to him while his tongue dipped deep. Her mouth held a sweet welcome, the tastes an evocative blend of needs and desires.

Haley clung to him, wanting to infuse all of her love into this one parting touch.

Finally he lifted his head, and when she didn't drop her arms from around him, he eased them gently away himself.

"I'd better go."

Haley laced her hands together to stop them from trembling. "Yes, of course."

He stared at her for a second, and then, with the same deft quickness with which he handled his switchblade, he cupped her neck and brought his mouth down on hers once more. It was a ruthless, hard kiss that was more desperately final than passionate. Haley didn't return it, for if she did she would surely fling her arms around his neck and cry to the point of being foolishly hysterical.

He stalked away with no parting words. She watched him climb on to the motorcycle and roar down the street and out of her life.

She picked up her bag and knocked on Alicia's door.

Unfortunately, Haley realized four days later, the newspapers didn't let her forget or even pretend to ignore what was going on in Mayflower Heights.

Seated in Alicia's sunny breakfast nook, she frowned as she read the latest reports of violence—and another drive-by killing.

"Cage made this all sound so cut-and-dried," she murmured. "They had fingerprints and they would make an arrest and it would all be over."

Alicia refilled their coffee cups and sat down opposite her. "He wanted you out of there, so naturally he would play down anything that might make you wary of going."

"Right," she said peevishly. "I was *informed* that I was leaving. My preferences had nothing to do with anything."

"I have to admit, Haley, that Cage wrestling control from you without a fight is quite a surprise."

"I gave in."

"Hmm, because you're in love with him."

She started to deny it, but Alicia shook her head.

"Every time we've talked about Cage, from the very beginning, you've always presented yourself as unmoved, unconcerned and totally in control of yourself." She took a sip of coffee, her gaze on Haley. "But you lost control that first night. I saw it and felt it even from across the room when you and Cage were exchanging, um, opinions?"

Amusement flickered in Haley's expression. "Sexual awareness."

"I knew there was another name for it."

"I, however, am putting that aspect of our relationship behind me," she said staunchly.

"No doubt with the same vigor as you've dealt with loving him, worrying about him, and the latest possibility."

"What latest possibility?"

"Going back to Mayflower Heights."

"I never said I was going to do that."

"But you will." Alicia got up and flipped on the small television. A local TV reporter was talking in low tones with background pictures of flashing blue lights, crowds of people and a police officer shouting through a bullhorn. Framed in the center of the screen was her apartment building.

Haley stared. "My God, what's going on?"

"I just heard it before you came into the kitchen. But from what I've gathered, the police and the Venoms are in a standoff on Standish Street."

"Where's Cage?"

Alicia shook her head. "They interviewed Norman and Al Pedenazzi, but neither of them knew where Cage was. I did hear that one of the Venoms had definitely been identified as Matthew's killer. Haley, wait! I wasn't serious about you going back there."

Already at the kitchen door, her eyes fearful but resolute, Haley said, "Back there happens to be my home, my neighbors, and—"

"And Cage?"

"I was going to say my life."

But as Haley rushed from the kitchen, Alicia murmured, "Maybe you don't realize it yet, but Cage is your life."

If it weren't for the Standish Street marker, Haley wouldn't have recognized Mayflower Heights. Despite the daylight, a haze of smoke from small fires hung over the homes and small businesses. Remnants of recent street fighting, of drug dealing, of destruction, lay scattered like the dregs of a lost war. Haley stared and closed her eyes in disbelief and denial.

Never in her most vivid nightmares had she seen anything like this. Any bonds of community restraint had been broken, any value that had once held this neighborhood together as a family of supportive friends and neighbors had been cruelly wrenched apart.

Mayflower Heights had become the inner city, a place that no one would live in by choice, a place of unending violence, where the only things permanent were hate and death—a place where tomorrow would be worse than yesterday.

She sniffled, rubbing her knuckles across her eyes. Had Cage grown up amid this kind of horror? If so, it was no wonder he'd been furious about Matthew being here, no wonder he'd viewed her idealism with such cynicism, no wonder he'd wanted revenge for Matthew.

She shuddered. How foolishly naive she'd been. She'd equated his inner city with her inner city when, in fact they were as different as a meadow and a jungle.

But the wonder of Cage was that, while he'd been blunt and angry and annoyed with her, while he'd viewed her efforts as a doomed-to-failure mission, he'd stayed and helped and been incredibly supportive. Yet, at the same time, he'd never allowed her to lose sight of the ever-growing danger.

Now, she stood amid the rubble and the ruins not only of her neighborhood, but also of the idealism that she'd so tenaciously held. How odd that she felt so little. She should be angry or heartbroken or desperate to resurrect her cause and start again, but nothing seemed very important now, nothing but finding Cage alive. Perhaps because she'd thought she had lost him when the pipe bomb had exploded and, having faced that horror once, she had no intention of facing it again.

Walking quickly now, she made her way toward the parked police cars. Glancing around for someone she recognized, she spotted Norman Polk. She worked her way to him, which got her a scowl when he saw her.

"You're supposed to be at Alicia's."

"Where's Cage?"

"Now, cupcake, this isn't as simple as the Association—"

"Damn it, where is Cage?"

"Jeez, I don't remember you having such a short fuse."

Haley closed her eyes and counted to five. "I guess I'll just have to find him."

Norman grabbed her arm. "You can't just go traipsing around here, cupcake—"

"Don't call me that!" she snapped, suddenly scared that he might not know where Cage was and furious that she'd lost her temper over something as trivial as a silly endearment. She swallowed and steadied her voice. "Norman, do you know where Cage is? Is he all right?"

Mollified, he said, "He's in your apartment building."

"But I thought the Venoms were in there."

"Yeah, well, some of them already gave up, but we know Boa is still inside."

"Boa. Oh, God. He's holding Cage hostage," she muttered, knowing it was true as surely as she knew her own name.

"Don't know. Cage snuck around the back and got inside about an hour ago, and we ain't heard nothin' since."

She turned to walk away.

"Hey, you ain't gonna do anything stupid, are you?"

She planted her hands on her hips. "Like what?"

"Hell, I don't know. Try some goofy move like trying to rescue him."

"Rescue Cage Murdock? Me? When the place is crawling with cops and guns and all the experts?"

Norman sighed with relief. "Good. Besides, this can't last much longer."

Norman went to refill his coffee mug, and Haley slipped into the crowd before he had a chance to stop her.

She knew the entryway that Cage had used to get into the building. Keeping in the shadows and away from the police, she worked her way to the fenced-in area where he'd stored his motorcycle.

High-minded ideas about rescuing Cage slipped into her mind, and her immediate reaction was to tell herself it was indeed impossible. Or was it? And what if she did try? Rules about who did what seemed silly, when a moment was crucial. Besides, no one would expect to encounter her, and that could be to her advantage.

Haley slipped through the entry door and entered the building. She searched around for the light switch, then decided it was better left off. She blinked and tried to focus as her eyes became accustomed to the darkness inside.

She felt along the wall, her hands encountering a huge gash, as if someone had flung a hatchet at the plaster. A door banged upstairs, and she quietly followed the sound. On the second-story landing she turned a corner and tripped over a sprawled figure.

She yelped, slamming her hand against her mouth to cut off the noise. The figure didn't move, and the silence in the building was eerie and ominous. A dim, naked wall light glowed at the far end of the hall. Haley stared down at the figure. He lay on his stomach, one arm flung out, a blackjack a few inches from his hand. The leather around the handle looked painfully familiar, and she swallowed. It was the same one that had been wedged against her neck. She looked closer at the figure, hoping, praying, it was Boa, but it wasn't.

That could only mean one thing. Boa had a more dangerous weapon, and he was somewhere in the building.

She shivered. Then, after taking a deep breath, she reached down and picked up the weapon, feeling immediately more confident. So much for the nonviolent approach, she thought ruefully. Maybe she had a streak of vengeance in her that had gone untapped.

She moved along the wall, slowly listening for sounds that might indicate where Cage was. Her worry made it hard for her not to shout his name.

She worked her way through what felt like a maze, but was actually just a few turns and twists. Alert for any sound, she slowly made her way back down the stairs. Then she heard a thump come from her apartment. With a tighter grip on the blackjack, she eased closer.

The door stood open, and she heard furniture scrape. Someone swore. By the time she got to her door, her heart was hammering.

She gripped the blackjack, stepped inside and gasped. Cage and Boa were locked in a tight grip, each trying to get an advantage over the other. Whether it was her motion or her gasp, suddenly Cage was aware of her presence.

"Get the hell out of here!" he shouted, then ducked when Boa swung a fist at his face. The moment of distraction worked against Cage, and Boa had him on the floor, his hands around Cage's throat.

"I'm gonna slice ya and dice ya, you son of a bitch," Boa snarled. "Gonna do it with a knife, so you know how it feels."

"Let him go!" Haley shouted, and then, as if only just realizing what she held in her hand, she rushed forward and swung the blackjack. But she hit Cage, who at that moment had managed to push out from under Boa. Unfortunately, the blackjack tore into his ribs, and he lost his grip.

Haley whitened with fear. Cage and Boa kept rolling and twisting for control. Her fingers were icy, and her heart was racing. She couldn't miss. She had to time her next strike exactly right.

She made her way out of Boa's line of vision, determined that her next swing would be precise and calculated.

Cage jammed his knee up, but Boa's hands were cutting off his breathing. Haley backed away, took a tight grip on the blackjack, and then moved.

She screamed, and for just a second the sound distracted Boa enough that when she swung the blackjack she caught his thigh. He yelled, cursing, gripping his leg. Cage broke the grip, shoved Boa away and rolled from beneath him. Boa howled, turning toward Haley. Cage grabbed him from behind, wrenching his arm up, high on his back. Haley backed up, her entire arm tingling from the velocity of her swing. Her fingers were white against the dark weapon.

Boa glared at her, the hatred so thick it made her scoot back a few more steps. He snarled, "You bitch. You're gonna pay for this."

Cage pushed him over to the window. His voice was low and deadly. "My brother's blood was splattered all over Standish Street. You shot him, didn't you? You waited until he came out of this apartment, and then you fired that Uzi at him like he was a piece of garbage."

"You're crazy, man," Boa said, and to Haley's amazement, despite his position, he sounded unconcerned.

Cage tightened his wrenching hold on Boa's arm. "We can do this confession of yours in a civilized way or my way. Your choice."

"Screw you."

In a chillingly cold voice, Cage said, "Matt was killed to warn off Haley, wasn't he? You figured she'd run like a rabbit if you came into her neighborhood and flexed some muscle. But she didn't, so you decided to get some of your friends and try a little gang warfare. Surround her and terrify her and then rape her."

"Hey, man, broads and whores and sweethearts all got the same stuff between their legs. Good for them to know why it's there."

Haley sat down hard on the couch, her arms pressing into her stomach as she fought her rising nausea. Matthew murdered just to scare her into leaving the neighborhood. As if he were of so little value, as if he were just a target to be used and disposed of. She should have known, and perhaps she had. Perhaps, even in the midst of the viciousness she'd known existed, she hadn't wanted to think anyone had that little regard for a human life.

Then, in the tense silence of the room, Haley heard the precise click of a switchblade. Her head snapped up. Cage held his blade in front of Boa's face. In the light from the street, the knife shone silver and sharp.

Cage was going to kill him. This was why he'd come to Mayflower Heights, this was what he'd wanted, despite all the help and advice he'd given the Association, despite the trips to Paradise Falls, despite their incredible lovemaking. It all came down to this. A moment between life and death.

Cage spoke in a low voice. "Then, after the Frazer brothers were arrested, you got together with the dealers and decided on a plan. First destroy the confidence of her neighbors, and then kill her." Cage turned the knife, the silver a deadly glint in the light. "We got it about right, Boa?"

"Cool it with the blade, man."

"Answer me, damn it!"

"Yeah, yeah, you got it right," he said in a strained voice as he tried to back away from the knife. "Don't cut me, man. Please."

"Cage..." Haley got up and went to him. She touched his arm, and almost drew back. He was rigid, and the heat in his skin was fierce. "I'll go and alert the police that you've got Boa."

"Not yet."

"Cage, please, you can't..."

"He's garbage. A stinking killer who'll kill again."

Fear gripped Haley, and when she spoke, her voice was barely a whisper. "But killing him isn't going to change what happened to Matthew. Killing him is only going to destroy *you*." She lifted the blackjack, her heart breaking, her love for him screaming through her. Yet she knew she couldn't let him do this. As much as she knew Boa was guilty, knew he probably deserved Cage's wrath, she couldn't let it happen. She couldn't let the man she loved destroy himself.

Pain burned in her throat. She gripped the blackjack with both hands, knowing that if necessary she would use it. "I can't let you kill him, Cage."

He stared at her, his eyes that wintry blue that so totally shut her out. "Why in hell do you care what happens to this bastard?"

She took a deep breath, feeling as if she were betraying every principle of idealism she'd ever believed in, but she said it, anyway: "I don't care if he lives or dies, but you matter too much to me to see you throw away your life for this scum."

Sweat poured off Boa.

Haley clutched the blackjack so hard the leather bit into her fingers.

Cage stared at her for long, tense seconds, and then slowly lowered and closed the blade.

Boa slumped visibly.

Haley had to sit down, so weak were her knees. Cage went to the window, dragging Boa with him, and yelled to the police that everything was under control.

Within seconds the police were inside and arresting Boa. Two other Venoms Cage had already dealt with were rounded up and taken away. Haley was surrounded by relieved neighbors and a worried and lecture-giving Norman Polk.

She tried to work her way through the melee to find Cage, but there was no sign of him.

Finally she lowered her head and cried.

Cage had gone.

Chapter 13

Two days after the arrest of the Venoms and Boa, the residents of Mayflower Heights had just about finished getting the streets once again looking presentable. Late in the afternoon of the third day, a few of Haley's neighbors had gathered outside Haley's living-room window.

Norman Polk had just come from Cage's apartment. Shaking his head in disappointment, he said, "He's gone."

"You mean gone as in he's not coming back?"

"Looks that way."

"But he didn't even say goodbye."

"Probably didn't want everyone beggin' him to stay."

"Yeah, you know how it is. Goodbyes can be tough. Besides, he got what he came for. Matt's killer."

"Wonder how Haley is taking all this," Norman said as he glanced up at the newly hung and planted window box.

"Hey, she should be pleased as punch. Mayflower Heights is lookin' good. For the time being, at least, we got some peaceful streets."

"Thanks to Cage."

"And Haley."

"Think maybe they were, you know, kinda sweet on each other?"

"Haley and Cage? As a couple, like in love and marriage?"

"Why not? It ain't as if romance can't happen in Mayflower Heights."

"He sure was shook up after the pipe bomb. And then going into the apartment house after Boa. Jeez, I was wondering if he was just plain nuts, but I can't say as I blame him for wanting to take on Boa."

Norman frowned. "Bastard's lucky Cage didn't slice him like cheese. We all knew how he felt about his brother."

"I was thinkin' that Boa should be thankful Cage didn't know who shot Matt when he had that blade poised to do some serious damage."

A few nods and some laughter moved through the group.

"I remember the way Cage looked at Matt's funeral. He had that same devastated grimness when he walked out of Haley's apartment the other night."

"Yeah, Haley hasn't talked much, but I heard from one of the cops that Boa was shakin' so bad he spilled his guts. The Venoms were used by the dealers to try and scare Haley and us off. Though that Boa scuz didn't deserve it, Haley saved his life."

"Yeah? I didn't hear that. What'd she do?"

"Took some doin', but she convinced Cage not to kill him."

A few seconds of silence settled over the group.

"The guy's a class act. Cage could have wiped the streets with Boa and the whole damn lot of them. Shows he ain't no dummy. Boa ain't worth throwin' away your life in prison."

"Well, guess things are gonna seem pretty quiet around here after the past few weeks."

"Yeah, but remember what Cage said when he showed us the drug stuff in the comic book. We gotta stay alert. Just 'cause the Venoms are locked up, that don't mean we're all safe and sound."

"But we've made progress."

"Yeah, no one can disagree with that."

Norman glanced toward Cage's apartment. "Sure wish he'd at least said goodbye."

In her apartment, Haley stepped away from the window where she'd been shamelessly eavesdropping. In the days since Boa's arrest, she'd overheard a dozen or more conversations on Standish Street. She'd listened just for the pleasure of hearing her neighbors chat about inconsequential things like the Boston Red Sox, who was running for political office in an upcoming election, who baked the best apple pie; not big things, but important things to her community. And she was more than encouraged by the enthusiasm of the Association for getting involved in a new drug awareness program.

Of course, there were still isolated drug deals going on, and some vandalism still occurred, but Haley felt as if Mayflower Heights had seized control of the drug-infestation problem, that the safe streets that she'd worked so hard for were now more of a reality than a dream. Paradise Falls, or at least the tranquility it represented, could exist outside her front door.

Yet she had this other problem.

Cage.

Not what to do with him, but how she would forget him. Her neighbors' comments and speculation about his absence weren't news. She'd known the precise moment he'd ridden away.

Hours ago, she'd lain in bed and listened to his bootsteps in her outside hall when he'd dropped the apartment keys into her mailbox. She'd heard him start the motorcycle and then roar away. She'd stayed still for a long time, her body rigid, her hands clenched, her eyes blinking to keep back the tears.

He could have said goodbye. He could have left her a note with the keys. He could have left a message with Norman.

But he had left as he had come. Suddenly, unexpectedly, and without fanfare. Maybe she was supposed to just shrug off his departure, as her neighbors had. Cage had gotten what he'd come here for. Oh, he hadn't exacted the revenge she'd feared he might, and for that Boa could count himself lucky. Haley shivered at the thought of what Cage might have done with his switchblade if he'd known about Boa that day he'd cut Boa's jeans.

But the police had assured Cage that the evidence was strong against the gang member, and the standoff in Haley's apartment, and his later confession of having killed Matthew, would no doubt send him to prison for a long time.

And so she now faced the days ahead. Alone. She wanted to forget him, forget that she loved him, forget that every time she closed her eyes his face swam before her.

Damn him. Or maybe she should damn herself for falling in love with a man who had told her from the very beginning that nothing could happen between them. She wasn't stupid, but she'd allowed her curiosity, her gratitude, her passion and, damn it, her heart, to get in the way of her good sense.

Haley sighed. "He's managed to have the strongest possible control over me, and he isn't even here," she muttered to herself as she took her watering can to the new window box. She'd planted some autumn flowers to welcome September. Perhaps the change of season would give her a change in mood. Summer passions would cool, nights would turn chilly, days would be busy.

And if she was busy, forgetting would be easier, she hoped. Her apartment building needed repairs, and she'd decided to do some extensive redecorating in her own unit. The Association had lots of plans for the fall, and she intended to be part of those.

Busywork, time-fillers, she thought grimly. All to avoid the one question she had no answer for. How would she get through the rest of her life without Cage?

In his brother's apartment, a real estate agent took pictures and noted details so that she could list the furnished condo for sale. Cage sat on the corner of the desk, talking to his superior in Washington.

Beside his thigh were the contents of his pocket. Cycle keys, crumpled bills, some change, and a folder from the

Paradise Falls Inn. Cage stared down at the picturesque setting on the cover. Without consciously realizing it, he traced his finger across the approximate place where their room had been located.

To his superior, he said, "Yeah, I've thought about it. In fact, I haven't thought about much else." Besides Haley Stewart, he thought, still unable to let go of her. Aloud, he continued, "Pedenazzi's idea of putting an agent in the area could work, and it would give them a boost of confidence. We've got to be as serious about what's going on in neighborhoods as we are at the border." Cage glanced up. "Hold on a minute, Leo."

"I'm sorry to interrupt you, Mr. Murdock," the real estate woman said.

"It's okay. What do you think?"

She beamed. "I shouldn't have a problem selling, despite the lag in the condo market. This is in a prime area that has gotten a lot of interest from aging baby boomers. Also, selling the furniture and the contents with the unit will attract those looking for a second home."

"Sounds good."

"Since you've already told me the price you're asking, all I need is an address where I can get in touch with you—and, of course, where the bank can send the check." She opened her notepad to a new page.

Cage said, "I want the check made out to the Mayflower Heights Association. And it should be sent to Haley Stewart, 35 Standish Street."

The woman's eyebrows almost reached to her blond hairline. "You're going to leave this beautiful condo to live on Standish Street?" she asked, not trying to hide the distaste in her expression.

Cage grimaced. Hadn't he asked his brother almost the same question? Only a fool would return to the inner city after he'd escaped. He shook off the feeling. He wasn't returning. Just the money was going to Haley, for the work she was doing.

Cage ignored her question and said, "Is there anything else?"

"Uh, yes, a number where I can get in touch with you when we have a sale."

"I'll call you in a few days."

She gave him her business card and then left the condo.

Back to his superior, he said, "Sorry, just a few loose ends to tie up here. Now, where were we?" They talked a few more minutes about Cage's suggestion of an agent or some kind of organized assistance from the DEA for the inner cities and in particular Mayflower Heights.

Agents Cage knew were suggested, but he had a variety of reasons why they were bad choices. Finally his superior suggested Frank, an agent Cage had worked with in the past, one who'd been looking for an assignment in the east.

Cage knew Frank would be perfect. Young, intelligent, quick, and he would work enthusiastically with the Association.

"Don't tell me. You got a problem with him, too?" his superior said when Cage didn't respond. "You know, Murdock, this was your bright idea, not mine. I'm considering it because I know that most of the time your instincts are dead-on, but a little mutual cooperation on your part would help."

"Sorry, it's just that Mayflower Heights isn't just any neighborhood."

"Really. And what in hell is different about it? From what you've told me it sounds like the drugs, violence and graffiti are pretty standard."

"Yeah, well, there's the antidrug association, headed up by the woman I mentioned—"

"The Stewart woman! Is that what in hell we're talking about? Some female crusader who thinks she knows more than the cops? What happened? She got herself in a mess, and she needs some muscle in there to get her out."

Cage took a few seconds while he pressed the phone against his chest. All his defenses roared to the surface, and it took all his concentration not to slam the phone down on its cradle. "Just forget I said anything," he growled.

"Look, Cage, I'm not trying to gut your idea."

"Maybe it was a lousy one to begin with."

"Or maybe you should be the agent who gets the assignment." His superior paused a second. "Got to get off here and get to a meeting. I'm already late. Get back in touch with me after you finish up with your brother's things. Meanwhile, think over what I said."

Cage dropped the phone onto the cradle, then swept the Paradise Falls Inn folder off the desk and into the trash. He shoved a hand through his hair and cursed. He hated the churning emotions that gripped and held him every time he thought about her. He hated that he'd been so gutless that he'd snuck out of the apartment before dawn so that he wouldn't have to say goodbye. And, most of all, he hated that he wanted to go back.

One woman.

How could one woman so totally turn him inside out? And he'd known she would. Hell, he'd known from that first exchange that he wanted nothing to happen between them. He'd even bluntly told her so. Pretty straightforward, so that no matter how he tried now to explain his involvement with excuses, he had none. He had no use for idealism, no use for inner-city living, no use for permanency, and yet here he was mired in feelings that were sexual and emotional and, instead of showing some signs of abating, were becoming more and more— He hesitated as his mind tried to avoid the word. Finally he realized grimly that *permanent* and *Haley* were entrenched inside him as if they were synonymous.

Why else had he said no to the agents that Leo had suggested? Any one of them would have done a hell of a job, and yet the idea of someone else there with Haley, working with her, seeing her delight when good things happened, holding her through the failures and disappointments...

He lowered his head, shaking it. Maybe Leo was right. Maybe he did covet the assignment and he was either too stubborn or too scared to ask for it.

For if he moved to Mayflower Heights, the entire foundation that he'd built his life on would be gone. He'd be back in the inner city, living there, working there, just as Matt had wanted to do.

Why? Hadn't he seen it the way it really was when Haley had gone to stay with Alicia? Stark, violent, curb-to-curb filth. Hadn't he heard someone call it the neighborhood from hell? Change a few details and it could have been the streets where he'd grown up. The streets where the old man had always told him he would die.

Cage walked over to the long set of windows that looked out over the city. Those moments when he'd come so close to killing Boa; if she hadn't been there, he knew he would have done it. And the revenge he'd wanted for Matt...

Oh, God.

Cage closed his eyes as he faced fully what had been slipping around in his mind for days.

He hadn't killed Boa, hadn't exacted the revenge he'd come for, but not because he'd suddenly changed his mind or become concerned about the consequences.

He had changed his mind because Haley had come into his life. For those few days after the pipe bomb, after he'd sent her to safety, Mayflower Heights had been hell. The neighborhood had deteriorated and darkened as if someone had turned out the lights.

Her presence had made the difference. Not clean streets, or police patrols, or the Mayflower Heights Association. Just Haley's being there.

And so it was in his life. Light or darkness. Haley or the rest of his life.

Because of her, he'd chosen to let Boa live.

Because of her attack on Boa with the blackjack, Cage had been able to wrestle himself free to overpower the gang member. No doubt Boa rued the day he'd ever tangled with Haley Stewart.

Isn't that what you're doing, Murdock? Cursing the day you got tangled up with Haley? She'd made him want to think about the tomorrows, long for a permanent relationship, but most of all, she'd become so important to him that a future without her stretched out before him, bleak and empty.

Cage went over to the desk, pocketed his keys and the crumpled bills, and glanced in the wastebasket. He reached down and plucked out the Paradise Falls Inn folder.

Paradise Falls, he mused, his own Shangri-la. She'd seen that potential in Mayflower Heights, but Cage had seen the reality in Haley Stewart.

He tossed the folder back in the trash and went to the telephone. He hoped to catch Leo before he'd left for the day.

Just as the sun displayed one of her sensational sunsets, Haley ended the meeting of the Association. She'd fielded the questions about Cage with a deft professionalism, she decided, and she was about to get some iced tea when she heard the motorcycle.

"Hey, it's Cage!"

She went still while a number of people went to the door. Within moments Cage was inside, shaking hands, answering questions and working his way toward Haley.

She pasted a bland smile on her face and stepped forward.

"How nice to see you again."

Why are you here, Cage?

"Things outside look great."

You look so good to me, baby, so good.

"Yes, we're getting the neighborhood back to normal."

My life has never felt so empty. I hate you. I love you.

"I noticed the flowers in your window box when I drove by."

I remember the way your breasts smell like roses.

"Fall is coming, and I—" Her voice slipped, and she quickly glanced down, cursing the rawness in her throat.

Cage leaned close and whispered, "Can we go somewhere private?"

She shook her head, raising it and hoping she at least looked calm. Clearing her throat, she said, "I don't think that's a good idea."

"Please?"

She blinked, her gaze meeting his wintry blue eyes. Except now they weren't wintry, they were worried, troubled, and—unless she was reading too much into them because her heart wanted to believe—she saw a desperation for her to comply with him.

She couldn't deny him, she knew it, and, holding on to some tiny glimmer of hope that he had returned because of her, she nodded. "All right."

The relief that spread over his face made her agreement seem startlingly profound.

He didn't touch her, but walked close beside her as they went outside. His motorcycle sat parked by the curb. They stood staring at it as if it held answers.

In unison they spoke.

"Cage?"

"Haley?"

"You go first," he said.

Already bracing for an answer she wouldn't like, she asked, "Why did you leave without saying goodbye?"

"Because I knew if I saw you I would want to stay."

"Oh."

"You expected me to say that, since there were no more reasons to stay, I'd left."

She nodded. "Or that goodbyes were for people who care about each other."

"And you thought I didn't care about you?"

"As one human being to another, I knew you did, but beyond that..."

Cage dragged a hand through his hair. "You think I'm still hung up about Matt. Hung up by the past and all those feelings of failure about him?"

"The bonds of family, of responsibility, are strong ones, Cage. I feel them for Mayflower Heights. For you and Matt, your bonds were blood and survival. Plus you were given total responsibility for him."

"Resented him, too, Haley." The blunt words weren't said with any attempt at excusing himself, making no exceptions. He studied her a moment. "You know, I think you knew before I did. That day we were doing the cleanup you said something about me feeling things I didn't want to feel."

Her eyes warmed. "I always thought from the beginning that you blamed yourself too much for Matt's death. I think the natural protectiveness that one sibling feels for another became a crusade for you."

He glanced away. "Maybe. But to resent your own brother..."

She touched her fingers to his wrist and felt the hard beat of his pulse. "Your father put an awful burden on you, Cage." At his sharp look, she shook her head. "Let me finish. In one breath he was telling you, or indicating by his actions, that you didn't matter, and then the next moment he was acting as if you mattered more than anything else."

Cage frowned. "What do you mean?"

"If you didn't matter to your father, why in the world would he have made you responsible for the brother who did matter?"

"I was the oldest. The one with the street-smarts—"

"The one he could trust. The one he knew would move heaven and hell to keep his kid brother from getting hurt. And you did that, Cage, for many years. But the time had to come when Matthew took responsibility for his own life."

"You know, the kid tried," he muttered. "Just hours before he died, he was trying to convince me that it was time I let him make his own choices." He paused and she saw again the deep love he'd held for his brother. "Actually more than Matt, I think I resented his maturity, his wanting to make his own decisions."

"Because you loved him and cared more about him than you did yourself."

He smiled then. "You always judge everything by some idealistic motive. Including this." He stared down at her. "But you know, I wouldn't change anything that I did for Matt. Sure there was some resentment, a few times when I felt like I was living two lives instead of one, days when I hated the old man for his favoritism...." His words trailed off. Finally, he added, "But I couldn't have, no, I should say, I *wouldn't have* done anything differently."

"Then you have no reason to feel guilty. Aren't you the one who told me that I couldn't save the world?"

"Yeah, along with a few other things that weren't so kind."

Looking into his eyes, Haley sensed that he'd put his feelings about Matthew into proper perspective, but there still remained too many hurdles between them personally.

Cage scowled. "A few minutes ago you were saying that I only cared about you as one human being cares about another."

Haley felt her tension return. "Please, Cage, I don't want to talk about what happened between us."

"Not talk about us or about me? Don't you want a chance to tell me that I've been cold, distant, too impersonal?" He shoved a hand through his hair and she wished he would tangle his fingers in hers. "I left because I was too scared to say goodbye to you."

She stared in astonishment at his honest confession, pleased that he hadn't given her a cop-out excuse. "Cage, I wouldn't have tried to make you stay. That would have been doing to you exactly what I accused you of so often. Trying to control you."

"Maybe that's what I wanted. Someone with whom I could say, here's my life. A hell of a mess, but you're the only one who's ever made me want to make it into tomorrow. The problem was, all the tomorrows without you looked like a long trip into hell."

"Tomorrows without me?"

"God, even the words sound odd." He took a deep breath. "Maybe I mean they feel foreign and complicated and...permanent."

Haley felt her heart speed up and pound so loud her ears throbbed. For the first time, she touched his arm, and felt the heat and beating pulse. He tipped her chin upward and she was lost in the intensity of his eyes.

"DEA is going to assign me to the New England region. I asked specifically if I could be based in the Mayflower Heights area. I told them about you and the Association, and they were very impressed with the level of community involvement. There's still some red tape and final approval from the director in Washington, but my superior says there won't be a problem.''

She listened, knowing she should be overjoyed. With direct help from DEA, and Cage here and on top of things, her desire and determination to make Mayflower Heights like Paradise Falls would be far more than a fantasy. It held the promise of progress and success in the future. But the other side would be constant exposure to Cage. She couldn't deal with that. She couldn't love him and keep it to herself. She just couldn't.

She stepped away from him, turning her back. Now she faced a quagmire. Refusing his offer and saving herself emotionally, or telling him his idea was wonderful for Mayflower Heights—and leaving herself. For surely she would have to do that. She couldn't live here and love him and not have him. ''Of course it would be wonderful to have you working on the drug problems, but I'm afraid that you and I working together wouldn't be a good idea.''

''Haley, listen to me.''

''No, you listen. If you think you're going to just come in here and expect me to—'' She paused, then shook her head to clear away any polite answers. ''No, I'll be blunt, like you always have been with me. I won't sleep with you. I won't be your sex-mate whenever you decide you want some excitement.''

He pulled her into his arms, kissing her despite her attempt to push him away. ''Sex-mate? Now that's one I haven't heard before.''

''Let me go.''

''What if I told you that, as sensational as sleeping with you is, I want more.''

She stopped struggling, her hands relaxed against his chest. ''More?''

''As in I want to love you.''

She scowled, leaned back and narrowed her eyes. ''Is this just sex dressed up in a prettier word?''

''No, it's love dressed up as in *I love you, Haley Stewart.*''

For a long, silent moment, she simply stared.

He grinned. "You looked as surprised as I was when I realized that all the agonizing and worry I've done about you was because I was falling in love with you."

She blinked, her heart racing with excitement. "Falling in love with me? All the time you were falling in love with me?"

He brushed his knuckles across her throat. The switchblade cut had healed completely. "I wanted to think all we had was this incredible sexual attraction, and to be honest, I'm not sure when I knew it was more. But that day you were surrounded by the Venoms, the terror I felt was so gut-deep I couldn't even name it. The escape to Paradise Falls was as much for me as for you. I needed to get away from here before I went back and finished the job on Boa."

She stared for a long moment, her hands still resting against his chest. "I thought you were going to kill him the other night."

He nodded grimly. "I probably would have. He killed Matt, and he tried to kill you, but when you said I would destroy myself if I followed through on the revenge, something inside me fell into place. Some piece that had always been missing. I don't even know what to call it."

She frowned. "But I told you a number of times that revenge would destroy you. Why did it suddenly have meaning?"

"Maybe because those other times I heard it but didn't believe it. And maybe those other times I just wasn't ready to accept that I deserve some happiness. But in those moments when I had the choice between exacting revenge on Boa and losing you..." His voice faltered, and he cleared his throat. Then, pulling Haley into his arms, he tucked her close, wanting to make her a part of him, to fill the emptiness. "Ah, Haley, knowing that I mattered to you, knowing that being with you had changed me, knowing that if I killed him I'd never see you again, never smell your skin, never taste your mouth, never love you..."

She slid her arms around him, her eyes damp with moisture. She had no words, no way to express the fullness of her heart.

He held her, feeling now as though his words couldn't come fast enough, the flood of feelings for her swamping him.

"You know," he said softly, "I've been in a lot of inner cities. Some have grown out of their violence, others have not, but here there was a vital difference. You. When I realized that Mayflower Heights only fell completely into hell after I sent you to Alicia's, I realized that you were the influence here. You were the one who held everything together. Then I took a look at my own future, the one I swore I didn't have, and knew that you were the difference in me. And if I didn't come back here and convince you that I love you, then I really wouldn't have a tomorrow that was worth a damn."

Haley whispered, "Oh, Cage . . ." Her voice shuddered, and her throat was raw, but happiness spilled through her like sweet summer sunshine. "I don't know what to say, except that I love you. I've tried to tell myself you were all wrong for me. That you were exactly the kind of man I wanted to avoid."

"Because of the control thing."

"Yes."

He tipped her chin up. "I don't want to control you, I just want to love you."

She stared into his eyes, the blue not wintry and distant, but warm and honest. She believed him and she trusted him, just as she'd instinctively done after the gang had surrounded her, and in the warehouse, and at the inn in Paradise Falls, when he'd left the room choice up to her. But, most of all, she'd seen her trust in him revealed when he'd walked away from killing Boa. Then Cage had had all the control, and he'd relinquished it.

She reached up and brushed her mouth across his. "I love you and I want you to stay and love me."

He tugged her into his arms once again, kissing her soundly. Haley threw her arms around his neck.

Cage rocked her tight against him.

Behind them, the Association members had gathered, their smiles broad with approval.

"See?" one of them said. "I told you romance was possible in Mayflower Heights."

"Oh, this is so exciting. Maybe we'll have a wedding."

"Haley and Cage married." The woman sighed. "Now that's the best kind of romance. Forever after."

Cage whispered, "We can't disappoint them, can we?"

"Absolutely not."

"Is that a yes, you'll marry me?"

"Oh, yes, that's a definite yes," she said as once again he drew her into his arms for a long kiss, a kiss that promised a beginning to all their tomorrows.

* * * * *